PAVEY BOULEVARD

Rie Anders

This is a work of fiction. Names, characters, organizations, places, events, and incidents are either products of the author's imagination or are used fictitiously.

Text Copyright © 2018 Rie Anders

ISBN: 1723908207

To Abby.

September 2016

The last flight of the day into Lake Union landed, and our Chief Pilot, Tom Wilde, secured the wings of the float plane and turned it over to our line guys. I'd worked for Kenmore Air, in Seattle, Washington, for almost eight years, since right after I graduated from college. Even now, I still haven't tired of watching the planes take off and land daily from the water. I love to hear the whir of the engines, and the splash when the pontoons finally make contact with the water. I always feel like an adventure is about to happen when I see the planes taxi out from the dock across the lake for take-off.

Tom walked up the dock with lighthearted steps. He was returning from a full day of flying back and forth to the San Juan Islands. I waved at him from the upper deck of the waiting area and smiled, welcoming him back.

"Hey Shaye, Mrs. Lansing left her book in the plane again today. Would you call her and tell her we'll have someone swing it by tomorrow?" Tom struggled through the door with his flight bag, Mrs. Lansing's book tucked under his arm.

Tom has been flying floatplanes for almost 40 years. He was raised in Alaska where floatplanes were an everyday form of transportation.

He is a distinguished looking older man, and is still fit and strong. His hair is gray and starting to thin, but it doesn't detract from his looks. He has also been like a father figure to me the last couple of months, since my father's death.

"Absolutely," I replied. "By the way, thank you for flying my mom up to Lopez Island last week. These past few months have been really hard for her, and it was nice that she could just relax, and not stress about the drive. I really appreciate it."

"Anything for you, you know that." Setting the book and his flight log on the customer service counter, Tom reached out to hug me. I gave him a quick hug in return, and stepped back so he could finish his flight paperwork. I knew he needed to close his flight plan soon, and then he would leave for the day.

Then he asked me, "Are you wrapping up for the day?"

"Yes. I have a few more changes to make to the marketing campaign for the new kayaking adventure series, and then I'll be finished for the day. I want to get it in front of Don to review before the weekend. I think he's going to be really pleased."

Don Sanders is the CEO of Kenmore Air, and between him and Tom, I have always felt supported and appreciated in my job. I started as a Customer Service Agent when I was 23, and was promoted to Marketing Director a few years ago. My unwavering love of Seattle, and my historical knowledge of the San Juan Islands gave me an added edge that helped people get really excited for a floatplane adventure.

"You've worked hard for this company, Shaye." Tom replied. "I'm proud of you." His tone was gentle and he looked at me directly so I would know he was sincere with his compliment. He was working for Kenmore when I arrived eight years ago, broken and lost, after my grievous summer on Lopez Island. He was always kind to me, never pushed for personal information, and kept me focused on my goals to build a career with the company, and a life in Seattle.

I smiled knowingly and said, "Thank you, Tom. I am so grateful for you and Don." I waved the book in front of him. "I'll make sure Mrs. Lansing gets her book."

I packed the book in my bag and headed back to my office to finish the proposal. After finalizing the changes, I grabbed my bag and laptop, locked my office, and headed out the back door to the parking lot.

It was a beautiful summer night in Seattle. The water reflected the last bit of sun, and looked like a river of gold. Earlier today it had been in the high seventies, and now the temperature was dropping to the fifties. It was the perfect end to a perfect summer day. My Ford Explorer was parked in my designated spot, and I smiled to myself with happiness, feeling content and at peace.

Pulling out of the parking lot, I headed to Elliot Avenue and drove over the Ballard Bridge to my two-bedroom craftsman house. The house had a low-hanging roof over the front porch, and thick stone support columns. It was small and cozy, and was perfect for just me.

I heard the phone in the kitchen ringing as I was unlocking the back door. I frantically tried to get the door open and shouted to no one in particular, "I'm coming, I'm coming!" No one ever calls me on my house phone anymore. My father became anti-technology when he moved to the Island full-time, so I guess I had kept it for him. I needed to think about disconnecting it.

I ran into the kitchen, dropped my bag on the granite counter, and answered the phone. "This is Shaye."

"Shaye, its Suzi Waters."

Suzi was the secretary of Marcus Reid, my father's attorney. "Secretary" sounds demeaning to her, and she prefers the term "Administrative Assistant"— very appropriate, since she runs the office like a colonel in the Army. Nothing is ever forgotten, or late, or misplaced. The irony is that she is only a hair over five feet tall, would almost fit in your pocket, and she's had gray hair as long as I have known her. I met her when I was just a kid, maybe five or six years old, and I know she wasn't quite 50 years old then. She never seemed to age or change. Even though I tower over her, I have always felt she would protect and defend me. She was as loyal as they come.

"Oh my God, Suzi! How are you?" She wasn't the type to waste time calling for a chat, so I knew she wouldn't answer my question.

"Girl, it is time to come back to the island." She didn't sound like she was asking.

I had a feeling she wouldn't want to hear me say I wasn't coming, but I had to try.

"I'm sorry Suzi, I can't right now. I have a job here, and a home, and I'm not able to come back. My mom came last week."

"Well darlin', I am not asking you to return. I am calling to tell you that the stipulations for the reading of the will state that you must be on the Island to hear it. Your Daddy insisted you be here." She was like a little dog that would not let go of a bone. In my heart I knew I would have to go, but I didn't want to.

With a heavy sigh of resignation, I responded, "When do I need to be there?"

She jumped right in with the answer. "Nine a.m., Monday morning. Mr. Reid will leave the Ford at the floatplane dock in front of the resort. I presume you won't have time to catch a ferry, and will be flying up?"

Wasting my breath asking her how she knew would have been pointless.

"Yes, I will fly up on Saturday. Thank you, Suzi, I will see you then." All the joy and serenity I had felt earlier today drained out of my heart. Avoiding the Island for the past 8 years had not been easy, but I had managed. I had only been back once with my mom to scatter my father's ashes, and even then, I had arrived and departed as stealthily as possible. I never planned on going back to visit, never talked with anyone from that summer, never asked about anyone. I had pushed the heart-wrenching unpleasant memories of my last summer on the island to the corners of my mind, and now I had to face my demons. I had to return to Lopez Island.

PART 1

May, 2008

The first time I saw Jason Reid that summer, he was sitting on the deck of the Islander Resort. It was my second night of work, and I was serving the tables on the deck of the bar.

He was drinking kamikazes with his friends, and by their laughter and the easy banter, you could tell everyone loved him. His dirty blond hair was messed from the wind and highlighted from the sun. It was also a little too long, but it suited him. His eyes were shielded by his expensive Ray-Ban sunglasses, and you could see by the smile on his face and the tilt of his head, he was happy and charming.

Wearing the typical Pacific Northwest khakis and an oatmeal colored collarless polo shirt; he exuded confidence and a little bit of arrogance. His friends were all sitting around the tables on the deck, but he was sitting posted on the railing. He had on Red Wing leather work boots, and hadn't even taken the time to tie them. He wasn't much taller than me, maybe 5'11", and trim and healthy. He never looked at me, spending most of his time with his arm around a short blonde in booty shorts and a flower print halter top.

I didn't think about him again, until I saw him at the local pub down the street from the resort. He was bartending when I went in a few days later to get a drink after work.

"Cape Cod, please," I said to him as I sat on a stool at the bar, and set my bag on the seat next to me.

"Cape Cod for the girl of the summer, coming right up." I jerked my head back and watched him swagger off, leaving me speechless.

When he returned, I quizzed him. "Why did you call me the girl of the summer? What does that mean?" I felt put off by his tone, but oddly flattered and intrigued he had given me a nickname.

"You are here for the summer, right? You aren't sticking around."

"Most of my childhood was spent up here. My family has a house on the South End, and I've been coming up here since I was five months old."

As he stared at me, I could now see his eyes were blue, breath-taking and sharp. They made me catch my breath, not by their ice blueness, but by what seemed to be frozen emotions.

He nodded at me, and then the absence of emotion was gone. Returning in its place was the carefree and charismatic guy I had seen the other day. "Well, ok then...girl of the summer." He smiled and laughed at his own humor.

I decided to introduce myself. "I'm Shaye Richards."

"I know who you are." He went about his work cleaning the glasses and stocking the beer.

Confused by his behavior I asked, "And you are?"

He put away the last of the clean glasses and leaned against his side of the bar. Lazily, he responded, "Jason Reid."

"Jason Reid. Jason Reid... Why do I know that name?" He had engaged in the conversation, and now I wanted him to continue.

He finally responded, "My dad is your father's attorney."

I almost jumped out of my seat. "That is why your name is so familiar to me. I remember now. We used to build driftwood forts on the beach in front of your house. You have an older brother and sister, don't you?"

He responded, "I do," and he sauntered to the other end of the bar.

He started a conversation with another customer, and his lack of direct attention indicated to me I was probably annoying him.

I was so happy to connect with someone from my childhood summers here, I hadn't been able to stop talking, and now I was determined to get his full attention.

I continued on, and had to talk a little louder since he was a ways down the bar. "Are they on the Island?"

He glanced at me and I saw his shoulders lower. Finally, he poured himself a soda and walked back my way.

He must have sensed I was just trying to be friendly because he relaxed against the bar to talk. "Evie works at the bakery, and Nick is in Seattle."

"Well, that's great! I can't wait to meet Evie." Now that I had his attention, I jumped at the opportunity to try and charm him. "I have the day off tomorrow. We should get coffee in the morning. Do you want to meet me at the Grind? The coffee shop? Maybe nine am?" I started to ramble, and he started to laugh. I realized he probably wasn't even awake at nine, so I proposed an alternative. "How about ten?"

He gave me a lopsided grin and said, "I can do that."

I stayed a little longer and finished my drink. Then I paid my tab, jumped off the bar stool, grabbed my bag and told him I would see him in the morning. I was looking forward to building friendships this summer, and feeling a little joyful at the possibility of maybe something more.

The next morning, I decided to ride my bike into town. It was a beautiful June morning on the Island. Pedaling down Fisherman Bay Road, I had a stunning view of the bay. The water was sparkling in the morning sun, and the cool morning air was hitting my face as I rode, waking me up before I even got to the coffee shop.

When I rode up, he was already there, leaning against his Bronco. He looked just like he had the other day on the restaurant deck, with his Ray-bans, hikers, and messy hair.

"Good morning." I smiled at him.

"Good morning." He smiled right back.

I put my bike in the rack provided by the Lopez Island bike shop, and we went inside the store. The coffee shop wasn't much larger than a studio apartment,

15

and was furnished with an eclectic mix of velvet couches and flower-print chairs. Books were available to borrow, and a patchouli candle was burning on one of the coffee tables.

We stood next to each other at the counter, as he ordered black coffee, and I ordered an iced mocha. We waited in silence as the barista made my drink, then he wandered out onto the deck that overlooked the other end of the bay and waited for me to join him. When my drink was finished, I grabbed a napkin and joined him on the deck.

He turned to me as I stepped out onto the deck. "So, girl of the summer, what are we doing here?"

"We are getting coffee." I wasn't sure how to respond to him, so I went with something banal.

"And...?" He straddled one of the chairs and sat down facing me. He really was quite boyishly lovely, and I was acting like a little girl with a silly crush. He took his glasses off and put them in the neck of his shirt. He was grinning as if he knew I might be into him.

"And, we are sharing a beautiful morning." I continued with the pleasantries, a smile starting on my face.

"And..." he asked again.

I grinned wickedly and responded, "And, you are going to ask me to lunch."

Now he busted out laughing and said, "Maybe."

I smiled.

"What are you doing on the Island, summer girl?"

I now understood he was asking something deeper, something more important.

16

Deciding to be honest, I responded, "I needed a change. I needed a break. I dropped out of school this last semester, and I needed time to think about what I really wanted to study. I was studying sociology, and now I have no idea what degree I want to pursue. My dad suggested I come up here to figure it out." I crinkled up my nose in a self-deprecating way, and said, "Actually, I don't think it was a suggestion." It seemed so childish saying it out loud to someone, but it was the truth.

"Are you going back?" He seemed genuinely interested, and his eyes had a little more warmth to them.

It seemed only fair I was honest with him, so I responded, "Most likely. I haven't thought about it much since I've been here. I have some time to make a decision."

He raised his coffee and said, "Well then, here's to figuring it out." I tapped his coffee mug with my iced drink, and laughed at the mischievous look on his face. He abruptly stood up and said, "Let's go see Evie."

We walked across the street to the bakery, and the sweet smell of cinnamon and sugar invaded my senses. The almond butterhorns, cinnamon rolls, raspberry scones, and lemon bars were so perfectly displayed I almost didn't want to eat them.

"Hey, baby brother!" A gypsy of a girl about my age popped out from behind the counter, and if it weren't for the eyes, I would have never thought she was his sister. Her dark black hair was long and curly, and pulled back with a rubber band and a bandana. She squeezed him, and he pulled her hair. She was almost as tall as me, but less curvy. She looked like a colt with ballerina arms, and the way she lit up when he walked in showed an immense amount of love. This had to be Evie.

"Hi, I'm Evie." She stuck out her hand, and I took it. Jason took over the introductions from there, letting her know I was Dan Richards's daughter and I was staying in my parents' house on the south end for the summer.

"I think we played together when we were really little. You're waiting tables at the Islander, right? I thought I saw you the other day." She was so full of life, so happy, her smile so infectious, I couldn't help but instantly like her.

I hesitated for a second. I didn't think Jason had seen me the other night, and I didn't want him knowing I'd seen him with the blond. "I—yes, I was working Sunday afternoon."

Jason hardly glanced back at me, he was so focused on the goodies. "Evie quit yackin' and get me a scone."

"He is such a brat. He's the baby, you know, so he gets whatever he wants." She rolled her eyes, and then winked at him.

He responded, "Yes, well, you are the only girl, so we are even."

"What does that make Nick?" She was still teasing him.

Jason responded, "A pain in the butt." He was smiling so I knew he didn't mean it.

Evie had walked back around the counter to get Jason a scone, and I asked her for a cheese croissant. Taking our treats out onto the deck, Jason talked with everyone that walked by. He asked about their kids, their day, and the weather. He included everyone in his greetings. I felt like a bit of a third wheel, since I didn't know many of them, but Jason made an effort to introduce me to most of the people that took the time to stop and talk.

We stayed for a while, and then he walked me back to the coffee shop where I had left my bike.

"Thanks for the coffee date. I had a really nice time." I suddenly felt awkward and not sure what to do with myself.

"About the girl you saw me with the other day," he started. I was surprised he decided to bring it up. "She's an old friend. We were together in high school and there is nothing between us." He looked so sincere and honest I decided to be the same.

"You guys looked very..." I trailed off as I struggled to find the right word without offending him, "close."

"She may want to get back together, but it's not going to happen. It's just easy."

Shock must have registered on my face because he instantly said, "Not easy like "she's easy." We're comfortable together, and she knows me really well."

I thought he was trying to tell me something, but now I was worried about being "easy" for him; so, I wished him a good day and jumped on my bike to ride home.

It was all I could do not to turn around, but when I got to the end of the drive, I lost the battle with myself and glanced over my shoulder. He had his Ray-bans back on his face, his arms akimbo, and a huge grin on his face. His smile gave me goosebumps, and I suddenly wanted him to kiss me.

I worked lunch shifts the rest of the week, and the following Friday he stopped in to tell me some friends of his were having a house party that night. He said it would be great if I could come. From behind me, my co-worker Jeff interrupted our conversation and asked if he could get a ride. Jeff was usually pretty quiet, and I didn't know much about him, but he was always friendly. He looked Italian or Mediterranean, I wasn't sure, with dark eyes and dark curly hair that he was always slicking back with olive oil from the kitchen. He was a little on the pudgy side, but kind of cute in a stray-dog kind of way. Jason glanced at him, and I could swear he rolled his eyes.

"No, dude, you cannot. Get your own ride," Jason said.

"Yes, Jeff, I will give you a ride," I said immediately, and smiled at Jason.

"Fine. See you tonight." Jason winked at me and walked out.

∞

The party was a large get-together, and the first of the season.

I drove into a large field to the left of the rambler style house and parked alongside a dozen or so other cars.

Jeff jumped out and headed straight to a large bonfire where they were keeping the kegs of Island Pale Ale, while I wandered into the house to look for anyone I might know. Other than Evie, and the summer staff at the resort, there were few people here I recognized.

I followed the cobblestone path that led from the front to the back of the house, and entered the kitchen through the back door.

Floral curtains and a lace runner on the table gave the house a country-chic vibe. Glancing at the kitchen cabinets, I appreciated the grained wood, and could tell, from my experience working with my dad in his woodshop, that they were handmade.

I grabbed a Heineken from a red cooler on the floor and continued exploring the house. The kitchen was open to a large family room, with a big leather sectional, shaggy brown carpet, and a rock fireplace. I took my beer and wandered in to sit on the hearth.

Two women sat on the couch: a girl who looked familiar to me, and Evie. "Shaye, come sit by me," Evie said. "Meet my friend Julie."

I walked over and sat down to the left of Evie, and looked across at Julie.

Evie continued with introductions. "Julie, this is Shaye Richards. She is living on the Island this summer, on the South End. Shaye, this is my oldest and dearest friend, Julie Hunter."

She looked me up and down, and I realized she was the blond who had been with Jason the weekend before. Julie was way more beautiful than I had remembered. She looked like a cherub angel, with flawless skin and thick dark eyebrows that were in stark contrast to her curly blond hair. I was glad I had made an effort to look my best. I was wearing my backless suede halter top and black palazzo pants, and my hair was braided down one side. My outfit gave me confidence in her presence.

Doing my best to be friendly, I said, "It's nice to meet you. Evie and Jason, and well, Jeff are about the only friends I've made so far, so I'm glad to have another one." Julie didn't look thrilled at the idea of befriending me. I knew if I was going to make it here this summer, I needed to be on the inside.

"It's nice to meet you too. Have you seen Jason?" She asked in a tone that was telling me to back off. This girl looked like she had the power to verbally shred me.

"I haven't."

As if conjured up by our discussion, Jason appeared through the back door. He tucked his messy hair back behind his ears. His eyes appeared brighter because of his navy blue T-shirt, and his ripped jeans showed off strong thighs. His usual red wing boots completed his laid back, easy look.

He made eye contact, wandered over to us, and immediately sat down to my left. His thigh was pressed up against the side of my leg, and he put his arm across the back of the couch behind me.

He looked over at Julie and said, "Hey, Jules, what's up? Where's your boyfriend, the bookworm?"

He was taunting her. She pinched her lips together, clearly showing she didn't appreciate his remark.

22

"Leave her alone, butt-head. He couldn't make it this weekend." Evie was protecting her friend, and Jason just laughed.

"I don't remember seeing him last weekend either," he mocked.

Lowering my chin, I chuckled under my breath. I didn't mean to laugh at her. I was laughing at the dynamics between the two of them. They were so close, and it was obvious by their level of comfort with each other that they had so much love for one another. Knowing each other for as long as they did, they didn't even realize how obvious it was to others how much they cared about each other.

Jason didn't let up. "I'm just saying, you could do better than Ghost Writer. Get it? He's never around and he's a writer?" He laughed, and Julie stood up to leave. If she'd had a drink in her hand, I think she might have thrown it on him.

Evie stood up to follow her. "You can be a real shit sometimes, brother mine."

"I love you too, Evie!" he shouted at her retreating back and turned back to me.

I smiled slyly at him and "tsked" him, clicking my tongue. "You are incorrigible. How much have you had to drink?"

He breathed in heavily, and then exhaled. "She's a flirt, and she's silly. She deserves better than him. She's not mad at me, she's mad at herself."

He didn't seem too worried about Julie or her feelings. Following his lead, I put her out of my mind. Our conversation went back and forth, banalities about the house, and the weather, and who the new head coach for the Seahawks would be. I asked him if he was working on the 4th of July, and whether he had a bicycle or not. He asked me what I wanted to be when I grew up, and that made me laugh, since we had already addressed that, and I still didn't have an answer.

He sat staring at me, and I felt the heat from his leg against me. His arm had moved forward, and he closed the gap between us. It was that small forward movement that gave me courage to speak.

"Do you want to kiss me?" The words popped out of my mouth before I could stop them.

"I'll kiss you," he said, but made no move forward. "I'll kiss you when you have some other guy in your car."

"Excuse me? When I have another guy in my car?" I asked incredulously.

"Yes." He just sat there, smirking.

"Another guy...with me...in my car?" I paused in between the words to make sure I was communicating correctly what I thought I heard.

"Yes," he said, and offered no explanation. He said it with such calm I could not tell if he was joking or not.

"That doesn't make any sense." I sat up a little straighter, and hoped my disbelief was evident in my voice.

He scooted back and crossed his arms in front of him. "Of course it makes sense. I can't stake a claim if another guy doesn't see it happen."

"Are you kidding me right now?" This conversation had become so ridiculous. I'd thought he

24

was smug before, and I was willing to overlook it since I didn't know him very well, but this was humiliating.

I put my beer on the coffee table and stood up. "I think, Jason, I will repeat Evie's sentiment that you, are a butt."

Walking back to the kitchen, I grabbed a bottle of water from the cooler and went outside to the back deck. The sun had gone down and the fire pit was glowing bright and orange, the embers rising like fireflies. Evie and Julie must have left because I couldn't see them anywhere. I didn't know if Jason had followed me out or not, and I tried not to look around so I wouldn't accidentally make eye contact with him. The air was chilly and I could smell the dampness of the soil. I saw Jeff walking towards me and realized I had forgotten all about him.

He asked me, "Are you ready to go? I have the morning shift tomorrow and wanted to make it an early night." I crossed my arms and sighed at him. I wasn't really mad at him, but I wished he would have told me earlier when he'd asked for a ride. I tried not to feel put out, because really, I was somewhat grateful to have an excuse to leave.

I responded flatly, "Sure, let's go."

We walked swiftly to where my car was parked, and I buckled up after I got in. Jeff followed me, and after he was in, I started the car. I was backing out when I heard a thump, like I had backed into a tree. I slammed my foot on the brake to stop the car, and I heard a rap on my window. When I looked, it was Jason.

I rolled my window down and said, "Christ, Jason, you scared me. What do you want?"

"Are you ready?" He bent down to eye level and had his hands on the window ledge.

"Am I ready for what?" I really just wanted to get home.

He reached in and gently grabbed the back of my neck. His mouth was on mine before I had a chance to say anything else, and I softened under the maneuvering of his lips. They were soft, and he kissed me with conviction. He tasted cold, and when he opened his mouth against mine, it was like licking ice cream. I was so caught up in the gentleness I didn't realize when he backed away smiling. He still had his hand on the back of my neck and was only inches from my face.

He quickly kissed my nose and released me. "Dinner tomorrow? Seven p.m.? I'll pick you up at your place." I was too shocked to respond, so I just nodded. He nodded back, smiled, stuck his hands in his back pockets and backed up. I guessed I had a date with Jason Reid.

Waking up the next morning in my parents' house on the Island, I replayed the conversation I'd had with Jason to make sure it really happened. His words had taken me by surprise, so it was difficult to comprehend that I actually had a date with him that night. Not having his number to confirm, I planned my day as if he would arrive at seven p.m.

After staring at the ceiling for a good ten minutes, and running my plans for the day through my head, I tossed back the comforter and gasped at the chill in the house. As quickly as I could, I dressed in layers to go out for a run. I put on my running shoes, grabbed my iPhone, and headed out the back door of the house.

Slowly jogging down the steep driveway, I turned onto the dirt road that connected to Island View Place. A stone and iron gate had been built at the end of the road that was usually kept closed and locked during the winter months. Very few people lived down this way, and the gate was only accessible by homeowners. During the summer months there were so many families and home-owners here that it would stay open almost into October.

The wooded area was divided into twenty, one-acre lots, and the houses were surrounded by Cedar, Douglas fir and Hemlock. The trees were far enough apart that I could walk a path through them to visit the neighbors, and close enough together to give me privacy.

I ran along the road, my feet hitting the pavement in time to my music. I was listening to an eclectic mix of Cold Play, Kings of Leon, Nine Inch Nails and various other alternative and pop bands.

The crisp morning air was refreshingly cold on my face, and I could feel my lungs expanding with my efforts.

Running up a small hill and around a bend in the road, I was greeted by an extraordinary view of the mainland. Through a break in the woods, because of the road winding down to a small private beach, you could see all the way across the Sound. I ran down the road to the beach, where I took a few minutes to stretch and catch my breath.

The air smelled divinely fresh and clean, with just a hint of the salt water scent. It was quiet moments like this that I allowed my mind to clear, and I could think, or not think, about what I was going to do in the fall. I wasn't ready to leave the island, but I knew I wouldn't stay. It was expected of me to go back to school. I put my headphones back on to clear those thoughts, and ran back to the house.

The driveway was steep and the house stood proudly at the top. With three stories, floor-to-ceiling windows, and a slanting blue steel roof it was surprisingly impressive for a "cabin tucked in the woods."

As a family, we built it together. I remember my brother and I hauling two-by-fours from the back of my dad's truck to a pile in the woods as my dad would hammer nails into the framework and put sub-flooring in. I took some pride in the outcome, even though it wasn't technically "my" house.

Once the house was completely framed, we would stay there, sleeping on cots in sleeping bags. Before that we would sleep in a tent on the property or, depending on my mom's mood, at the resort.

In the mornings, my mom would make pancakes or oatmeal over a Coleman burner for breakfast, and then we all had to work until noon. After our work was done, my brother and I would run through the woods playing Indians or building forts in the forest. Sometimes we would take the aluminum dinghy out into Mud Bay. We would drop crab pots and row back out later to see if we had caught any crabs that might, or might not, pinch our fingers.

Shaking off my memories, I entered the house through the back door, careful not to rattle the stained-glass window my dad had hung on the back. It was beautiful, but constantly banged against the built-in glass window of the door.

I put on a pot of coffee and went to take a shower while it brewed. When I was dressed, I went back into the kitchen and noticed I had missed a call from my mom. I grabbed a cup of coffee and went into the living room to call her back. I settled in an oversized chair in the living room, facing the floor to ceiling windows that looked out into the woods of weeping cedars.

She answered on the first ring, so I guessed she was waiting for my call. "Hi, Mom, sorry I missed you, I was in the shower."

Launching right into her diatribe of instructions, I don't think she even heard me.

"Now, remember your father and I are coming for the July 4th holiday. I don't want any dishes in the sink, and there needs to be clean sheets on the beds."

When my parents weren't here, I slept in the Master Bedroom. It had the best view, and a deck that was perfect for reading or napping. Sometimes I would pull a futon out onto the deck and sleep outside. Now that they were coming, I would have to sleep in the downstairs guest room.

She continued, saying, "Your brother and Caitlyn might be coming too, so you may need to sleep in the bunk beds."

Maybe not the guest room, then. I understood I was the youngest and not married, but it still made me feel like a child when she relegated me to the kid's room.

"Ok, I get it Mom."

My mom amused me. She was always so organized and prepared. She probably already had a list of things I needed to do before they got here.

"And I need you to get a few things for us before we get there." And there you go. She was so utterly predictable, and I loved her for it.

"Hold on a minute, I need to get a pen." I walked into the kitchen towards the shelf where my parents kept all the pens, notepads, and a large glass jar filled with candy.

I grabbed a pen, took the cap off, and prepared to write. "Okay, go ahead."

She rattled off a few things, and asked me to get some wine from the local vineyard as well. After the list making was complete, she asked me how I was doing. It was always business first, but the love invariably followed.

"I'm good. Work is good, not too stressful. I'm making some money, and my coworkers are friendly. Some of the tourists are a little demanding, and it is weird to not be the tourist, but it's good. I'm good Mom."

"Have you seen the Reids yet?" she asked.

"Actually, I have a date with Jason tonight."

There was a brief pause on the other line. Thinking maybe she didn't know who Jason was, I continued, "Jason Reid? Mr. Reid's son?"

She hesitated for another minute before she added hurriedly, "Yes, yes, I know, sweetheart. Remind me, and is he the younger or older son?"

Ah. She hadn't paused because she didn't know who Jason Reid was. She'd paused because she didn't know which Reid he was.

"Jason is the youngest. Evie is the middle sister, and Nick is the oldest. Evie is really great. We've hung out a few times and I really like her."

"If I remember correctly, Jason was a bit of a wild boy. I seem to recall Martha mentioning she was always trying to get him to calm down a bit."

"What do you mean by 'calm down a bit?'"

"Oh, he was always just a free-spirit, really— jumping out of the barn into bales of hay as a kid, tractor racing, dirt bike racing. I think he was on a rodeo circuit for a while, but I don't know the specifics. Be careful sweetie, this could be just a summer thing for him." Her concern for me was endearing, and I assured her I would be careful.

"It's just dinner Mom," I assured her, and wanted this conversation to end, so I asked, "When will you and Dad Arrive?"

Her 'Mom tone' disappeared, and she switched back to her 'efficient voice.' "We are catching the five o'clock ferry Friday night, so we should be at the house by seven."

"Ok, I'm working during the day so I should be home to meet you."

"Invite Jason to dinner Friday night, it'll be good to see him," she said to me.

"We'll see how it goes."

"Ok, baby girl. You be good and we'll see you in a few days." My Mom was a southern girl, born and bred, and her quirky endearment never got old.

"See you Friday, Mom. Love you."

"Love you too, baby girl." She hung up and left me smiling.

It was still early in the afternoon, so I took a book and my coffee and went outside to read. The air felt cool and fresh, and after a short period of time, I fell asleep.

When I woke, the sun had dropped down in the sky and I was starting to get cold. It was getting close to time for my date with Jason, and I needed to get ready.

He hadn't told me where we were going, so I chose a rayon wrap dress with cap sleeves, and nude flat sandals. I usually had my hair pulled back in a ponytail or in a messy bun for work, so I decided to be different and leave it down and wavy.

At exactly seven o'clock, I heard his Bronco coming up the driveway. He had some kind of loud, dual exhaust system on the truck, so it wasn't difficult to hear him coming.

As he was walking up the steps, I saw he was dressed similar to every other time I saw him. It made me laugh because he was so unpretentious and laid back.

I opened the door, and he was standing there, smiling. "Are you ready?"

That one phrase made me grin, remembering the last time he'd said that to me.

"Yes I am." My response this time was different, and he dropped his chin to his chest and chuckled.

I stepped out onto the porch and shut the door behind me.

He put his hand lightly on my back, guided me to the truck, and said, "Let's go."

Walking around to the passenger's side, he opened the door for me.

"Where are we going?" I asked, once he had climbed into the driver's side.

He reached for his seatbelt and said, "You are so anxious. It's a surprise. Relax."

I glanced at him sideways, but he kept his eyes on the road.

We rode in silence for a few minutes with the radio playing Tim McGraw's "The Cowboy in Me." It reminded me to ask him about the rodeo circuit at some point.

When he got to the bottom of the hill and turned south, I realized he was driving towards the Island South End Marina.

There wasn't much there except a small grocer, a Whole Foods Café, and a fueling dock for boats. There were about 40 boat slips, and most of them were full this time of year. People who wanted privacy and quiet, as opposed to the resort lifestyle, usually came here. When we got to the dock, he jumped out of his truck and ran around to help me out. I saw him grab a bag of something out of the back. I was hoping it was dinner; I was starved.

"What's in there?" I asked.

"Wow! Nosy. You can't relax can you?" he responded.

"I am just making conversation. You haven't said a word." I said, trying to be self-deprecating, but I wasn't sure he bought it.

"That's fair." He paused long enough to acknowledge my statement, then continued, "Can you wait just a bit longer until we get where we're going?" He was smiling.

I tried not to look chastised and said, "Sure."

We walked down the dock, and when we came to a 60-foot cruiser, he leapt aboard. At first, I was confused as to why he was getting on the boat, but then I saw the name: "M&M's." I realized it was for Marcus and Martha, his parents.

He turned and looked at me expectantly, as if waiting for the questions he knew were coming. I remained quiet and raised my eyebrows at him. That got me a laugh, and an answer.

"Yes, it is my parents. Yes, I have permission. Yes, I can drive it. Yes, I brought you dinner. Yes, I will kiss you later." And with those parting words, he turned and disappeared into the cabin of the boat. I was starting to seriously crush on this guy.

He started the engine, backed the boat out of the slip, and headed out into the cove. It was a beautiful night, and without the city light pollution, I could see so many stars twinkling and satellites gliding across the sky.

Once we got out into deeper water, he dropped an anchor, disappeared down to the lower deck, and reappeared with the questionable bag. He pulled out a bottle of Lopez Island Chardonnay and a six pack of Blue Moon beer. I asked him about Julie.

"Julie's parents own the vineyard, but you knew that. Her family has been here since, like, 1890 or something." He looked upward to indicate he meant "forever." "We went to high school together, and were just, I don't know, together. It wasn't anything dramatically romantic. We just always seemed to be together. People thought we were cute as a couple, and eventually we agreed." He paused and glanced away.

He opened the wine and poured me a glass. "I feel more protective of her now, more than anything. She picks the shittiest guys, and they always leave her."

He paused again, and as he opened his beer, I commented, "I think she may feel differently towards you."

He looked up at me and responded, "No, I don't think so. She's just lonely, and I'm familiar."

I had thought I wanted to know about their relationship, but the conversation was starting to depress me, and the last thing I wanted to be tonight was sad. So, I changed the subject.

"I heard some crazy rumors about you."

He leaned back on the bench and put his arms across the back, dangling his beer from his left hand. "Oh yeah, and what would those be?" His eyes were crinkling, and he seemed amused by my statement.

I was flirting with him, and said, "You have left a trail of broken hearts all over the Island."

His eyes twinkled at me. "Not true."

"That you were on a rodeo circuit for a while?"

He threw his head back and laughed boldly. "Well, that one is *not* a rumor."

"Tell me about it."

"We all rode horses when we were young. Nick was a good rider, but not adventurous. I think he always felt like someone had to be the responsible one. Evie was a crazy-wild barrel racer." He rolled the word crazy, and his eyes, but the tone was full of admiration. "She was gorgeous on that horse, but she didn't love it the way I did."

He paused for a minute and stared vacantly at his feet in reflection. I could see the wheels turning in his head, and waited patiently for him to continue. "I would get out there in the arena and cut, and every time I just wanted to cut cleaner and tighter. It became everything to me."

"What is cutting?" I knew nothing about horses other than you needed reins and a saddle to ride one.

"It's an event where I try and get two cattle out from a herd, and I'm judged on my ability to handle the cattle and prevent them from returning to the herd. It is used a lot on ranches to get cattle out that need to be branded." He shared his explanation with so much enthusiasm. "My horse was a great cutting horse, and could anticipate what the cattle would do. I loved it."

I asked him, "Why did you quit?"

"The competition was fun, and I was really good." He puffed his chest and laughed at himself. Continuing, he said, "But the traveling was exhausting. Three years felt like ten, and I missed my family, so I decided to come home."

He looked so sexy leaning back against the seat, and I wanted to lighten the mood so I decided to flirt a bit. "And now here you are." I crossed my legs and smiled at him.

"And now here *you* are," he replied. "With me, on the boat, in that little dress." He moved closer. "Does the tie open your dress all the way, or do I just slip underneath it?" He was so silly and playful I couldn't help but laugh.

"Are you trying to change the subject?" I asked him demurely.

"I'm trying to get your dress off." He slid over next to me and lifted me into his lap. He was nuzzling my neck, so I relaxed and just let him kiss me.

Kissing Jason was sweet and fun. He was playful, and even though I knew he wanted to, he never really tried to get my dress off.

We ate bread and cheese and the fruit he had brought with him, and we continued kissing and drinking wine on the deck of the boat. When it started to get cold, I knew it was time to go.

He held my hand on the ride back to my house and after parking alongside my car, he got out and walked me to my door. I stood on the top step and he stood below me.

"See you tomorrow?" he asked.

"Yes. I work during the day, but I'll stop by after work."

"Ok, good." He was smiling up at me, so I leaned down and kissed him sweetly.

"Thank you for a lovely night."

"You are very welcome." He reached up and gave me another swift kiss before turning back to his truck. "See you tomorrow."

I waved at him as he backed out, and then I let myself into the house. He waited until I had shut the door gently behind me before he drove away.

The next day I worked the lunch shift and then headed down to the bar to see Jason.

Jason, Evie and a few others that I recognized from the party the other night were there, and I hung out with them playing pool and listening to music.

About an hour after I arrived, Jason came over and dropped down into the booth next to me, his arm reaching across the back of the booth. Leaning in close, he whispered, "You should let me come home with you tonight."

I turned to look at him, and his eyes felt like lasers piercing into me.

"I should not let you come home with me," I responded coyly.

"Seriously?" He was acting put off, but his cheeky smile told me he wasn't really upset. He laughed when he said, "You are killing me! You wore that flirty little dress last night and now you show up looking like this today. How can you deny me the opportunity to rub my hands all over you?" His voice was soft so others wouldn't hear him, but his tone was teasing, so I knew he wasn't really hurt. After work I had changed into flip-flops, jean shorts, and an off-the-shoulder tie-neck blouse. My legs were tanned from all the biking I had been doing, and I could tell by his covert glances that I was a distraction to him.

His soft tone was giving me butterflies, and I wanted to get to know him better. We had such a nice time the night before, and I felt confident he might not be just a fling, so I asked, "Why don't you come to dinner later this week? My parents are coming up, and my mom said I should invite you to dinner."

"You mentioned me to your mom?" And there it was, that cheeky grin that made him so attractive to me.

"I mentioned we had a date. She said it would be nice to see you and I should invite you to dinner." I stated this in a matter-of-fact tone so he couldn't tell how nervous I was.

"In that case, I will be there." He kissed me on the cheek, pulled his arm out from behind me and went back to the bar.

∞

Later that week, when my parents arrived, I helped them get settled. We unpacked groceries and duffle bags from their GMC Yukon, and I set the table for dinner. Jason was coming at seven o'clock, so there wasn't much time for me to get ready by the time we got everything unpacked.

Jason arrived just a minute before seven. I heard his truck engine echoing off the bay before I saw him drive up the driveway.

I greeted him at the door. He had brought a six pack of beer and a cheesecake.

"Cheesecake?" I reached out and took it from him.

"Doesn't everyone like cheesecake?" he asked. I opened the door wider so he could come in, and took the dessert from him.

My mom came around the corner from the kitchen and took him in a hug. "Jason, look at you! I haven't seen you since you were a little boy. How are you?"

It was a rhetorical question because she just kept rambling. "Come in, come in. I see you brought dessert. That was so thoughtful of you."

She asked about his parents as she slid the cheesecake into the refrigerator. "I would love to see them this summer. Your mom and I used to spend so much time together when you were younger. Of course, Shaye won't remember that, because she stopped coming up when she was 15. Or was it 14, honey? I don't remember." I looked at Jason and rolled my eyes.

Jason chuckled and responded politely, "They are doing just fine. As a matter of fact, my mom mentioned to me today they wanted to invite you over for dinner some night while you're on the Island."

She was pleased to hear that, and responded, "Fabulous! I will give her a call this week."

Walking into the kitchen, my dad made a beeline toward Jason and shook his hand. "Jason, how are you son?" At a few inches over six feet tall, my dad towered over Jason.

Jason didn't seem fazed at all by my dad's height. He shook his hand and said, "Sir, nice to see you." They wandered off into the living room while I helped my mom finish preparing dinner.

The evening went by quickly, and there was never a silent moment. Jason told stories about himself and Evie as children ,and we laughed about Evie making Jason have tea parties with her, and how she still incessantly teased him. He didn't talk much about Nick, so I knew very little about him. Jason mentioned he was doing an internship with a law firm in Seattle and was coming up this weekend, but other than that tiny bit of information, he didn't say much about him. I wasn't sure if it was because there wasn't much to say, or because they didn't get along. I would find out over the next few days.

After dinner, Jason and I walked down the steps into the woods where my dad had built an outdoor living area. Hanging from the branches were white Christmas lights that made it look like a fairy house. It was intimate and private, and I enjoyed the peace.

Sitting down on a gliding bench, Jason brought my feet up into his lap. I turned and leaned against the padded arm-rest as he spoke. "That was a really nice dinner. Your mom is really sweet."

I responded, "And my dad is really scary?"

He laughed and repeated, "And your dad is really scary."

We sat on the bench for about twenty minutes, holding hands, gently gliding back and forth.

He was making circles in my palm, and I asked him, "When is Nick arriving?"

He slowed his thumb and responded, "I'm not sure, maybe on the noon ferry tomorrow. He is driving up, and depending on ferry traffic, it could be later."

"You never talk about him. Do you like him?"

"I love him. He's my brother." He must have sensed that wasn't really an answer, and he sighed. "He's my older brother, Shaye, so he's... well, he's older.

He has his life in order, and he's a little over protective. It doesn't mean I don't like him."

I searched his eyes for more, but he wasn't offering anything else.

He pulled his hand out of mine and said, "I should get going so you can visit with your parents. Tomorrow is going to be a really long day."

We stood from the bench and walked back up to the house. He said good-night to my parents, and then I walked him to his Bronco.

"Remember, I am working the bar tomorrow night and it'll be a late night." There were going to be two bartenders on the fourth, especially since it was a weekend.

"I'll be fine. I think I'm going to hang out with Evie and Jeff."

He stopped in front of the door and opened it. He put his left hand around the back of my neck and pulled me in for a kiss. "Remember," he smiled mischievously, "Julie will be there too."

"Oh Yay! I love having holes burned in the back of my head." I laughed, and he climbed into his truck and shut the door.

I waved good-bye and wandered back up to the house. Tomorrow was going to be a very long day.

The fourth of July was a truly festive holiday on Lopez Island. The islanders were really proud of their firework show, and every year tens of thousands of dollars were spent on the fourth largest pyrotechnic display in Washington State.

When I woke that morning, I smelled coffee brewing, and I wandered out to the kitchen to get a cup. My mom was sitting out on the deck enjoying the morning, and I assumed my dad was getting his car ready for the parade. A few years before, he'd refurbished a 1935 Ford Tudor Sedan. It was black and silver with suicide doors and a greyhound hood ornament. Every year he drove it in the local parade. Second only to his love of the house, the "Silver Streak" was his pride and joy.

I took my cup of coffee and walked out to join my mom. "Good morning," I said to her, leaning down and giving her a kiss.

"Good morning, sweetie. Did you sleep ok?"

"I did."

"Jason seems nice."

I wasn't sure what kind of response she was searching for, so I simply answered, "He is."

Other than the caution she had expressed earlier this week, nothing had happened at dinner to cause her concern.

We sat in silence drinking our coffee, listening to the birds chirping and the leaves rustling from the light breeze blowing through the trees. The mood between us started to feel heavy, as if we were in a standoff to talk. I won, because she spoke. "Do you think you could be serious about him?"

"I don't know mom, it has only been a few weeks and two dates. It's just fun right now. Can we please not talk about this? It is too early to have a deep conversation."

She sighed and said, "Just be careful sweetie. He seems like a very nice young man, but there is something unsettled about him. I have the impression he is still searching for something."

"Well, that makes two of us, because I am certainly not making much forward progress in my life by living up here this summer." I knew she meant well, but it seemed as if she was projecting her feelings about me onto Jason. "I appreciate your concern, Mom, and I love you. I will be careful." I stood up, kissed her on the head and started back inside. "And now, I am going to help Dad get ready for the parade."

Walking out the back door, I followed the dirt path over to the garage. "Hi, Dad, you almost ready?" He was putting the American flags on the clips he had put over the windows.

"Hey, kiddo. I will be ready in about fifteen minutes. I need to grab another cup of coffee, and then we can head down to the starting point."

For such a big guy, he was acting like a kid at Christmas. He loved showing off his car and I couldn't blame him; it was a beautiful, sleek, sexy car.

I went back inside. I knew I wouldn't be coming back to the house today, so I grabbed my work clothes and a change of clothes for later, and threw them into a backpack.

After the parade, I would grab lunch with my parents and then I was working the dinner shift. My shift would start at three o'clock, so I would be off early enough to celebrate. Most of the diners would stay on the deck for the firework show, but I was meeting Evie at the pub.

Standing in the kitchen, my mom was washing out the coffee pot and putting away the toaster. "Mom, we're leaving."

"Okay, sweetie. What time should I meet you guys for lunch?" she asked.

"I have to be at work by three so why don't you meet us at Foolish Amy's Pizza Garage at one?"

Amy was born and raised on the island, and left after high school to attend Colorado College in Colorado Springs. Her college boyfriend went back to Denver after they graduated, and the next thing she knew he was getting married to his high school sweetheart.

She came back to the Island and started making pizza out of her house as a business. She would even deliver on the Island, zipping around in her 1989 SAAB Convertible.

Then she opened up a small diner in her parent's garage. Her brick-oven-cooked pizza grew so popular she was able to open up a restaurant in the strip, centered across from the grocery store and a few doors down from the bakery. The name came from her self-deprecating humor, and the fact that she started in her parent's garage.

"See you then," she replied.

Settling into my dad's car, Dad and I drove to the starting point of the parade. All the islanders loved to get involved in the parade. There were old cars, hippies on bikes, a lawn mower drill team, the school band, the local band on a flatbed truck, and various other decorated floats.

It was fun to ride with my dad and throw candy at the onlookers. When we got into town, I saw Evie waving frantically from the bakery, and I waved back.

The parade ended at the Post Office. My dad parked the car and we walked over to Amy's garage. My mom was sitting on the deck wearing white shorts, a blue T-shirt, and a white baseball cap with a sequined American flag on it. Her Jack Rodger's sandals showed off her red toenails. Her patriotic outfit made me smile. My mom loved the island, but she was a city girl at heart.

As I approached, I noticed she was deep in conversation with another woman, and didn't even see me standing near the table.

"Hi Mom," I said.

"Oh, hi, sweetie. Where is your father?" she asked.

"He got side-tracked talking to a friend across the street and will be over in a minute." I added sarcastically, "Or an hour, since he talks to everyone."

"OK. We can order without him if he doesn't show up soon." She pulled a chair out for me and said, "Why don't you sit down, Shaye. This is Mrs. Reid. You met her years ago."

I smiled and sat down between her and my Mom.

"It's nice to see you," I said kindly. "It has been a long time but I do remember you." She was a lovely lady. Her hair was cut in a short bob. It was black with streaks of gray. Evie had the same dark hair. Both Jason and Evie had her piercing blue eyes.

I stayed with them as they talked idly about the weather and the summer. I pulled out my phone and checked the time. I took a picture of the Sound and posted it to Instagram with the tagline, 'Just another day in paradise. Happy 4th.'

My dad finally approached from inside the restaurant. He walked up and gave Mrs. Reid a hug and a kiss on the cheek, and then sat down next to my mom. He grabbed her hand and waved down a waitress. The waitress nodded in acknowledgment and came over with water and menus.

Looking up at her, I asked, "What is your special pizza today?"

"We have a deep-dish pesto veggie. It is super good."

I opened my eyes a little wider at her elementary language, tried not to laugh, and then looked to my parents for approval.

They nodded their agreement, and I said, "That's sounds great! Make it a large, and I will have a diet coke, please."

She took our menus and went back inside.

Mrs. Reid was still with us. She'd mentioned earlier she couldn't join us for lunch, but would keep us company until the Pizza arrived. Nick was coming for the weekend and she wanted to get the house ready.

She directed her next question to me. "How are you enjoying your summer here on the Island?"

"I'm enjoying it. I'm waiting tables at the resort, and all the staff is really friendly. I've made a few new friends, and have hung out with Jason and Evie a few times." I just threw it out there to see what would happen. I certainly didn't want to keep anything a secret. She was also good friends with my Mom, so it wasn't as if I could pretend he didn't have dinner with us last night.

"Yes, your mom mentioned he had dinner with all of you last night. I am happy to hear that. He hasn't been back on the island very long, and I'm glad he's connecting with you." She took a sip of her tea, and raised her eyebrows a bit, a small smile forming on her lips.

A moment later, the pizza arrived and Mrs. Reid excused herself. She pushed her chair away from the table and reached for her purse hanging on the chair back. Looking at me before she rose, she said, "It was nice to see you, Shaye. I hope I see you again soon."

"It was nice to see you too."

She turned to my mom and said, "Colleen, lets plan dinner soon."

"That sounds lovely. See you soon."

My parents and I ate our Pizza and enjoyed the sunshine and quiet. Later today, when the sun started to set and the fireworks were preparing to go off, the Island would go a little crazy. This was a nice quiet break before the late-night partying began.

When we finished our lunch, they told me they were going to watch the show from some friends' house on the hill, and that I should be careful tonight.

"You rode here with your dad—how are you getting home?" My mom sounded concerned.

"I'll get a ride with Evie or Jeff. I will be fine, Mom, and if I need to, I will just stay the night with Evie." I hugged them both good-bye and started walking to the resort. It was only a mile from the town and took me fifteen minutes to get there.

The afternoon and early evening passed by quickly. People were coming in for dinner and staying for the firework show, so the tables didn't really turn.

My last table finished up about nine p.m., and now they were just ordering drinks. I asked if I could go ahead and close out their bill and transfer their drinks to the bartender. They were fine with that, so I closed out my shift and went to change my clothes.

Just as I was walking through the restaurant to the bar, Evie came bouncing through the door, saying, "Shaye, have you finished working yet?"

"I thought I was meeting you at the bar."

"I was anxious and wanted to make sure you were moving fast."

I chuckled at her enthusiastic behavior. "Just give me a minute to change my clothes."

"I'm going to get Jeff, and then I'll give you both a ride." She went towards the kitchen looking for Jeff.

"Cool. I'll meet you back here. But hurry up—I want to watch the fireworks from the bar." Being this far north in the United States, we had to wait until almost ten o'clock to start the fireworks show. It made for a long night, but left little time for partying.

Jeff, Evie and I rode down to the bar in her Jetta, and when we walked in, the bar was already crowded, mostly with locals. There were a few tourists, but they seemed to be friends of the locals, and already fit in.

The band was playing, and Jason was behind the bar serving drinks. He was joking around with the customers, and I could tell by the laughter and joy on his face that he was definitely in his element.

Julie was sitting on a barstool, and when she saw us, she stood on the rung and waved. I knew she was harmless, and I really hoped I would grow to like her.

"Hey, summer girl!" Jason saw me and smiled. "Cape Cod?" he yelled over the music.

I could barely hear him above the music, so I mouthed, "Yes, please." He looked so happy it made me smile. He wouldn't have any time to talk to me tonight, but I liked being near him anyway.

He put my drink in front of me and knocked on the bar with his knuckles indicating it was on the house. I smiled at him and wandered over to the table where Evie, Jeff and Julie were sitting.

Just as I reached the table, Evie jumped up and said, "Upstairs!"

Jeff stood up and made eye contact with Jason. He made a circle above his head, indicating another round, and then pointed upstairs. Jason nodded back, and we made our way to the side door that led to the steps to the upper outside deck.

The fireworks were just starting as we got up to the deck, and a waitress appeared with our drinks a few minutes later. As I stared up at the explosions of light and color, I thought of previous fourths when I was a child: riding in the back of a pick-up truck, parking alongside the bay and making a bed out of blankets in the back. The Fourth was always cold, and summer always seemed to begin the very next day.

Evie was screaming with delight, and Julie could be filing her nails for all the attention she was paying to the brilliance in the sky. Out of the corner of my eye, I saw Jeff staring longingly at her.

Interesting. I guess I had misplaced the affection. It was Julie he was crushing on. Laughing, I said to myself, "This should be fun to watch."

The firework show went on for about twenty minutes. Each burst was brighter and bigger than the last, with a huge finale of booms and lights that seemed to go on forever. Once the last explosive star faded out, we could hear horns and hollers from the boats in the bay. Everyone had enjoyed the show, and now was when the partying began.

"C'mon, let's go back downstairs. I want to dance." Evie grabbed my hand and dragged me down the steps and back into the bar. She signaled Jason for another round and we headed to the dance floor.

We danced and drank and danced some more. Later, when I reflect back on that night, I think I knew then that my world would change monumentally. All the events of my life had been so simple, so predictable. This summer had been a shift in my, and my parents, best laid plans, and I felt like I was going off-script.

I could see heads turning and heard, "Welcome home," and, "How are you doing?" The air around me thickened, and the hair on the back of my neck stood on end. Somehow, I knew Nick had arrived, and my reaction to his presence was visceral. I hadn't even seen him, and yet I knew something intense was about to happen.

When I finally turned and saw him for the first time, my chest constricted and I couldn't get a breath. Something in me shifted, and it was almost as if it was pre-ordained that my life would never be the same. Even if I had known the outcome of that summer, I couldn't say for certain I was mature enough to have made different decisions.

Staring at him, I tried to process my sudden, overwhelming emotions. Feeling like a weight just landed on me, I put my hand to my collar bone and took a deep breath. This was insane. He was beautiful. He looked like Jason, but taller, sexier and more masculine.

His faded jeans, gray T-shirt, and Eddie Bauer vest gave him that "Seattle look," and he would have been clean shaven if it wasn't almost midnight. I couldn't look away from his face, with his short, blond-tipped hair and kissable mouth—I was simply mesmerized.

His face was perfectly symmetrical, with a straight nose and a mischievous grin. His teeth were perfectly straight and white, and I noticed a dimple in his cheek. Everything about him was calm and strong. He appeared confident, but not arrogant.

If I hadn't already known he was studying law, I would have taken him for just another pretty, island summer boy. Guys were slapping him on the back, and the girls were working their way towards him, like moths to a flame. His eyes were sensuous and carnal, and he was looking at the girls as if they amused him. I could understand why they were hovering around him, waiting their turn for a hug and a greeting.

Panic rose in my chest, and I looked for a path out where I wouldn't run into him. I needed to get myself together before I met him, and I knew I would. The band kept playing, and Evie hadn't even seen him yet.

The irony of this moment was not lost on me, and I felt like I was being tested. Evie finally noticed that I had stopped dancing, and she turned to look in the direction of my gaze. She screamed in delight and ran to him, leaving me behind.

Taking this time to pull my thoughts together, I skirted around the crowd of people dancing and headed towards the bathroom. By the looks of Evie and Nick, they would be awhile catching up with people, and I would have time to calm myself.

When I reached the bathroom, I washed my hands and took a few calming breaths. Reaching for a paper hand towel in the silver dispenser to the right of the sink, I wet it under the faucet and then pressed the towel to my cheeks.

"What on earth, Shaye?" I said out loud. It had to be the alcohol. "How many drinks have you had?" I was talking to myself in the mirror and was thinking the number was five, but it might have been six. I couldn't add back that far.

I took another minute to center myself, talking myself back down to a normal place. I shook my arms out to my side and stood up straight. Taking one more calming breath, I headed back out to the bar. Scanning the bar and dance floor, I tried to locate Evie, Jeff or Julie. Julie, lord, I forgot all about her. Where had she gone? My thoughts started scattering again, and I needed to keep myself together. I couldn't think about her just then.

I saw Evie and Nick at the end of the bar, and I took another deep breath and relaxed my shoulders. Nick leaned against the wall with his left leg bent and his foot braced against the wall. Jason was not behind the bar, and I saw Pete hand Nick a Mirror Pond Pale Ale.

"Shaye? Over here!" Evie was smiling and waved me over. I was praying I wasn't shaking.

Evie was sitting on the very last bar stool so she could talk to her brother. There were two other guys talking with them. As I got closer, she jumped off the bar stool so she could yank me along faster than my snail pace. She hopped back up on the stool and pulled me to her side.

"Nick, this is my and Jason's friend, Shaye." The way she said "Jason" indicated we were more than friends. And the way he raised his brow indicated he understood her tone.

He was even sexier up close, and I knew my eyes were darting back and forth between him and Evie. I didn't want to look at him for too long.

Where Jason had piercing blue eyes that could appear cold, Nicks blue eyes were warm, and observant. The eyes gave away his intelligence, and he looked at me as if I was keeping a secret from him. He smirked, and I could tell he was going to get me to talk. The way I was reacting, I would have told him whatever he wanted to hear.

He smiled, reached out his right hand and said, "It is very nice to meet you, Shaye." I shook his hand and felt a rush from my palm, through my heart, and down to my core. I could have sworn I saw his pupils dilate, and his smile dropped just a bit. His hand tightened for a fraction of a second, and I felt a pull towards him before he released me.

When he spoke, I felt my skin warm. Everything about his voice washed over me, and I thought I was going to pass out. To make matters worse, I'd had way too many vodka cranberry drinks, and my tongue was stuck to the roof of my mouth. Nothing about this meeting made sense.

Evie prattled on, not noticing my discomfort. "Shaye is Mr. Richards's daughter. Daddy's client? She came up for the summer and is working at the resort."

He cleared his throat and appeared to have pulled himself together before he spoke again. "Right. Mom mentioned that to me this afternoon before I headed for the ferry. How is your summer going?"

Evie's prattling had given me time to pull myself together as well, and I said, "It's going really well. I'm doing a lot of biking and relaxing. It's really peaceful on the South end of the Island."

Jason appeared while I was talking and noticed his brother for the first time. "Nick! You made it! I was starting to worry you wouldn't make a ferry tonight."

He hugged him and asked if he could get him another beer. Nick responded he was good. Jason then said, "Did you meet Shaye? Our summer girl?" I rolled my eyes a bit, suddenly annoyed that he kept calling me that name. He made it sound as if I was disposable, but I just smiled.

"I have," he responded, and then continued with, "I didn't know we had a summer girl. What do we do with her in the fall?" Jason laughed and went back behind the bar. Nick winked at me and smiled, letting me know he hadn't missed the dismissive introduction.

Ordering another round of drinks and then grabbing my hand, Evie said, "C'mon, let's go dance." Turning back to her brother, she said, "Nick, behave tonight. I don't want to clean up the trail of broken hearts when you leave."

We danced a few more dances and had a few more drinks. I managed to avoid any further conversations with Nick but I knew where he was for the rest of the evening. As it neared one in the morning, I needed to get home. I walked up to the bar and waved for Jason's attention.

"Hey, beautiful, you okay?" He looked genuinely concerned, and I was grateful he didn't call me "summer girl" again.

"I think I had too much to drink. Can you call me a cab?"

"Nonsense!" he said to me, and yelled down to the end of the bar. "Nick, Shaye needs a ride home. Can you take her?" Nick was still standing in the same spot talking to a bearded guy without any shoes on. I died a little of embarrassment.

Speaking softly to the guy with the beard, Nick pushed himself off the wall and walked down to me and Jason. "Time to go, summer girl?" and I knew he was laughing at me.

"You don't need to take me home." It was bad enough being in a crowded bar with him. Being in the confines of a car would be so much worse.

"It's not a problem. I have been up since six this morning, and it was time I headed out too. Let me say goodbye to Evie, and we'll go."

I turned back to Jason, but he had already gone back to the customers. I crossed my arms on the bar and dropped my head to my forearms.

I felt myself nodding off on the bar when I heard, "Are you ready?" It startled me. I flipped around and Nick came into focus.

For a split second I thought he was going to kiss me. There was no way he could have known that is what Jason had said to me before he'd kissed me. So, I brushed it off. Although I might have sounded a little too breathy when I said, "Yes, I am."

He led me to where he parked his black BMW 5-series sedan. I slid into the tan leather seats and buckled in. Despite his appearance tonight, it suited him.

We drove in silence for a mile or two before I couldn't take it anymore. I blurted out, "So, I've been seeing Jason." He didn't immediately respond, so I continued, "Your brother? Jason? I've been dating him."

He laughed a little and said, "Yeah, I got that."

I couldn't tell by his tone if he was making fun of me, or if he thought my outburst was cute.

I gave him directions to the house and we went another few minutes in silence. I thought I heard jazz music on the radio, but I couldn't remember the name of the musician.

"It's just that I thought you should know who you were driving home." The alcohol was clouding my judgement and I could hear myself slurring, but I continued on. "I mean, as soon as you walked in the bar, I couldn't breathe and this has never happened to me before, and you are just so lovely and I feel like I need to touch you, and I can't because I'm seeing Jason, and well... you are just so lovely."

Nick looked at me quizzically, trying to gauge my level of drunkenness, I was sure. He had a smile on his face, as if he was endeared and equally entertained by my fragmented sentences.

I felt my head loll back on the headrest, and I think I heard him say, "You are lovely too," but I can't be certain because I fell asleep.

The next thing I knew, we were in front of my parents' house, and Nick was rubbing my arm, whispering, "Shaye, wake up. Shaye, you are home."

I slowly opened my eyes and saw him leaning towards me. I reached up to touch his face. His cheek was scratchy and warm, and I leaned over a little in my seat as if to kiss him. He was smiling at me with amusement, and I suddenly realized where we were. I snapped my hand back, rolled my head over and up, and saw my Mom on the back deck. I closed my eyes and groaned out loud, "Oh, God."

Nick chuckled and got out of the car. He walked around to open my door and helped me to the steps. He walked me up the steps to my mom, and said, "Good evening, Mrs. Richards."

She was very kind when she responded, "Hello Nick, thank you for bringing her home."

I think I said good night and then walked into the house. My mom followed me in and shut the door behind me. Stumbling towards the bathroom, I heard her say, "Honey, that wasn't Jason."

I shut the bathroom door behind me, responded miserably, "Yes, Mom, I know," and proceeded to get sick.

The next morning, I was quite certain that I had died, and that the banging coming from the kitchen was the clamor of the gates of hell being wrenched open. I slowly pried open my eyes, and immediately threw my forearm across my face to block out the light.

A few minutes later, my mom walked in with some water and an aspirin. "Hey, baby girl, you ok?"

I realized then that the banging wasn't coming from the kitchen: it was in my head.

"Yes, I'm fine." I groaned, and she sat down on the side of the bed next to me. She looked at me with concern.

"Stop looking at me like that. I just had too much to drink."

The bedroom window was open, so the cool morning air flowing into the room was helping clear my head. I rolled over and closed my eyes again. Lying on my left side facing the window, I felt the cool air on my face and inhaled deeply to get some of it into my body.

She shifted a little bit so she could get my attention and catch my eye.

"I know you did, sweetie, but you don't drink much, and then Nick brought you home and you got sick in the bathroom. It's unusual for you, and I want to make sure nothing bad happened last night. Did Jason do something?"

I groaned out loud and pulled the pillow over my face. "Oh, my dear God!" My mind had been a complete blank until that moment, and then it all came flooding back. "I met Nick last night."

"Yes, he brought you home. Do you want to talk about it?"

I was so grateful she was here now. I removed the pillow from my face and kept my eyes closed. "Jason didn't do anything to me. He was working. I drank too much, and Nick offered to bring me home. That's it." I could feel her staring at me, so I opened my eyes. "And I might have told him he was lovely." I groaned again, and she chuckled softly.

"Well, lovely he is, my word."

"Oh, for goodness sake, Mom."

She laughed at me. Changing topics, she informed me my father had left earlier in the day by float plane, and she was going to try and catch the three-thirty ferry.

"Why did he leave so early?" I hardly ever got to talk to my dad. Sometimes I wondered if he even had a clue what was going on in my life.

"He has a board meeting early tomorrow and wanted to be prepared." She stood to leave. "Get up when you can, and if you don't get up, I will come say good-bye before I go."

"What time is it?" My phone had died, and there wasn't a clock in this room.

Looking at her watch, she said, "It is just past noon."

"Noon!" I almost shouted, but I remembered just in time that it would hurt my head, so I whispered loudly. "Thank goodness I have the day off today. Okay, I will get up in a little bit. Will you please bring me my charger?"

She left the room and returned a few minutes later with my charger from the kitchen.

When the battery showed 5%, I turned it on and saw I had three missed calls. Evie called to make sure I got home all right. Evie called again and said she had talked to Nick and knew I got home all right. The third call was from Jason, asking if he could come down and see me later that night.

I was debating who to call first when a text came in from Jason asking if I was ok. I decided to call him first.

"Hey, how are you?" He sounded genuinely concerned.

"I am a little hungover, but I'm ok." I felt guilty talking to him. I knew I hadn't done anything wrong, but I still felt ashamed of my unexpected emotional reaction to Nick.

He asked me if I would like some company that evening. "I could bring some dinner and stay in with you."

"That sounds really nice, but can I take a rain check? My mom is leaving later today, and I really want to spend some time with her." I didn't tell him she was leaving within the hour, which made me feel even worse.

"Sure, I understand." He continued, "I'm thinking about getting a group together later this week to head down to the park and camp for the night. Does that sound like something you would want to do?"

He sounded hesitant, as if he were afraid that I would say no.

"I'd love to, thank you for inviting me." It would be good for the two of us to spend time as a couple with other people.

"Great! Well, I will let you go. Get some rest. Tell your mom I said hello, and I will catch up with you tomorrow."

I hung up and decided I was too tired to call Evie. Besides, she already knew I'd made it home safely. I nodded off again, waking when my mom came in to kiss me good-bye. "I love you, baby girl."

She ran her palm down the side of my face, and I said, "I love you, too, Mom," and fell back asleep.

∞

Later that week, leaning on the hostess stand at work, I saw Nick crossing the street to the resort office. I hadn't seen him or spoken to him since the fourth of July.

He glanced my way and waved. Resisting the urge to duck behind the desk and hide, I waved back. He stopped short, looked both ways, re-crossed the street, and jogged my way.

"I'll be right back," I said to Anna, the hostess. The lunch crowd had not arrived yet, so the restaurant was quiet. Still, I didn't want to have this conversation in front of her.

I met him halfway across the parking lot. His eyes were shielded by a pair of dark Ray-Bans, but I could tell he was smirking at me.

"Hello!" He greeted me with enthusiasm, and for a moment, I thought he was going to hug me. I stuffed my hands into my back pockets so I wouldn't reach out to touch him.

"Hi there. Where are you headed?" It was such a lame question, since I could see he had been heading toward the resort office.

Taking his glasses off, he tucked them into his T-shirt. "I need to meet with the owner about some legal papers for my dad. I left the internship in Seattle and decided to spend the rest of the summer here working for him."

Oh, this was really bad. I'd been counting on him leaving soon, and my heart picked up at the thought of him being around.

"Wow! Well, that's good. That's, well, great."

His grin slowly grew.

"I am sure he really loves having you around." I continued talking quickly so I could get this conversation over with. "Hey, listen, I wanted to thank you for taking me home on the Fourth. I know you didn't have to, and I am very grateful."

"It wasn't a problem. Shaye, it was my pleasure." The way he said 'pleasure' sent heat waves through me, and I felt my chest constrict.

"Great. Well. Again, thank you, and I will see you around." I turned to head back to the restaurant.

He reached for my hand to stop me.

His hand was warm, and I felt the heat run up my arm. I turned back and looked at our hands.

Just as quickly as he grabbed me, he dropped his hand and put it in his pocket. He looked slightly embarrassed when he asked, "Are you planning on camping at the park later this week?"

"Yeah, I think so. Are you?"

"I am. A friend of mine from the law firm is coming up. I thought it would be fun for her."

I almost gagged. Her?

"Great." I choked the word out. "And again, well, great. It should be a good time." I was stumbling over my words and feeling like a complete idiot. I started back to the restaurant again and pointed to the door. "I really need to get back, Nick. I'll see you later."

"See you later, Shaye." With that, he turned and headed to the office.

When I got back to the hostess stand, Anna was showing a group to a table in my section, so I didn't have time to really process Nick's news. I tried to ignore the butterflies in my stomach, and greeted the table with a professional smile, determined not to let him distract me from work.

The day passed too slowly. It was a typical gray Pacific Northwest day, and there weren't many tourists on the island that week.

I kept wondering who this girl was that Nick was bringing to the island, and then I had to keep reminding myself that I was with Jason. At least, I thought I was with Jason. We were talking every day and had met for coffee a few times this week, but nothing was official.

Later, when I was just getting off work and walking towards my bike, Jason pulled up in his Bronco. He jumped out, walked over to me and scooped me up. He carried me over to the rock hedge and set me down. He was so adorable I couldn't help but smile.

This was where I was supposed to be. This was who I wanted to spend my time with. Right?

He stood between my legs, stuck his face down into the crook of my neck, and started kissing me. "Yum, you smell so good." I could feel him smiling against my neck.

"I smell like a burger and fries."

He laughed and said, "Even better."

"What are you doing here?" I wasn't expecting to see him, and it was a happy surprise.

He backed up a bit. "I am on my way to work and wanted to check in with you. Are you camping with us at the park this weekend?"

"I am," I declared with a cheeky grin.

He stepped back from me abruptly, seemingly satisfied with my answer, and I almost fell off the hedge. "Great! I think Julie and her douchebag boyfriend are coming, and Evie and Jeff. Nick said he was bringing a friend from Seattle, and there are a couple of my friends from the rodeo who are thinking about coming up."

I was a little disappointed in the cast of characters, and didn't really like the way he referred to Julie's boyfriend; but I was still looking forward to camping, and hopefully getting to know Jason a little better through his friends.

My only reservation was that it was hard to pin down what I was to him. One minute he was in my face, cute and flirty, and the next we were group-dating. Maybe my mom was right: maybe this is just a summer thing for him. I don't know why that bothered me so much, but his abrupt pulling back from me just now felt like he was closing himself off.

"I'm on my way to work, but I can give you a ride down to the bay if you'd like."

"I'm fine riding my bike. Thank you though. Talk to you later?"

"Okay," he leaned forward to kiss me on the cheek. "I will pick you up Friday at 3 p.m.?"

I nodded and said, "Perfect."

∞

Friday arrived, and Jason pulled into the driveway a little after three. I saw him coming up, so I grabbed my backpack and walked out to meet him. He had called earlier to tell me he had the tent, the sleeping bags, and all the camping gear. "The only thing you need to bring," he had said, "is you."

As I walked around to the passenger side of the car, I noticed there were two people in the back seat. When I opened the door, I saw it was Nick, and a tall, dark-haired girl. She was wearing capris and a silk top. I really tried not to laugh, but I was sure she didn't know what camping was.

"Hi, I'm Shaye." I introduced myself when I got in.

Nick took over the introductions, "Shaye, this is Jackie Burnett. She is a colleague from the firm I was with earlier this summer."

"It is nice to meet you. Is this your first time on the island?" I forced myself to be pleasant and pasted a smile on my face. I didn't want her or Jason to pick up on the internal struggle I seemed to have with myself when Nick was around. There was no reason to be snarky to her.

Despite her choice of camping attire, her tone was enthusiastic and friendly when she responded, "It is. Nick talks about this place so much. I had to see it for myself. It is lovely, and I am so excited to sleep in a tent." Her enthusiasm made her sound kind of dense, but she was an attorney, so I knew that wasn't the case. Nonetheless, I promised myself I would make her feel welcome.

"I am sure you will have a great time. Jason, did you bring the supplies to make s'mores?" My voice came out way too manic, and I thought to myself that I really needed to calm down.

He turned and looked at me with his brow furrowed and slowly drawled out, "Yes," and then turned back to the road. I heard Nick chuckle behind me.

Jackie was talking in the back seat about some project at work. Every now and then, she would make a comment about the hay in the fields, or ask me a question about myself. I could feel Nick staring at me as Jackie talked. It was taking all my willpower not to turn around, smack him on the head, and tell him to knock it off.

Jason had picked a beautiful camp site at Spencer Spit State Park. It was just up from the beach, and had room for four to six tents. There were two picnic tables, and a fire pit with three logs around it for benches.

As soon as the Bronco was unpacked, I got to work setting up Jason's and my tent. I felt Nick's eyes on me, and it was racking my nerves. Jason and I had not slept together yet, and I still felt I wasn't ready. I wasn't sure how I would handle it if he had expectations for tonight.

Shortly after we arrived, Jeff, Julie and Evie showed up. Julie looked sad. Again. When she told us that her boyfriend was not coming, I started to wonder if the guy even existed.

Jason's friends rolled up right behind them in a Ford F-250 truck. They were loud, and their obnoxious behavior indicated that they most likely had started drinking earlier in the day. Jason greeted them, and there was a lot of back-slapping and hugging. He opened a beer, and one of his friends brought out a bottle of tequila.

"Jackie, are you doing ok? Can I get you anything?" I asked her more as a distraction for me than any actual desire to help her.

"I'm good, thank you."

Just then, Jason called out for her, "Jackie, come here. Come meet my friends." She smiled, grabbed a wine cooler from the Igloo, and walked over to where they were setting up the grill. I stood there dumbfounded as he ignored me and introduced Jackie to his friends. What the heck?

I scanned the campsite, and my eyes connected with Nick's. He just shrugged and took a drink of his beer. Nick was apparently okay with this, but I wasn't. I tried to shake off my feelings of disregard, and wandered over to join the group.

"Hey guys, I'm Shaye." I glanced around at all of them and raised my beer in a toast.

"Shaye, I thought you met everyone. Everyone, our summer girl, Shaye. Shaye…" He arced his arm around the circle and said, "Everyone. Then he laughed, threw his arm over my shoulders, and tucked me into him. I relaxed knowing he had not intentionally ignored me.

There were lots of laughs, and Jason's friends told all kinds of funny stories about him. Nick had been manning the grill and making sure everyone was fed. Jackie had joined in the boys' drinking games, and was getting really drunk.

At one point, I noticed her eyes were starting to close. Evie must have noticed this too, because she said to her, "Jackie, c'mon, let's get you to bed."

Apparently, Jackie agreed with her because she stood up and mumbled, "Ima, Ima… Evie? Yes. I… I think I need to go to bed now."

I think she was trying to say she was a bit drunk, which was an understatement. Evie wandered off with her, one arm wrapped around her waist for support.

They had only walked a few feet when Jackie ran crookedly over to the bushes and threw up. It was difficult not to laugh at her, but I didn't. I'd had my moments, and she would probably be embarrassed in the morning.

Jeff and Julie were sitting near each other talking quietly, and Jason was drinking and laughing with his friends. Nick was cleaning up the grill and washing our plates. Feeling somewhat disconnected again from the group, I grabbed a jacket and wandered off towards the beach.

The sun had set, and the air had grown cold. There were about twenty boats moored in the bay, and their lights were twinkling off the water. Over the water, I could hear laughter and music coming from the boats.

I sat on a piece of driftwood, took off my shoes, and buried my toes in the sand. The waves lapped at the shore about fifteen feet in front of me, and I enjoyed the ambient sounds of the night. I sat quietly, staring at my toes in the sand for a few minutes, and listening to the water and the laughter floating across it.

Then I heard, "Can I join you?"

I didn't need to look up to know Nick was standing behind me. His voice was soft and tentative.

I turned my head and said, "Of course."

He had also put on a fleece jacket and a beanie cap, and looked entirely too huggable. He was wearing khaki pants and Keen sandals. He sat down next to me, took his sandals off, and buried his toes in the sand next to mine.

I put my hands on my knees and rested my chin on the backs of them. I looked at our feet and tilted my head a little so that I could see him. "It feels good doesn't it? It's so cold just a few inches down."

The night and stars surrounded us, and the moment felt intimate. It felt like it was just the two of us here together, and I was resentful that I would eventually have to go back to the camp.

Reaching out, he put his right arm around me and pulled me to him. It felt strange to allow him to be so familiar, but it also felt right. I rested my cheek on his chest and closed my eyes. He felt so good and warm, and I wanted to stay there forever. It didn't even occur to me that this was wrong.

"Jason seems to be having a good time." He spoke, completely ruining the mood.

I sighed heavily and pulled out of his arms. I said, "Yeah, I guess so." Our bubble had already deflated, so I continued, "Jackie does too."

He laughed, and said, "Yeah, no, not so much now. She is going to be hurting tomorrow."

We sat in silence for a few minutes, staring out at the bay. Each of us in our own thoughts, but our bodies close enough to touch.

"What's your story, summer girl?" His voice was quiet, and the tone was lazy. It sounded to me like he would have leaned back, if he could have without falling off the log.

"You do not get to call me that!" I responded a little too vehemently.

He reached for me again and said, "Shhhh. Quiet." Chuckling as if he already knew the answer and wanted to tease me anyway, he asked, "Why not?"

"First of all, it's not your name for me. And second, I don't like it. It makes me sound..." I paused, searching for the right word, "...temporary." I hadn't really understood why I disliked the name until I said it out loud.

"Temporary to the Island? Or temporary to Jason?" His perception helped me be a little more honest with myself about the situation.

I untucked myself from his arm. "Both, I guess."

"Well, do you want to be permanent?" he asked me.

"Permanent on the island? Or permanent to Jason?" I wasn't sure what he was asking.

"I would have to say that if you are going to be permanent to Jason, the island is a given." He sounded sad, as if he didn't want to hear my answer. He also knew his brother well, and knew Jason would probably never leave the island again.

"I don't know right now," I admitted. "I need to think about finishing school. I had started the summer knowing I would go back in the fall, but I wasn't expecting this." He didn't ask me what 'this' was. I don't know if I expected him to ask me what I meant by my statement. If I thought he would give me clarity with an answer, I was wrong.

"You might want to figure it out." He looked out at the water and his tone was aloof. He took a drink from his beer. It angered me that he sounded so detached.

"Are you the vetting crew deciding if I should be with Jason or not?" I didn't do a good job of hiding my displeasure at his tone.

"No, it's just that you seem like the kind of girl that could break his heart. He's an island boy, and needs an island girl." He stated this so matter-of-factly I couldn't tell if he even cared or not.

Now I was pissed off. "I'm not asking for your opinion."

"And yet, here I am, giving it."

It was starting to feel like he was lashing out at me for not bending under his verbal assault.

"Don't be an ass, Nick. I was just starting to like you." I felt tears pricking the back of my eyes, and it was all I could do to keep them from falling.

Our feet were still buried in the sand, and his leg was pressed up against mine. He was looking at me, and my fleece was all of a sudden too hot.

"I think, Shaye," he leaned in, put his mouth to my ear and whispered, "that you started to like me a while ago." He was so close I could feel his breath as he spoke. If I turned my head just a few inches, I could put my lips to his. I felt entranced and isolated in this intimate bubble we had created.

"And that is the reason you need to tread lightly with his heart." His words were like ice water, and I jerked back.

I stood up and brushed the sand off my legs. Grabbing my shoes, I turned and said, "I'm heading back. You should see to your girlfriend."

When I arrived back at the campground, I saw that everyone had turned in, except Jason and his friends. They were laughing heartily, and the Jack Daniels was almost gone.

"I'm turning in," I said to him.

He responded with slurred words, "Ok, 'night beautiful."

Once I was in our tent, I undressed and put on a pair of flannel pajama bottoms and a T-shirt. A short while later, I heard Nick say good night, and he went to his tent.

I put my fist to my chest and pulled my knees up. I was fairly certain nothing was going to happen tonight with Jason. I was also most definitely certain liking Nick was going to be detrimental to my heart.

The month of July flowed by slowly and easily. Flocks of people came to the island and stayed for weeks or weekends. Nick was around, but working with his dad during the days, so I barely saw him. Not seeing him gave me some breathing room to get to know Jason better, to spend time with him. I also had time to put this relationship triangle in perspective. Maybe I had just imagined the feelings between me and Nick. Maybe they were only one-sided.

Jason and I biked and kayaked, enjoying the beautiful island weather together, and I felt calm when it was just the two of us. He was funny, and not so gregarious when we were alone. I felt as if he felt safe with me, and didn't need to try so hard to be engaging.

One night near the end of the month, Jason and I had dinner together at the resort. It was a high tide, and the air was still warm. The sun was setting, and the breeze smelled like salt water, hyacinths, and the wild sweet peas that grew alongside the roads all across the island. I have always loved the look of them.

We were sitting on the deck of the Islander staring out at the harbor and talking about the tourists. I had my feet in Jason's lap, and he was doing his best imitations of Evie and Julie. Strings of fairy lights across the deck were creating a warm, inviting ambience.

"Speaking of Evie." I sipped my wine, enjoying the relaxing foot rub Jason was giving me.

"Are we speaking of Evie?" Jason laughed at me and squeezed my foot.

"I think she has a thing for Jeff."

"Can we not talk about that? I don't want to think about my sister having a crush on anyone." He smirked at me.

"I think Evie has a crush on Jeff, but I saw Jeff and Julie talking one night, and they looked really close."

Jason looked thoughtful for a minute and then sighed. "Poor Evie. Julie does this all the time, goes after every new guy, regardless of who she crushes in her path. I know it's not intentional, and Evie doesn't see it because Julie is her best friend, but just once, I would like Julie to meet someone emotionally stronger, and intellectually smarter, than her. Someone that won't put up with her shit."

I had nothing to say to that, since I wasn't Julie's biggest fan anyway. It was safer if I just kept my mouth shut.

We sat silently for a while, listening to the night sounds and the chatter from inside the restaurant bar.

Jason cleared his throat and said, "I'm thinking about maybe moving to Seattle in the fall and taking classes at a community college."

This was not the conversation I had been expecting, and I didn't immediately respond. I waited to see if he would continue; I didn't need to wait long.

"It has been a fun summer, but I think it's time I started thinking about what to do next. One of my Dad's clients owns an airplane charter company, and he mentioned he could get me on as a line guy while I get my business degree."

I didn't know much about airplanes, but I knew that corporate charters were very expensive. Jason seemed a little unsure about the opportunity, though, and I wasn't entirely convinced he really wanted to leave.

"What is your hesitation?" I asked him.

He responded quickly, "None. I think it's a great idea." Pausing, he then added. "Do you think we could keep seeing each other in Seattle?" He was so endearing and sweet. His tone was a long way from the cocky guy I'd kissed at the beginning of the summer.

I pulled my feet off his lap and leaned over to whisper, "I would love that."

Part of me felt nervous about his declaration. I had not yet decided what I was doing in the fall, or even how I felt about him. I felt a bit like I was betraying him with my words.

For the most part, I had enjoyed spending time with him, but he was still running hot and cold. We weren't together every day, but people on the island knew we were dating.

I had seen him unexpectedly at The Grind, a few days prior with Julie, and since he sometimes worked the bar late at night, I felt like there were things he was intentionally keeping from me. The fourth of July flashed through my mind, and I saw the moment when I couldn't find Julie, and Jason wasn't behind the bar.

I wanted to see him in Seattle, but I didn't want him to make decisions for himself based on us.

We continued to talk while we finished our dinner, and then he drove me home. Walking me to the door of my house, he reached around me and put his hands on the back of my shorts. With his mouth in the crook of my neck, he said, "You should let me stay."

I still wasn't ready for that level of intimacy with him. I wrapped my arms around his shoulders and said, "Soon."

He started kissing his way up my neck to my ear, down my cheek and jawline. His kisses were feather soft and warm. When he reached my lips, I sighed and relaxed into him. Pulling his hands up to my hips, he drew me gently to him. I tightened my hold on him, and then he slowly released me.

"Okay, then. I think that about does it for tonight." He laughed uncomfortably and ran his hand through his hair. Strands were sticking up, making it messier than it already was.

I smiled coquettishly and said, "Okay, then."

He turned to leave, smiled back at me and said he would see me the following day.

I woke the next day to pouring rain. It hit the steel roof like ping pong balls, and I didn't think it would let up for most of the day. Since I was working the lunch shift again, I decided it would be best if I drove my car to work.

The grey sky darkened the house, even at eight in the morning. Nestled in the trees, the house felt cocooned and sheltered from any light. Sometimes I liked days like this. I wished I could waste the day curled up with my coffee and a good book. But not today. Today I had to get to work.

As I had predicted, the rain did not let up, and the restaurant was slow. I left work a little after four and stopped in at the bar to say hi to Jason. It seemed that everyone else had the same idea.

Evie had closed the bakery early and was sitting with Jeff and Julie in a booth. Nick was there playing pool with a couple of local construction workers who were supposed to be laying concrete, but couldn't because of the rain.

I hadn't seen Nick since the camping trip, and my chest constricted at the sight of him. He wore brown Sperry loafers, jeans, and a blue camp shirt. The shirt was untucked, and he had rolled up the sleeves. The top two buttons were undone, and I could see his collar bone. He leaned over the pool table to take a shot. I got a glimpse down his shirt and could see the hard cut of his chest.

My mind went blank, and I found myself staring at him. I was so drawn to him, and it was confusing me. Dragging my eyes away, I knew I couldn't stay long that afternoon, or I would say something stupid and make a fool of myself in front of everyone.

He looked up and saw me, gave a jerk of his head in greeting, and raised his beer to his mouth. Staring at his mouth, my own started to water. I saw his eyes crinkle in understanding.

"Hey, Summer Girl, did you bring the rain today?" Jason asked me light-heartedly. He startled me out of my lustful haze.

I sat down on one of the bar stools and tried to act normal. "Right? I think I am going to head home shortly and make it an early night."

"Sure thing. Cape cod for you?" He was already mixing the drink for me.

Evie walked over and hugged me from behind. She rested her cheek on my back and wrapped her arms around me. I reached up to hold her hands in front of my chest.

"Where have you been? I've missed you." She had obviously been drinking for a while because I'd just seen her a few days ago, but she made it sound like it had been forever. She released me and stepped to my side. "Jason, I need another Guinness."

"No, Evie, I don't think you do." He laughed and poured her another one anyway. "Last one Evie, and then Jeff is taking you home."

She slurred her words a bit, but for the most part was just having a good time. "You are the best brother ever!" She grabbed her beer and asked me to come join them.

"Ok. But I can't stay long. I've had a long few days, and I really just want to tuck in." I didn't feel bad about saying that. I knew I would be fast asleep in a few hours.

I stayed for about forty-five minutes, talking to some of the locals at the bar, and then I said my goodbyes. Nick was at the other end of the bar. We hadn't talked to each other at all. He caught my eye as I was standing to leave, and I saw a question in his eyes. I chose to ignore him and walked to my car.

About ten minutes later, my car started slowly rolling to a stop. I panicked for a moment before realizing I'd forgotten to fill up my tank. The needle read E. I had run out of gas. I lowered my head to the steering wheel. "Crap, crap, crap!" I said in frustration.

I had been riding my bike so often I had forgotten about filling up my gas tank. There were only two gas stations on the island: one at the south end, and one at the grocery store. I was right in between both of them. It was still raining, and the last thing I wanted to do was get out and walk in either direction for gas.

I pulled my phone out of my bag and called Jason to see if Jeff had left yet with Evie. At least my phone still had a charge.

"He left right after you, Shaye." Jason said. I heard him yell down the bar, "Hey, Nick, Shaye rank out of gas on Hillcrest Road. Can you go get her?"

"Jason, no, it's fine. I can walk." The questioning look Nick had given me earlier was too much for me to process, and I didn't want to be near him right then.

I heard Nick mumble something in the background, and then Jason was back on the line. "Nick will be there soon. He's going to stop and get you some gas."

"Okay. I will be here. I'm right across from the old school house." I knew Nick would see my car, but I felt like I needed to say something that didn't give away my trepidation.

"See you tomorrow," Jason said, and hung up.

Fifteen minutes later, Nick showed up with the gas can. He must have left right after I hung up. It had stopped raining enough that I could get out of the car to talk to him.

"Thank you so much!"

His eyes were smiling at me as he said, "You are welcome. But you should make sure you fill it up first thing tomorrow."

He unscrewed the gas cap and started pouring. He had put on a blue fleece pullover, and he looked so good in it I wanted to hug him.

I was trying not to wring my hands. "I've been riding my bike most of the summer. It didn't even occur to me the check the gas level."

"I see that." He was patronizing in an endearing way, and he smiled at me.

When the can was empty, he tapped the spout on the filler neck so that he wouldn't spill on my car.

"I will follow you home. Make sure you get there safely." He wasn't flirting or angry, just resolute.

"Ok. Thank you."

He followed behind me to my house and pulled his car in behind mine.

I stood on the cement slab of the lower deck, and watched while he stepped out of his car. I felt a tension between us, but it wasn't uncomfortable.

"I was going to put some pasta on for dinner. Would you like to stay?"

"That sounds good. Thank you." He smiled, put his hands in his front pants pockets, and followed me in.

"Do you want me to open a bottle of wine?" He was pulling his jacket up over his head, and I watched as he turned and hung it on the coat rack. I saw a glimpse of his abs when his jacket pulled his shirt up slightly, and I felt myself get warm with longing. This was probably a really bad idea, but I couldn't bring myself to ask him to leave.

Instead I responded, "That would be great, thank you."

I told him where the glasses were. I could feel him behind me in the kitchen, and the room felt small and intimate.

I was standing at the counter putting the pasta in the pot when he came up behind me and put my glass on the counter to the right of me. His front was just inches away from my back, and I could feel the heat from his body. It was making me dizzy, and I was having difficulty focusing.

"Be careful. Don't spill your wine," he said softly and then backed away. Out of the corner of my eye I saw him walk into the living room.

"This is a beautiful house. Your dad built it, right?" he asked in a more conversational tone. All flirtation was gone, and for a moment, I was relieved. I needed time to get my thoughts together.

Grateful for neutral conversation, I spoke loudly so he could hear me, "He did. Well, we all did. My brother and I would carry the plywood and beams. We had to work until noon, and then we could go play until dinner. I still take credit for building it, too."

The pasta was cooking, so I grabbed my glass of wine and went into the living room to join him. I took a seat on the couch and watched him.

"I remember you," he said. "Your dad was at the house doing some business with my dad. You had a friend with you. I guess you must have been about twelve? I almost ran over you on my horse. I came around the corner, and you were in the middle of the road. You and your friend had gone for a walk."

"Oh my god! That was you! We thought we imagined you. You came around that corner so fast, and then disappeared into the woods. We thought we could follow you, but we lost the path." I laughed, remembering what we'd thought of him. "We were enthralled with you. You looked like a Norse god sitting on that horse. How funny!"

He watched me intently. We were staring at each other, and I realized my mistake in telling him my thoughts. I had become too comfortable with him.

Unfolding my legs from underneath me, I stood from the couch. "I'm going to check on dinner."

In the kitchen, I grabbed two large bowls from the cupboard, and when I turned, Nick was there to take them from me. He held them while I dished out the pasta, which I dressed with a sundried tomato and olive oil sauce.

We took our bowls and our wine to the kitchen table, and he lit a candle. We made small talk about the eclectic collection of rooster sculptures and art that my parents had, and he told me about growing up on the island. He asked me what I was studying in school and we kept the conversation relatively safe.

After a few minutes, he asked me about Jason.

"What do you want to know? He's your brother, don't you talk to him?" I tried to keep my tone light and non-committal. Spinning up some pasta onto my fork, I took a really big bite. If I had food in my mouth, I wouldn't be able to say very much.

"Are you happy with him?" His right hand was swirling his wine glass, twisting it back and forth with his pointer finger and thumb, and he was leaning back in his chair.

His hands were distracting, and I was transfixed with the movement. His fingers were long, and my eyes traveled up to his forearms that were sprinkled with blond hairs. I had heard him, but I didn't want to answer, so I took a sip of wine and twirled my pasta around in the bowl. Finally, I put my fork down, and the stainless steel clinked against the bowl.

"It's only been a few weeks, Nick. He is a great guy, and we have fun together." I leaned back in my chair, mirroring his position. Someone looking in through the window might imagine we were gearing up for a fight.

He leaned forward. "That's not what I asked you. Are you happy with him?"

Pausing a moment before I spoke, I realized I wasn't going to answer, so I stood up and said, "Are you finished?" I didn't wait for his response before I grabbed his bowl and took our dishes to the sink.

He must have sensed my need for some space because he stood up, picked up his wine glass, and wandered into the living room. Evidently, he found the stereo, because I heard Diana Krall playing, and knew he'd found my playlist.

I took my time washing the dishes and putting them in the drying rack before I grabbed the bottle of wine and my glass and went into the living room.

He was facing the wall of pictures again. I sat down in an oversized chair and tucked my legs under me. There was a picture of me on the wall holding an eighteen-pound King Salmon. My dad took the picture when I was fifteen.

"This you?" He jerked his head towards the picture.

I laughed and said, "Yes. My dad took me to Alaska for a fishing trip. I caught that on my first day."

"It's cute. You look cute." He corrected himself— in case I thought he'd meant the fish.

Smiling, I said, "I got that."

He took a few more minutes to look at the pictures, and then turned towards me. For just a few moments, he just looked at me and said nothing. I did my best to hold his gaze and took a sip of my wine.

"He doesn't really seem like your type," Nick said. The comment didn't catch me off guard because we hadn't closed the conversation from dinner.

I looked at him seriously and said, "The fish?" Then I laughed.

"You know what I mean." He sounded displeased with me.

I was getting annoyed with the questions about Jason. "I don't think you know me well enough to know what my type is."

"I think someone with a bit more stability and drive would suit you better." He put his left hand in his front pocket and widened his stance a bit. It was an arrogant pose; I felt a chill.

"That's kind of a judgmental thing to say about your brother, don't you think?" I said, reaching to my right to grab a blanket.

"I love my brother dearly, but he hasn't been the most motivated individual. He drinks too much, and he values partying with his friends more than thinking about his future."

"Maybe he figured you had the responsible characteristic covered." I snapped at him. I had already thought all the things Nick was saying, and yet I still felt like I needed to defend Jason.

"Maybe." He relaxed his pose and lowered his gaze. "I know he's the baby, but I think my mom coddled him too much. She always allowed him to run loose. My dad was much more difficult on me and Evie."

"Do you resent him?"

He responded quickly. "Not at all. I just want him to be happy."

I felt a surge of adrenaline as I asked, "Wouldn't I make him happy?"

He raised his eyes to mine and stared intently. "I'm sure you would make anyone happy."

My breathing sped up and I felt like we were treading on dangerous ground. I didn't break eye contact with him, and he continued "The question is, would he make you happy? You seem a little more grounded than him."

I chuckled. "That's funny, considering I dropped out of college and have no idea what I am doing in the fall."

He continued to look at me, this time with kindness, and something else I couldn't name. "You'll figure it out, Shaye."

My name sounded reverent on his lips; my chill was suddenly gone, and the blanket felt too warm. Other than the music playing softly, neither of us made a sound.

He walked slowly towards my chair and sat on the coffee table in front of me. I felt hunted, but I couldn't look away from him. I could see my chest rising and falling in front of me, and still, he held my gaze. His legs spread, he rested his arms on his knees, linking his hands.

My head started to spin, and I felt the need to say something. "Well. Thank you for... thank you for helping me today." I tried to sound casual, but it was coming out choked, and I heard a sound come out of the back of my throat.

Nick slowly leaned forward. "You are very welcome, Shaye."

"I, well, thank you again. I will walk you out."

It was an empty threat. I tried to unfold my legs, but Nick was too close. I couldn't stand up without bumping in to him.

"No, I don't think you will, Shaye." He leaned in closer, and I think I stopped breathing.

I wanted him to kiss me right then, but I waited to see what he would do. He slowly took my wine glass from me and set it on the table to my left. When the glass was firmly on the table, he leaned in to kiss the side of my neck.

I closed my eyes. It felt decadent and sensual, and I let my head roll back. His mouth slowly moved up to my ear, feather soft kisses drowning out any reasonable thoughts.

He kissed his way to my cheek, cradling my other cheek with his hand. His mouth was soft, and his lips were branding me. He kissed the corner of my mouth, and then slowly backed away.

Taking my other cheek in his right hand, he looked me in the eye and said, "Tell me to stop."

There was no way I could find the words to tell him to stop. I shook my head slightly and said, "No."

"I'm going to kiss you, Shaye." The way he said it made it seem like he was promising so much more than just a kiss. It sounded as if he was going to give me the world.

I responded, "Yes."

Taking that one word as permission, his mouth crashed into mine as he kissed me hungrily. He plunged his tongue into my mouth, and I felt dizzy and hot. He tasted like wine and sin, and he was delicious. It wasn't soft or gentle. It was hard and full of life and passion and promise. It seemed like he had been restraining himself all night, and now he was free to take what he wanted from me.

There was nothing that would stop this onslaught of sensation. This had been building since we shook hands in the bar, and I felt as if we had been waiting for each other forever.

Kissing his way down my neck, he hesitated—as if realizing he didn't want to rush this.

Slowly, he unbuttoned my shirt and pushed it aside. He wrapped his arms fully around me and buried his head in my chest, kissing and nipping his way down my front. My bra unsnapped, and I felt him pause.

He sat back and gently pulled my shirt and bra from me. I felt exposed and worshipped at the same time. He held his hands gently at my sides, looking at me sweetly as if giving me permission to stop. I leaned back in the chair and simply said, "Please."

He undid my pants and slid them off of me. I sat up a bit so I could pull his unbuttoned shirt down his shoulders.

He was kneeling in front of me now, and I once again reclined back in the chair. He kissed slowly down my belly, and rubbed his fingers under the top of my panties. My skin was hot and flushed, and I wanted to touch every inch of him at once.

I reached out to unbutton his pants, and he stood to pull them down. His boxers went with the pants, and I inhaled sharply. He was beautiful, and right now he was mine.

Kneeling down again in front of me, he blew softly on my belly. "Tell me what you want, Shaye," he said as he moved his mouth lower. His left arm circled me, and his right hand glided up the outside of my leg. He bent down and licked the inside of my thigh.

"You, I want you."

That was all he needed to pull me from the chair to the floor and rip my panties off with both hands. There was no waiting. He pushed into me, and I gasped, throwing my head back and wrapping my arms around him. His body was a cocoon above me. I felt small and protected and completely consumed. He immediately slowed and held me.

Cradling my face, he kissed me chastely and said, "You are so beautiful. So lovely." I opened my eyes to him and my heart lurched. The words I had spoken to him previously were now so clear I almost cried.

Moving more urgently, he repeated, "Tell me, Shaye. Tell me what you want."

I felt a bolt of lust. "You. Just you. I want you." My words were hitching in my throat and they became a mantra. "I want you."

In my one moment of sanity, I realized this was why I hadn't been with Jason. I didn't feel connected to him like I did to Nick. I couldn't explain it. I didn't understand it. But being with Nick was consuming me. With Nick, I felt like I had come home. I couldn't tell where he started and I stopped.

As he moved faster, I felt like I was burning up. Every nerve I had was being touched, and I felt like I was going to explode into a thousand pieces.

Nick reached down between us to touch the sensitive spot that would push me over the edge. I tensed, and he put his mouth to mine, capturing my scream. My orgasm crashed through me, and he followed right after. Every part of me felt shattered, and I thought I would have to figure out how to put the pieces of my heart back together.

He fell onto me, and then gently placed kisses all over my cheeks, my eyes, my lips, and my chin.

We lay on the floor quietly, catching our breath. When he'd recovered, he stood and pulled me up, wrapped the blanket around me, and carried me to the couch. He looked at me thoughtfully and said my name softly. Then he got up and walked down the hall to the bathroom. When he returned, I was crying.

"What have we done?" I pulled my knees to my chest.

He sounded abrupt when he said, "We don't need to talk about it right now. Let's just be together, ok?" He was pulling up his pants. "We don't need to figure this out tonight."

Nick knelt in front of me, running his palm over my hair and kissing my head, as my phone rang. I pushed him to the side and got up to answer it. It was Jason.

"Hi, yes, I got home safely. Sorry I didn't call you." I listened to him talk for a minute, and then he asked for Nick. "Yes, he's right here."

I handed the phone to Nick, "It's for you."

"Hey man, you off work soon?" He was acting like hanging out with me was totally normal, although, I couldn't exactly expect him to say, "Hey man, I just had sex with your girlfriend on her living room floor."

Jason must have been talking because Nick was silent and staring at me. His stare grounded me in place in front of him, and I stared right back.

He continued looking at me as he said, "Ok, I'm headed back now. See you in a bit." He clicked the end call button and handed the phone back to me.

"You have to go." I didn't know if I was asking a question or making a demand. Either way, I knew he was leaving. Now that I had come out of my sexy fog, I knew it was for the best.

Nick had finished dressing and was walking to the door. "We'll talk later, Shaye." He looked me in the eye to make sure I understood what he was saying. "Shaye? We'll talk later, OK?"

I nodded and followed him to the door to walk him out. When he had driven away, I shut the door and said, "Good night, Nick."

I woke the next morning and tried to focus on me and what I needed to do next. I didn't want to think about Nick, so I started to think about going back to school.

I thought I might have missed the deadline for fall registration, so I decided to ride my bike into town and head to the library, where I could use the computer to confirm what I needed to do to sign up for fall classes.

I arrived at the library just as it was starting to rain. I logged on to one of the computers to check my student status, and read that I had two more weeks allowed for late registration.

Checking the class schedule, I found the ones I needed and made a note to sign up for them later. It was raining harder, so I wandered the aisles looking for a book to read while I waited for it to stop. Curling up in a chair by the window, I saw Nick's BMW pull up.

He got out of his car and jogged up to the door. As he pulled it open, I felt a gust of wind come in with the cold. He walked in and shook the rain off his coat. He turned to his left and saw me by the window. I pulled the book up to cover my face, knowing he had already seen me. It was futile to ignore him, but I tried. When I peeked over the top of the book, he had taken the seat across from me and was grinning.

"I saw your bike," he said. "Do you need a ride somewhere?" His eyes were crinkling in at the corners, and a slight smile was on his mouth. My mouth went dry, and I stared at his lips, thinking about how soft they were and how badly I wanted him to kiss me.

I did my best to resist him. "No, thank you. I am going to wait it out, and then ride home." He chuckled softly because this was the Pacific Northwest, where it never seemed to stop raining.

Standing up to leave, he said, "Ok, then," and turned to walk out.

I was left staring at his back, utterly confused by what had just happened. He hadn't said anything about the night before.

I wanted to scramble to the window, but instead, I watched him covertly, so he wouldn't see me as he drove away. I continued to stare out at the rain after he was gone. Lost in my thoughts of him and Jason and school, I saw him drive back into the parking lot a few minutes later. He stepped out of his car with two coffees in his hands.

"Oh my God," I muttered to myself, "he is bringing me coffee." I sat up a little straighter in my chair and caught his eye as he came through the door.

"I thought since you were going to be awhile, I would join you." He handed me a cup. "Coffee?"

I took the coffee from him warily. "Thank you."

He smiled down at me and left me to wander through the stacks in the library.

I sipped my coffee slowly; it was warm and smooth. The combination of the rain, the quiet of the library, and the sweet coffee calmed me, and I realized I could stay here all day, and just be near Nick. I felt a flash of guilt, but pushed that feeling down. I just wanted to enjoy the moment.

He came back to the window with a James Michener novel, sat down across from me, and began reading.

He didn't talk to me. Every now and then, I looked up at him, and he would smile. This was both disconcerting and comfortable at the same time.

The rain started to let up, and I thought I should be heading out. Wrapping up the chapter I was reading, I closed the book.

I took a minute to just look at Nick. He was wearing his heavy Timberland boots, cargo pants, and a North Face windbreaker. I felt my heart constrict, and wanted to scream at him, 'What have you done to me?' I wondered what his reaction would be if I actually said it out loud. I didn't, though. I wasn't sure I really wanted an answer—not yet.

He was engrossed in his book, and it took him a moment to realize I was staring at him. When he looked up, he stared right back at me, his eyes kind and accepting—patient.

"Are you ready to go?" he asked, as if he had known all along that I would want a ride home.

"Yes," I said simply.

We walked to his car, and he grabbed my bike and put it on his Thule bike rack. We rode in silence on the way home, and I didn't feel that we needed to say anything. There was so much that could have been said, but it just didn't feel necessary right then.

Pulling into my driveway, he got out and took my bike off the rack. He walked it over to the house and put it under the deck.

I got out and walked towards the front door. "Thank you for the ride. I really appreciate it."

"Not a problem," he replied with what I was coming to see as his standard answer. I was standing on the second step up to the back deck, and he was at the bottom with his hands in his front pockets.

"You always seem to be rescuing me." I tried to keep the mood light by not saying anything that would ruin it.

He smiled up at me and said, "Happy to help." He paused for a moment before he continued, "Did Jason talk to you about the beach cookout this weekend?"

What the heck? Had he seriously just asked that? My head was reeling from his question. He sounded as if this was just another regular day when he had just given his brother's girlfriend a ride home.

We had just had a peaceful afternoon together, and now he'd ruined it by bringing up something that obviously Jason should have mentioned to me. My eyes stung and I felt dismissed, as if he was trying to shame both me and his brother—like I wasn't good enough for Jason to have mentioned it to me. And it was as if he was trying to be the more appealing brother by bringing it up first. I clenched my fist at my side and tried not to cry.

"No, actually, he hasn't mentioned it." I waited to see if he would continue.

"He will. My parents are hosting a crab bake. Some friends of theirs, Evie, Julie, you and Jason." He paused for just a beat and then said, "I think Jackie is coming."

Was he trying to get a reaction out of me? Now I really wanted to slap him. I pursed my lips. "Why is she coming back? I thought she had a miserable time when she was here before."

Nick smirked at my jealous outburst, and I instantly regretted it.

Speaking slowly, he said, "We were working on a project together in Seattle before I left, and she thought we could finish it this weekend. She also thought she would give the island another chance, as long as she didn't need to sleep in a tent."

I almost asked where she would be sleeping, but I caught the green monster just in time to say, "Well, that sounds like fun. I'll wait to hear from Jason."

The moment turned awkward. He said, "Great! Well, I will see you later then," and he walked back to his car. He waved over his head, got in the car, and drove away.

I was so pissed off.

I walked in the door and slammed it so hard, the stained-glass picture hanging on the back of the door almost fell off. He obviously had not felt the same way I had the night before. Or had he? And this was his way of protecting himself? This was awful. I felt so stupid and used.

Taking a deep breath, I tried to calm myself, and plopped down on the couch to think this through. Staring out the windows into the trees, I thought to myself that he sat with me all day today, he brought me coffee, and he was so sweet to me last night. This was *something,* right? Oh my God! These jumbled thoughts were hurting my head.

My phone rang, startling me. I looked at the screen and saw that Jason was calling. I picked it up and pretended to be glad to hear from him.

"Hey babe, Nick just called. He said he gave you a ride home and mentioned the cookout?" Now I was pissed at Jason because it sounded as if I was an afterthought to him. "Can you make it?"

Think quick, Shaye, I thought to myself. At this point it was the last thing I wanted to do. It was something that sound fun though, and I wanted to go to the party.

I pasted a smile on my face. Fake it till you make it, I guess. "Yes, that sounds really fun." I hoped I sounded cheerful.

"The bar is getting busy and I need to go, but I'll call you later to talk about the details, ok?"

"Ok. Have a good night."

He said a quick good-night and then hung up.

Over the next few days I calmed down a bit, and realized that despite the complicated feelings I was having around Nick and Jason, I really wanted to go the party. I really wanted to be around Evie and enjoy my time on the island.

∞

The night of the cook-out arrived, and I took my time getting ready. Jason was coming to get me so that I wouldn't have to drive.

I washed and blow-dried my hair, so it was thick and full. It hung to my shoulder blades, and I curled the ends so that the waves would add some bounce. I put on liquid eyeliner, mascara, and lip gloss, and kept the rest of my face clean. I wanted to look fresh-faced and beachy.

I decided to wear the wrap dress I wore for my first date with Jason. It was feminine and pretty, and perfect for a night on the beach. My mom had left her fancy Jack Rogers sandals behind, so I borrowed them and went downstairs to wait for Jason.

Once again, I heard his truck before I saw him. I watched as he got out of his Bronco and came up the back steps. He walked up to the door, and my heart constricted at the sight of him. He was wearing Sperry Top-siders, khaki shorts, and a tucked-in button-down shirt. He looked like Nick, but not, and my heart broke for what I had done.

I opened the door. When he saw me, he dropped to his knees, "Fuck me!" he exclaimed. "You look beautiful."

Laughing at his theatrics, I said, "Get up. Don't be silly."

He grabbed my face gently and said, "Seriously, Shaye, you are stunning." Then he kissed my cheek.

"Thank you." I smiled and shut the door behind me. "Are you ready?"

He laughed at our inside joke and walked me to the car.

The Reids' house was a two-story at the end of a long drive just above a long stretch of beach. The circular drive was around the back, and when I entered through the French doors, my eyes were immediately drawn to the view of the ocean through the floor-to-ceiling windows.

There were two bedrooms in the back, and the great room, kitchen, and dining area were in the front. Immediately to the right when I walked in were stairs which led down to a game room and two more bedrooms. The roof was slanted, so the windows reached up twenty feet from the floor. Off to the right was the master bedroom, and a large deck that spanned the entire front side of the house. Off the front of the deck were steps that led down to the beach.

We walked into the great room, and I could see a group of people already down on the beach and about ten more people on the deck. I immediately saw Nick and Jackie leaning against the railing. She had her left arm around his waist. He had his right hand behind her on the railing and in his left hand what looked like a gin and tonic. He saw us, said something to his guest, and headed our way.

"Jason. Shaye. Good to see you." He was acting like the host of the party. He shook Jason's hand and patted him on the back. Then he leaned in to give me a half hug and kissed me on the cheek.

Jason responded, "Hey, Nick, is that Jackie?"

Nick said it was. "She thought this was the kind of party she could get into. The camping wasn't really for her." Nick and Jason both laughed, and I reached down to grab Jason's hand. He held it tightly and I felt safe. It helped dampen the hurt of what I perceived to be Nick's rejection of me.

Thirty minutes later, Jason and I walked down to the beach where Mr. Reid was cooking the crab. I greeted him with a quick hug and thanked him for inviting me. "Call me Marcus, Shaye. No need to be so formal." He grinned broadly, and I noticed that he too had a gin and tonic in his hand.

"Thank you for having me over, Marcus. Your home is beautiful." I immediately loved this man, and felt so welcome.

There was a tiny woman next to him who looked familiar to me, but I couldn't recall her name. I introduced myself to her hoping she would do the same. "Hi, I'm Shaye Richards."

"I remember you, darlin'. I'm Suzi Waters, this old guy's assistant." She pointed at Marcus with her thumb. She continued in a bold voice, "You used to run around the old office over by the post office when your daddy would come in to visit. In and out, in and out. We almost installed a doggy door for you—you were about to wear the hinges off the frame." Her voice was bigger than she was, and I suddenly remembered being enveloped in her hugs.

My smile was stretched across my face, and I was happy I had decided to come to the party. This woman alone brightened the night.

The party was loud and boisterous. I took my sandals off so that I could feel the sand between my toes. The sun sparkled off the water, and the wind blew gently. It was a balmy night, perfect for a beach cook-out, and I basked in the party atmosphere.

I felt the wind pick up, and a few strands of my hair got stuck on my lip gloss. Pulling it off my lips, I flipped my hair back and glanced up at the deck. Nick was leaning against the railing and he caught my eye. The sun was setting and it reflected gold off the windows, a backdrop to his beautiful face. He looked at me longingly and apologetically. It was a brief glance, but it was enough for me to know that he knew I was feeling hurt. I wanted to go to him, but Jackie was never more than a few inches from him. She was always holding his arm or touching him and laughing. Whatever Nick thought Jackie wanted from him, he was very wrong.

I waited for an opportunity to get Nick alone to talk. We needed to talk. The longer we waited, the heavier my heart felt. Jason had left me alone on the beach to talk to Suzi, and we were still there talking like old friends as the sun set on the horizon.

Suzi and I walked up the steps together to join the rest of the party. Everyone had moved to the upper deck or inside the house. She said an early good-bye, and I hugged her at the door.

"Don't be a stranger, little girl. You come to the office and I will bake you some cinnamon rolls. That Evie may have taken my recipe, but my buns are still the best." I laughed out loud at her and said I would do that.

The party wound down around ten o'clock, and most of the Reids' friends had left. Julie and I helped Mrs. Reid clean up the kitchen, while Jackie and Evie were talking on the couch. Nick, Jason, Marcus, and someone I had not met were on the porch talking.

"Who is the man talking with the boys?" I asked.

Julie responded that it was her boyfriend. "His house is just down the road at the other end of the beach, and he walked over a while ago."

"Oh my God, you mean he does exist?" I teased her. I was drying a dish and put it down on the counter to be put away.

"Seriously, Shaye? I was just starting to like you." She tried to sound hurt, but I knew she wasn't. I laughed at her attempt to continue pretending she didn't like me.

Mrs. Reid interrupted us. "Girls, go sit down. I can finish up in here."

I dried my hands on a kitchen towel and followed Julie into the great room. We sat down, and Jackie instantly turned to me.

"Hi, I'm Jackie," she introduced herself. I looked at her quizzically and laughed a little. I wasn't surprised she didn't remember me. She hadn't said a word to me the entire evening.

"Yes, it's nice to see you again, Jackie." I was pleasant, but I enjoyed poking her just a bit to remind her we already met.

She looked at me with feigned confusion, then said, "Oh, that's right, you were camping with us. You look different in a dress." I looked at her wondering if she had really forgotten who I was, or if she was just being a bitch. Then I looked at Evie as if to say, 'Is she for real?'

Evie laughed. Playing the peacemaker, she said teasingly, "Yes, our Shaye is quite stunning when she tries."

The guys walked through the doors from the deck, and Jason announced we were all going to the bar. Evie jumped up excitedly, and I mumbled with mock enthusiasm, "Yaaay."

Julie walked over to her boyfriend, and then turned to us to say, "I think we are going to pass." Her boyfriend looked smart, and not remotely her type. Not that she was dumb, just that he was quiet and reserved. He didn't talk to me at all, and I never saw him smile or laugh. He was shorter than me, and his goatee and glasses made him appear much older than us. I wondered what the attraction was. Julie seemed meek around him, not her jubilant, snarky self.

As I watched the dynamic, Julie turned to Evie's mom. "Mrs. Reid, thank you for a lovely party. You guys are the best." She hugged us all goodbye, and then they left.

"Nick, I'll ride with you and Jackie, if that's ok," said Evie.

"That's fine. We are all headed back this way later anyway, so that works."

My stomach knotted up, and I pasted a smile on my face. I guess my question as to where Jackie would be sleeping was answered. I knew I had no right to be jealous, but it was hard to accept that it was possible Nick had got what he wanted from me and was moving on.

"Ok, let's go." I was acting overly cheerful, and I knew I needed to tone it down.

Jason was already out the door. Evie had bounced out in front of me, and Nick and Jackie were following behind me. My feet felt like they had cement blocks on them, and I felt Nick's eyes on my back.

I got in Jason's Bronco and took a deep breath as I shut the door. I thought to myself, 'I can do this.'

When we arrived at the bar, the atmosphere was lively. I couldn't help but have a good time. Kings of Leon was playing on the bar stereo, and Evie and I were singing along to 'Use Somebody.' I was feeling flirty and happy, and Jason had wrapped his arms around me from behind. I felt like everything just might be ok.

Out of the corner of my eye I saw Nick playing pool; Jackie was sitting in the corner looking like a sour puss. She seriously did not belong here, and I kind of felt sorry for her.

An hour or so later, I was sitting in a booth with Jason and Evie when Nick and Jackie came to say their good-byes.

Jackie was hanging on Nicks arm, and Nick said, "Evie, you need a ride?"

Evie looked at Jason for confirmation, and Jason said, "Yes, she does. We were getting ready to go as well."

I felt Nick's eyes on me, and I couldn't look at him. I looked at Jackie instead, and she had a smug smile on her face. I am not prone to violence, but her attitude made me want to pull her hair and slap her.

"Shaye, come see me tomorrow at the bakery. I get off at 3, and we can go kayaking. I want to flirt with the guys at the kayak shop." Evie was drunk, and I couldn't refuse her.

"Sure, hon, I will see you tomorrow at three." I made a mental note to call her tomorrow and confirm. I didn't think she would remember her invitation when she woke up in the morning.

We all walked out to the parking lot and hugged good-bye. Evie was still singing 'Use Somebody,' only now she was much more vocal. I was trying so hard not to laugh.

Jason and I drove back to my house. He had his hand on my knee, and I was covering it with both my hands.

We got to the house, and he followed me inside. He immediately walked in to the kitchen, opened the refrigerator, and grabbed a beer. I didn't really pay much attention to how much he had been drinking at the bar, but now I saw that maybe he'd had more than I thought. He cracked open the beer and headed into the living room. As soon as I walked in behind him, flashes of me and Nick flew through my mind. I paused and crossed my arms. I felt tears pooling in my eyes.

Jason turned and walked back to me. Putting his hands under my dress, he reached up behind me and squeezed my bottom. I knew he wanted to have sex, and I needed to figure out a way not to.

I gently pushed him off of me. "I think I had too much to drink, Jason. Do you mind if we wait?"

Apparently, he was drunker than I'd realized, because my excuse didn't faze him. He planted himself on the couch, covered his eyes with his forearm and said, "Sure. Do you mind if I stay here though? I don't think I should drive home."

"Of course you can stay here." I grabbed the blanket from the back of the couch and covered him up. I leaned down, kissed him on the forehead and said good-night.

I texted Nick that Jason was too drunk to drive, and had passed out on the couch.

He responded immediately, *thank you.*

Upstairs, I washed my face and brushed my teeth. Staring at myself in the mirror I started to cry. "What am I doing? What on Earth am I doing?"

I heard noise in the kitchen, and it took me a minute to remember that Jason had slept on the couch last night. I got out of bed, put my bathrobe on, and walked downstairs to see him.

He was leaning against the counter in the kitchen, barefoot, with his shirt unbuttoned and untucked. His hair was a mess, and he had his hands clasped behind his head. He looked like he was trying to hold it up.

"Good morning." I walked over to him and put my arms around his waist. Since I was almost as tall as him, I only needed to turn my head a little to the left to kiss his cheek.

He wrapped his arms around me, buried his head in my neck and said, "Good morning."

"Did you sleep ok?" I leaned back so I could look at him.

"Yeah. Kind of." He chuckled, and I knew he had a headache. He was waiting for the coffee to brew.

I grabbed two mugs from the cupboard and asked him how he took his coffee.

He responded, "Black."

We brought our coffee out to the back deck. He sat with me for about ten minutes, and then he said he needed to get going.

"Do you work tonight?" I asked him.

He blew on his coffee and said, "Yes. Five until closing." He took a sip and then said, "What do you have planned today?"

"I was thinking about riding down to Watmough Bay and going for a hike." Watmough Bay was one of my favorite places. It was quiet and isolated, and it fit my mood today.

He nodded and said, "That sounds like a good day." He was quiet, and the silence stretched on for longer than was comfortable. He looked at me with his piercing eyes and waited a few seconds before looking away.

We finished our coffee, and I brought our cups into the kitchen. He had buttoned up his shirt and was slipping on his shoes.

"I'll try and come by later tonight," I said to him as he was walking to his truck.

He turned back to me and kissed my forehead. "That would be great."

After he left, I took a quick shower and put on a pair of running shorts and a blue tank top. I put some snacks and a sweatshirt into a backpack, and headed outside to get my bike. I rode down the hill to Cattle Ranch Road. I made a right on the road that would lead me to Watmough Bay. A few minutes into my ride, I heard a truck pull up behind me, so I slowed and eased over to the side of the road. The truck drove past me, and when I looked over at the driver, I saw that it was Nick.

I slowed to a stop. Nick pulled the truck in front of me, stopped, and slowly got out.

He looked at me and said, "Hi!" His eyes were shaded behind his Aviator Ray-Bans, but I could tell he was smiling. He was always smiling.

I dismounted from my bike and responded simply, "Hello."

"Where are you headed?" he asked easily.

I responded a little too snippily, "Where's what's her name?"

He threw back his head and laughed, "Oh, Shaye, what am I going to do with you?" And then he grabbed my bike and put it in the back of the truck.

I tried to stop him and said, "What are you doing?"

He just kept walking, "Get in, Shaye. I'm coming with you, but I need to change my clothes." He got in the truck with my bike in the back, and calmly waited for me to get in.

I sighed heavily, but realizing I actually really wanted to spend the day with him, I walked to the passenger side and climbed in.

"Where is your car?" I asked conversationally.

"My dad needed some yard supplies, and I said I would stop and get them for him after I took what's her name to the airport." He glanced at me sideways.

I didn't want to give away my emotions, so I responded simply, "Huh," and continued to stare straight ahead.

But I couldn't resist one more little jab. "I guess she can't handle island life."

He laughed out loud and said, "I guess not." He paused a moment and tried to catch my eye. I refused to look at him, and he said, "Or, she didn't want the competition."

My breath sped up, and I glanced at him quickly. He reached over and grabbed my hand, raised it to his lips, and kissed my fingertips softly.

He pulled the truck over to the side of road so he could look me in the eye. "I'm sorry Shaye. I have been trying to stay away. I wanted to talk to you last night, but there was just never a good time. I wanted to give you and Jason space, if he was what you wanted, but I just..." he paused. "I just want to be near you. Please let me spend the day with you."

"Jackie is a Bitch," I said to him.

He laughed and said, "I just poured my heart out to you and that's all you have to say?"

I shrugged and said, "I guess you can hang out with me today. I mean, really, you have already taken me captive."

He kissed my fingers again. "Thank you for your graciousness."

He held my hand until we got to his parents' house so he could change his clothes.

He lifted my bike out of the back of his dad's truck, said, "Wait here, I'll be right back."

I saw him run into the house and come back out a few minutes later in shorts and a T-shirt. He walked to the garage, and I saw him push some buttons on the side of the wall. The garage opened and I saw a dirt bike and a couple of other road bikes hanging from the ceiling. He reached up and grabbed one, walked out of the garage, and shut the door behind him.

"Ready?" He looked like a little boy.

"Ready!"

We rode our bikes down the driveway and headed along the bay road. It was a beautiful sunny day on the island. Watmough Bay was about four miles from Nick's parents' house, and we made it there in about thirty minutes. We left our bikes in a bike rack at the head of a half-mile trail and started the walk to the beach. Nick reached out to hold my hand, and I let him. Last night I had felt safe from Nick, holding Jason's hand. Today, I felt claimed.

As we walked, I talked about my decision to go back to school. He talked about receiving an offer from the firm where he had been interning at the beginning of the summer.

"Nick, that's great!" I exclaimed "What a wonderful opportunity for you."

We walked under the trees, and the sun was making shadows on the path in front of us. I was comfortable and calm walking with him.

He responded, "It is. My dad also asked me if I wanted to stay and work with him."

I felt a quick flash of panic. He sounded as if he was asking for my permission, or for my input.

I responded non-committedly, "That would be great, too. I'm sure your dad would be very happy if you stayed."

We arrived at the beach, and I sat down on a large log. Nick picked up some rocks and started skipping them across the water.

"I remember more of you now—from when I was younger." I said to him after a few moments of watching him.

He turned and grinned at me. "That's a good thing."

I picked up a stick and started drawing in the sand between my feet.

"I remember riding my bike to the general store to get ice cream." I continued, "I was probably nine or ten, so you would have been about, what—thirteen or fourteen?"

"I guess, yeah." He was still picking up rocks and skipping them across the water.

"I remember that your grandparents owned the store. You were working there in the summer, and you always seemed so official and acted as if you owned it." I was smiling now because I could picture him being all serious back then.

"I do own it." He turned and winked at me.

"Well, aren't you a cheeky one?" His arrogance made me chuckle, and I turned my face up to the sun. Without opening my eyes, I asked him to tell me about himself.

"What do you want to know?"

"Why did you choose Gonzaga?"

"Scholarship. Next?"

"Favorite color?"

"Blue." I snapped my head down and opened my eyes to look at him. He smiled at me, and I knew he was referring to my eyes.

"Favorite food?"

"Easy, cheese tortellini with tomato vodka sauce."

"Yum! That sounds good." Now I wanted to eat. I continued with my interrogation of him. "Favorite superhero?"

"Iron man."

"Typical. Favorite sport?"

He turned and walked back towards me. He stood in front of me, blocking the sun, reached down, grabbed my face with both hands and said, "Kissing you." He had obviously stopped listening to me. "You are so beautiful."

"Stop. You can't say those things, Nick." I didn't say it with much conviction.

"Yes, I can. And yes, you are." Then he leaned down to kiss me. The kiss was soft and sweet, and I melted under him. I reached out and put my hands on the back of his thighs to keep myself from falling backwards.

His full lips were gentle, and he waited until I relaxed before tentatively reaching out with his tongue. Slanting his mouth and making a sound in the back of his throat, he deepened the kiss. I let my head fall back while he maneuvered his mouth on mine, and soon, I stopped thinking.

I relaxed even more, and he went on thoroughly kissing me. He slowed the kiss, and then nipped my bottom lip before pulling back slowly. His hands trailed slowly down my arms, and he took my hands.

He spoke softly to me, "Come on. Let's climb to the top."

Pulling me up off the log, we walked over to a path that led up to the top. We climbed to the cliff that overlooked the bay that was the southernmost point on the island. I felt the sun on my face, and my leg muscles burned from the climb.

When we reached the top, the view was breathtaking. We could see 360 degrees around the sound, taking in where the straits of Juan de Fuca flowed south into Puget Sound. Someone had built a swing and hung a hammock, and I got in the hammock to rest and stare out at the water.

"Are you going to tell him?" Nick asked suddenly.

I looked over at him. I wondered if he brought me all the way up here because he knew I couldn't run easily from the conversation.

I wasn't going to pretend I didn't know what he was talking about. I was calm when I responded. "What am I supposed to tell him, Nick?"

He said quickly, "About us." His eyes were dark, and he wouldn't look away from me.

"I know, 'about us,' Nick. I mean, what exactly do I say to him, and how do I say it?" My heart was hurting, and I felt tears starting to form. "Do I say, 'you are a great guy, Jason? I had a great time with you, but I had sex with your brother, and I think I'm falling in love with him?' Is that what I say?"

Nick looked at me sadly, and I continued, "He seems to be drinking more than when we first met, and I'm kind of afraid to tell him."

My stomach knotted, and I was surprised by my own words. I had one arm over my stomach, and I put my other arm over my eyes. I hadn't sorted out my feelings towards Nick in my own mind yet, and now that they were out there, I hurt even more.

All of a sudden, I burst into tears and just sobbed. I couldn't stop crying. My heart felt like it was fracturing, and Nick was the only one who could put it back together.

Nick carefully climbed in beside me on the hammock. His demeanor towards me had shifted from confrontational to comforting. He put his arm under my head and pulled my legs up over his lap. He smoothed his palm over my forehead until my tears slowed.

"Are you going to stay with him?" Nick asked softly after I had worn myself out.

"Stop, OK? Stop." I whispered because I couldn't talk. "I don't want to talk about this right now. It's a beautiful day. Can we please just enjoy it?"

We swung gently back and forth in the hammock, and after a while, I fell asleep. Nick woke me with kisses on my face. His hand was resting on my belly under my shirt. I reached up to cradle his face and brought his mouth to mine. I was lost to this man in my half-awake state, and I wanted to go on kissing him forever.

I needed to figure out how to manage this triangle without hurting all of us in the process.

I pulled back from his face and said, "We should head back."

He nipped at my lower lip. "No."

Laughing, I said, "Be careful getting out so we don't..." we flipped over and landed on the ground, "...fall." We both burst out laughing, and he pulled me under him for another kiss.

Holding hands, we carefully hiked back down to our bikes.

Heading out of the parking lot, we rode along the back roads to avoid cars on the main road. We rode slowly, enjoying being together, until we reached the turn to his parents' house.

Slowing to a stop, we stood straddling our bikes, staring at each other with unspoken feelings.

"Thank you for spending the day with me." My words sounded trite even to my own ears.

"You are welcome." He seemed a little distant from me, and I wanted to make sure he knew how much I had enjoyed our day. We had resolved nothing, and I felt opportunity slipping away from me.

"Are you going out tonight?" he asked.

"No, I think I will stay in. It has been a long week, a long weekend, and my parents are coming up next weekend. I need to get the house ready." I was smiling at him, hoping he understood that I needed some space to think.

We were standing in the road where someone might see us if they drove by. He wasn't going to kiss me again. That wasn't the way either one of us wanted our relationship to be discovered.

Looking at me intently he said, "I want to be with you, Shaye."

I put my fingers to my temples and closed my eyes. "Do you? Really?"

"Yes," he said adamantly.

He waited a few moments for me to continue, and when I didn't, he smiled sadly at me and said, "Will I see you tomorrow?"

"Uhm, I..." I couldn't answer him.

"It's okay Shaye. I do understand."

"Nick. Just give me a few more days. Please? Can we wait until my parents leave next weekend?"

"Ok, Shaye." He sounded disbelieving.

He put his foot on a pedal to ride off and I desperately wanted to reach out and touch him.

"Nick."

I felt a deep sense of loss. I was aching with the need to just attach myself to him and announce to everyone that he was mine. Instead, I watched him ride away.

My parents arrived a few days later, and my mom decided she would host a dinner party. She invited the Reids, a local couple that owned a small café in the village, and the neighbors that lived next door.

Evie, Jason, and Nick arrived together, and I did my best to avoid both Nick and Jason, skirting around them in the house and avoiding eye contact.

Jason was entertaining everyone with stories about some of the local bar patrons, and Nick was on the back deck talking with my dad and Marcus about business.

I opened a bottle of wine and went into the living room to grab Evie. "Walk with me."

Evie and I walked down to the fire pit, sat down on the gliding bench, and talked quietly while we drank the wine right out of the bottle.

"Sooooo, how's Jeff?" I said, teasing her a bit, and hinting that I knew how she felt about our friend.

"We aren't together, Shaye." She answered as if she was annoyed at me for asking. "I think he has a thing for Julie."

I realized it wasn't annoyance in her tone, it was resignation. "Oh my God! Does everyone on the island have a thing for Julie?"

"Shaye, Julie and Jason were over a long time ago." Her tone indicated I had nothing to worry about with Julie. She seemed to think I was still annoyed by her, which was exactly the opposite of the truth.

"Evie, Julie has grown on me. I wasn't referring to her and Jason. I was actually trying to make a joke. She is kind of smoking-hot." I had to clarify my opinion, and said, "From a purely objective perspective, of course."

She wasn't laughing, and I realized she must really like Jeff. Her response hadn't been flippant, it was melancholy.

"Oh, Evie, I am sorry—you do like Jeff." It wasn't a question, and she looked at me with confirmation in her eyes. I put my arm around her, pulling her to my side. I looked up to the deck where everyone was milling around. I raised the wine bottle in the air and yelled up to them, "More wine down here, please!"

Jason had been leaning against the railing and heard me shouting. He turned and looked at us, shook his head, and said, "Be right down."

A few minutes later, Jason arrived with a bottle of Cabernet.

"Where are your glasses?"

Evie looked at him and laughed. "We were just drinking from the bottle Jason."

"Well, that's classy," he mocked us, chuckled under his breath, and took a drink from the bottle.

We stayed there for a while, passing the bottle back and forth. It did feel a little trashy, but at least my Mom couldn't see us.

A few minutes later she yelled down to us that dinner was ready. "And bring the glasses up, I don't want them to break."

The three of us looked at each other and just burst out laughing.

Dinner was served family-style, outside on the deck. We all sat around the large table that my dad had built. Nick sat across from me, and Jason to my left. My dad was at the head of the table, and my mom was to his right.

Citronella candles had been placed strategically around the deck to keep the mosquitos away. Fresh flowers decorated the table, and my mom had placed tapered candles into empty bottles of wine. She had started burning them earlier in the evening, so wax had already dripped down the sides.

Jason seemed to be getting louder and more boisterous with his stories, and I caught my Mom's eye across the table. With eyebrows slightly raised, she was looking at me with question in her eyes. I raised my eyebrows back at her, indicating I wasn't sure what she wanted me to do about it.

I looked away from her, took a sip of my wine, and glanced at Nick. He was talking to our neighbor about putting out crab pots in the morning. He must have sensed me looking at him, because he turned and smiled sweetly at me. His smile alone made me feel safe, and I wanted to just get up and leave with him. I quickly glanced at my Mom and saw she had noticed.

"Nick, I heard you might be staying on the island after law school?" This came from my mom, and I wondered what angle she was playing.

He directed his attention to my mom and was polite as he responded. "That's right. I was offered a position with the firm in Seattle, but I am giving serious thought to staying on the island and working with my dad.

Marcus added, "I need someone to start taking over these clients for me. I don't want to work forever."

My dad joined in and said, "I agree, Marcus, well said."

Jason raised his beer and said, "To Nick! And the future of Reid and Reid." He was smiling, but it was strained, and there was a hint of bitterness in his tone.

Despite my feelings towards Nick, I cared about Jason, and hearing such bitterness hurt me. He'd had too much to drink, and wasn't acting like himself.

There were cheers around the table of, "To Nick." We all raised our glasses and toasted. My dad was caught up in the happiness of his friend, Marcus, and didn't seem to notice my anxiety.

When dinner was finished, Evie and I cleared the table and took the dishes to the kitchen. My mom made coffee while I washed, and Evie helped me dry.

A little after nine, all of the Reids left, along with the couple that owned the restaurant. The neighbors who lived in the house through the woods stayed for a bit and talked with us around the fire pit, before walking back on the path that connected our two properties.

I went back into the house and was washing my wine glass in the sink when my mom came in and stood behind me. I could sense her standing there, but she didn't say a word.

I finished rinsing my glass and put it in the drying rack before turning to look at her. She was leaning against the counter with her arms crossed and her eyebrows raised. They were even higher than they had been at dinner.

"What are you doing, Shaye?" she asked me.

"I was washing my glass, and now I think I might go to bed. Do you want to go to the farmers market tomorrow?"

"Don't avoid my question, and don't change the subject!"

"I don't know what you are asking me." I was fidgeting. I knew what she was talking about, but I didn't want to answer her. I tried to step around her and go to my room.

"The Reids are good friends of ours. If you are messing with that boy, you need to stop."

"Mom, I am not messing with Jason. He's a good guy, and he just had too much to drink tonight."

"I'm not talking about that one." Her eyes were drilling into me.

"You mean Nick? Nick is a pain in the ass. He is smug and arrogant and keeps rubbing that annoying girl from Seattle in my face." I was trying to convince her, since I already knew that Nick wanted to be with me. I said the last part a little too strongly, and I saw my mom's face relax.

"Oh, Shaye. Baby, be careful." She could read me so well I started to tear up. "This can't end well."

"I'm not messing with Nick, Mom." I was talking through my tears. I wiped them off my cheek with the tips of my fingers and crossed my arms in front of me. "I'm not. I am trying to sort out my feelings before someone gets hurt. I promise."

"When did this happen?"

I was certainly not going to tell her we'd already had sex. She would decide I wasn't too old for grounding, and I would be on the next ferry home.

"Probably on the Fourth, when I met him in the bar. It was instant. At least, for me it was. I think it was for him too." I paused, remembering that night. "He didn't pursue me, Mom. He tried to stay away so Jason and I could have a chance. But I don't think he can. We just fit together. We just kept finding each other."

She crossed the kitchen floor and took me in a hug. She rubbed my back, and eventually I stopped crying. "Go to bed, baby girl. Perhaps things will be clearer in the morning."

"I love you, Mom."

"I love you too, sweetie. Go to bed." Her anger had been replaced with love and concern, and I felt so glad she was there.

∞

The next morning, my mom and I drove down to the bakery before heading to the Farmers Market. Evie was working, and smiled broadly at us when we came in.

"Shaye, give me a minute and I'll join you on the deck." She was busy helping a customer and told us to go ahead and grab a coffee.

We went out to the deck with our coffee and waited for Evie to join us. I was feeling wrung out from the night before, and my mom's quiet company was soothing. I watched the little birds jumping on the chairs and railing, and chirping for treats, their little dark eyes flitting back and forth cautiously.

Through the window, I saw Evie remove her apron and hang it on a hook, and then she came bouncing out to the deck. In one hand, she had a plate with two gooey cinnamon rolls, and in her other hand, a bottle of water. She sat down on the railing with a heavy sigh and handed me the plate.

"Hi, Mrs. Richards." Evie was so sweet and full of life. She was innocence and kindness wrapped up in a ball of energy, and I was so glad she had become my friend.

"I had so much fun last night," she continued. "Your house is so beautiful, and you were such a gracious hostess."

She responded, "You are very welcome, Evie. I am glad we're getting to know you so well this summer."

Taking a drink from her bottle of water, she said, "I think I drank too much wine, though. I'm struggling to get through my day!"

"We all have our moments," my mom said, and I smiled at her gracious response.

We had been sitting for a few minutes enjoying the morning and our coffee, when Nick drove up and parked in front of the deck. He stepped out of his car, and I couldn't help but grin. He was wearing his Timberland hiking boots, cargo shorts, and a navy T-shirt. He put his Ray-Bans up on top of his head and gave us all a huge smile. My heart expanded at the sight of him, and it became very obvious to me that I needed to talk to Jason soon.

"What a nice surprise: all the pretty girls." He leaned down to give Evie a kiss on the top of her head and then leaned over to kiss my Mom on the cheek. He came to sit down next to me, but didn't give me a kiss.

I turned to look at him with an over-exaggerated wounded expression on my face. "Where's mine?" I said, and flitted my eyelashes at him.

I thought he would laugh. Instead, he leaned into me, and using his fake chivalrous voice he said, "Why, Ms. Richards, I believe the kiss I have for you is not meant for public display. I think it is more appropriate for a, shall we say, more intimate environment." He was teasing, but it caused my face to heat, and I could not look at Evie or my Mom.

"Seriously, Nick?" Evie said, "Don't tease her like that. She was only kidding."

Nick leaned back in his chair so that it was up on the two back legs and laughed out loud. "My apologies, Shaye, you can have a kiss too." He dropped the chair back to the deck, leaned in to kiss me on the cheek, and stayed for a fraction of a second longer than appropriate. I felt my eyes close, and I breathed him in for just a minute. He smelled so good—warm, like sunshine and pine.

He leaned back in his chair again, a cat-that-ate-the-cream smile on his face, and I needed a moment to catch my breath.

"Excuse me for a minute." I stood from my chair, and, unable to look anyone in the eye, I said, "I will be right back."

I headed around the corner to the bathroom. I needed to be more guarded when he was around. I was acting like it was ok to flirt openly with him, and that wasn't fair to Jason. I needed to talk to Jason soon.

After a few calming breaths and splashing cold water on my face, I returned to the table. Having armed myself with a pep talk, I felt more composed. Nick was talking with my Mom, and Evie had gone back into the bakery.

"Hey, did Evie go back to work?"

"No, she was going to join me for lunch, but now she's ditching me for a nap." He was grinning up at me with a knowing smirk. "Your mom invited me to join you at the market, and then we can all have lunch together."

"Of course she did." I glared at my Mom, and she just sat there, smugly sipping her coffee.

"Well, then. Should we get going?" she said.

Nick left his car in front of the bakery, and we walked across the street towards the farmers market.

The market was located behind another row of shops in a pavilion area that was used for concerts and outdoor plays. We strolled through the market and looked at the hand-made crafts by local artists, Nick and I following closely behind my mom.

I stopped to admire some beautiful hand-blown glass ornaments, and Nick stood behind me. My mom had moved on and was talking to a woman that made jam and pickles. Nick and I moved off to the side of the vendors and watched all the tourists shopping. They all looked so happy and carefree.

Nick asked me, "How are you today?"

He looked happy. I felt like shouting to the world he was mine. Being with him today felt so right, and I wanted to hold his hand, but it wasn't time. We needed to do things right.

"I'm good, but you can't flirt openly with me. It's not fair."

"I want to be with you, Shaye. I want us to get to know each other better, to give what I'm feeling a chance. What *we* are feeling a chance." He said 'we' a little louder than he meant to, so he lowered his voice again. "We don't even need to do it here. We can be in Seattle, we can be in Oklahoma or the Ozarks. I don't care." He was talking with intention, but quietly so that no one would overhear us.

Glancing at him sideways, I saw he was serious. His blue eyes were looking into mine, so I said, "I want to be with you too."

His grin grew wider, and he looked like he wanted to fist bump someone.

We were standing shoulder to shoulder. "My mom asked me about us last night."

"Your mom did?" He sounded surprised. "She asked you what's going on with us?" He turned slightly towards me, and I glanced at him.

"Not in those exact words, but she caught me smiling at you, and she saw something. She told me to be careful."

"You know I want to just pick you up and kiss you right now, right?"

I glanced back at the lady selling pickles, and saw that my mom was still looking at the different jars of jams and jellies. Talking sideways to Nick, I said, "I want that, too." I felt a rush of anticipation. I knew he wouldn't, but it felt good to say it out loud.

"Give us a chance, Shaye. This is right. We are right together"

I saw so much feeling in his eyes, and I didn't want to pretend anymore. In that moment, I felt calm and resolute. "I know, Nick. I know."

I wanted to turn and hug him. Now that I had really come to a decision, I couldn't wait to be with him. My eyes pleaded with him to be patient. "I'll tell him, I will. Please, just let me do it when I'm ready. We had a great time before you showed up. I really like him. I care about him, and he's your brother. If we are going to make it, I need to do it right."

"Girl, you are killing me," he groaned, and I could tell he wanted to scoop me up and kiss me. Now that I had told him I would talk to Jason, he seemed willing to wait.

My mom walked back over to us, and we both just smiled at her. "Those smiles can lead to no good," she said. We both just laughed.

I looped my arm through hers, and we walked to lunch, with Nick following behind. I glanced over my shoulder at him and smiled. He smiled back and patted his chest over his heart. I felt light and happy and hopeful.

∞

The bar was full that night, and Jason had the rare Friday night off. I had driven myself to the bar, determined to keep a clear head and find a good time to talk to Jason.

Evie, Julie, and I sat in a booth while Jason moved back and forth between us and the bar to do tequila shots with a friend. Earlier in the day, the friend had shown up from off the island. It annoyed me that I couldn't get Jason to focus on me, and that he was drinking so heavily again.

Nick was playing pool with Jeff, and I caught his eyes on me every now and then. We both seemed to be waiting for a good time to talk. I sensed he was on edge.

Julie sighed heavily and interrupted my thoughts. "UGH! I cannot wait until the summer slows down. I am so over doing tours at the winery. I love this place, but I am free labor to my parents, and I am just... so... over it!" She paused in between the words to emphasize her displeasure.

"You have a beautiful piece of land, Julie. You should feel blessed." I said, hoping to make her feel better about the work.

She sighed again and rolled her eyes at me. "Okay Pollyanna, you just keep trying." She raised her glass to her mouth and took a long drink of her Jack and Coke. I realized her mood had to do with more than just the vineyard.

I had not seen her boyfriend since the night at the Reid's house. I wanted to ask her if everything was ok, but tonight was not the night I was going to get myself involved in her drama. I had enough of my own.

Jason came back to our booth and slid in next to me. "Hello, my pretty girl." He leaned into me and kissed my neck.

I saw Nick walk up to the bar and ordered another drink. He glanced our way, and I could tell he was getting impatient with me. This was not good. I could feel him watching me, and I started to panic. Jason was trying to pull my legs onto his lap and stroke my thigh.

I tried to extricate my legs from his lap and said, "Jason, please, stop." I tried to be polite, but he kept laughing and trying to pull my legs back up.

"Jason, knock it off." Julie came to my defense. I mouthed *thank you*.

"I'm just playing around with her," Jason snapped at her. "Let her speak for herself, Julie."

"I think you've had too much to drink, Jason. It is impairing your ability to see what is right in front of you."

My head snapped around, and I shot a questioning look at Julie. She shrugged her shoulders, smirked sideways at me, and took another drink.

I moved to push him out of the booth so that I could get some air. "Excuse me Jason, I need to get out for a minute."

He over-exaggerated my shove, pretended to fall over, and moved aside so I could get out of the booth. After I stepped out, he slid back into the booth and slouched down in the seat. I heard him call to the bartender and his friend to bring the table another round.

On the other side of the pool table was the door that went out to the side deck, and I stepped into the shadows to take a breath.

A few minutes later, I heard the door open and shut behind me, and I turned to see Nick.

"Shaye!" he said, and he wasn't smiling. "What the heck, Shaye? How long are you going to let him do this?" His voice was low and came out as a growl. "I can't keep watching this go on!"

"Please don't snap at me!" I said. I was shaking, and I didn't know what to do. I wrapped my arms around myself, "It's harder to tell him than I thought. I am hurting about this."

He came to me and gently grabbed my upper arms, "Please, Shaye, I am tired of this game. I want to be with you, and I know you want to be with me, too. I know you do. We can figure this out together." I could hear the longing in his voice. "Tell him tonight."

"It's not that easy!"

"Yes, it is!" He was angry, but kept his voice quiet so he wouldn't bring attention to us.

"You are his brother. I didn't see this coming. I came to the island for a break. I don't know how to tell him." I was pleading with him to understand.

He moved his hands from my arms to my face and pulled me close to him. "Yes, you do. We will do it together, Shaye."

I lifted tear-filled eyes to him. "Nick, I need time. Just a few more days. Please."

Now he was angry again, "No you don't! You know! You want me, and I want you, too." He pulled me to him and kissed me hard. I wrapped my arms around him and kissed him back. It was so perfect, I almost wept with resignation.

He backed up a few inches and said quietly, "Please Shaye. I want to be with you. I didn't plan this, either. I came back for the weekend, and when I saw you in the bar, I was captivated by you. I saw you on the dance floor when I came in, and it completely caught me off guard. I couldn't wait to talk to you, to hear what your voice sounded like, to touch your skin. I didn't know then that you were with Jason. Oh my God! What a horrible moment that was." He was caging me in, and I felt the longing in his voice. "I changed my mind about the internship the next day just so I could be near you. I know it wasn't right, but I couldn't stop wanting to be near you. Waiting for you, waiting for the right time, was torture."

I reached up and put my hands on his shoulders. I reached up to smooth back his hair. "Just give me another few days, Nick. He's really drunk and I want to tell him in private. Please." I knew I sounded desperate, but he wasn't going to let up.

"Shaye, I think I love you." He put his forehead on my forehead, "I don't want to be without you another day." He kissed me again, softly and said on my lips, "Please."

We were so engrossed in each other that we didn't hear the door open again.

"Are you fucking kidding me right now?" Jason stood just a few feet from us. He threw his hands up in the air and made a circle as if he could retreat from what he just saw.

I stepped out of Nick's arms and said, "Jason?"

"I know I'm not seeing this. Because my brother wouldn't have his tongue down the throat of someone I thought was my girlfriend." He was slurring his words a bit, but they were clear to me. "Would he? Shaye?"

I felt that verbal punch, and it made me sick to my stomach. "Don't be crass, Jason. Let's go back inside." I wasn't doing a very good job of calming him down.

Jason looked right at Nick. "Seriously, Nick? What the hell is going on?" Jason was drunk, but he looked wounded.

"Jason, can we talk at home? Let's go home." Nick was calm and focused. He sounded as if he wanted to protect all three of us.

"Fuck you, Nick!" Jason pointed his finger at Nick, and then directed it at me, "and fuck you, too, Shaye." Jason turned to leave through the side gate that led to the parking lot.

"Jason, stop! Please, let me talk to you." I ran a few steps toward him. I could tell he was in no shape to drive, and I wanted to keep him here until Nick could talk him down.

He said, "Nope, I'm outta here," and kept walking.

"Jason, you've had too much to drink. Please don't drive." We were both following behind him, trying to slow him down.

"Later, *brother*." With those parting words, he ran to his truck, jumped in, and sped off.

Nick turned and commanded, "Stay here, Shaye. I will come back to get you."

"Be careful. The fog has rolled in. It'll be hard to see where you're going."

He ran to his car and took off after Jason, and I went back into the bar.

My head was spinning, and I couldn't believe what was happening. I hadn't expected the situation to spiral so quickly out of control. Walking back into the bar, I looked around for Evie and found her sitting in the booth. She waved me back over.

"Hey, where did Nick and Jason go?" she asked as I approached her. "I saw Jason drive off, and then Nick was running across the parking lot after him. Are they coming back?"

"I'm not sure." I tried to be as non-committal as possible with my response. But tears were starting to form, and it wasn't going to be long before they fell.

Evie was now more lucid than she had been a few minutes before, and she said, "Oh, Shaye, what happened?"

I wanted to tell her that I thought I might have feelings for Nick. I wanted to tell her what had happened.

Instead, I glossed over what was happening and said, "I was outside talking with Nick, and Jason came out. We were close and quiet, and I think he misinterpreted what he saw." I felt shifty for lying, but I couldn't tell her the truth. "I tried to calm him down, but he stormed off. Nick said he would be right back."

Evie didn't look surprised as she reached for my hand. "Everything will be ok. Don't worry. They will figure it out." She held my hand and bit down on her lower lip. Her eyes were flitting about. I could tell she was worried, but was being strong for me.

No one else in the bar seemed to realize anything was out of the ordinary. The bartender brought Evie and me another beer. We sat in the booth together, silent and reflective. The speakers in the bar blared music, and we made casual conversation without really even listening to each other. Evie pulled out her phone, and I saw her texting.

Twenty minutes later, we saw an ambulance drive past the bar. Evie and I both looked at each other in surprise. Then, Evie jumped up and yelled for Jeff. She started gathering her things, shoving them in her bag and talking quickly. She was looking frantically around the bar.

"Jeff! Come here!" She was already gathering her messenger bag and throwing it over her shoulder. "Shaye! Give Jeff your keys. We need to find out what's going on."

Evie looked briefly at me for confirmation that I understood, but I just stared blankly at her.

She repeated herself, this time she was more demanding. "Shaye! Give Jeff your keys!" Her actions were too fast for my brain to keep up.

"Nick said he would be right back," I said. Evie looked at me as if I had lost my mind.

Evie was running ahead of us, and then back to drag us along. "Jeff, hurry!"

We ran out into the parking lot. "Shaye, where did you park?"

I was moving in what felt like slow motion as I looked around for my car. "Along the road, I think." I told him my keys were in the car.

I was dazed by my and Evie's fear. It was so thick, I thought I could reach out and touch it. It was making it hard for me to concentrate.

We found my car, and Jeff got into the driver's side. He waited for me to get in and buckle up, and Evie jumped in the back seat.

He drove out of the bar parking lot and along the bay road towards Evie's cottage. As we rounded the corner and headed up the hill, we saw flashing lights and saw a helicopter trying to land in the road. I felt my eyes widen and my heart beating a million miles an hour.

"Faster, Jeff, faster," Evie screamed at him. She sat in the back seat, holding on to the front seat backs, with her head between the two seats so she could see out the front window.

Jeff had barely come to a stop at the top of the hill before Evie was scrambling out of the car. The fog was thicker now, and I could barely make out Jason's Bronco up ahead. It looked like it had completely wrapped around a tree. I stepped out of the car, and my eyes searched for Nick.

Evie saw him before I did, and she began running and screaming, "Jason! Jason!"

I was frantically searching the crowd of people for Jason, my mind incapable of comprehending what I was seeing. The lights from the emergency vehicles bounced off the trees and the pavement. Surrounded by fog, the scene was eerily surreal.

Nick heard Evie's scream, and he turned from talking to an EMT and jogged to her before she could get to the site of the crash. "Evie, No!"

Evie wailed and fell into Nick's arms as she watched the EMTs carrying Jason to the life-flight helicopter.

I started to take a step, and Nick caught my eyes over Evie's head. I saw so much pain and anguish in his eyes that I felt my legs give out from underneath me. I dropped to my knees and silently sobbed. My chest ached; I felt like my heart was being ripped from my body. I knew I was on the hard cement, but I don't recall how long I sat there. I felt a hand on my back and turned to find Jeff reaching for my elbow to pull me up.

"I don't understand. I don't understand." I said to Jeff. "What happened?"

"Let's go, Shaye. I'll take you home." He was so quiet, so calm. With the lights from the emergency vehicles flashing all around me, and the helicopter lifting off, it all felt like a dream.

"I don't understand. What happened? How did this happen?" I felt light-headed and couldn't catch my breath.

Jeff walked me to the car. "It looks like he took the corner too fast, Shaye. He probably lost control."

I saw him look to his side and nod to someone. I looked up in time to see Nick and Evie walking over to the ambulance. Jeff opened the passenger door and helped me inside the car.

"Wait. Evie's bag." It was still in the back of the car. I reached behind the seat and handed it to Jeff.

He jogged over to Evie. She was sitting in the back of the ambulance with a blanket wrapped around her and her head on Nick's shoulder. She was crying.

I saw her lift her head, take the bag from Jeff, and glance over to the car. I had my hand over my mouth, my eyes mournful, and Evie put her hand to her heart. She nodded to me, and then turned to Jeff and said something, which looked to be 'thank you'.

Jeff got in the car and slowly backed away from the scene. When he was able, he turned and drove to the other road that would lead to my house.

Jeff drove slowly and carefully in the fog. We drove in silence until we got to my house, and I saw the ambient lights on in the kitchen.

"Oh, my God." I said out loud. "I forgot my parents were here." I dropped my head in my hands and started to cry all over again. It seemed like days ago that I was having lunch with Nick and my Mom.

I couldn't bring myself to get out of the car, so I just sat and stared out the front window. "Thank you for bringing me home, Jeff."

"Shaye," was all he said.

I turned to look at him with tear-filled eyes. I couldn't hold back, "It's my fault." I had to tell someone. I didn't want to own the feeling that I was responsible for his accident. The weight of the guilt was consuming me. I put my fist to my chest as if I could rub the pain away, but it was buried too deep inside. I almost told him about me and Nick, but he spoke before I could continue.

"It's not your fault, Shaye." He reached for my hand. "You weren't driving the truck."

"Do you think he'll be ok?" My eyes were pleading with him to say yes. He looked at me with sad eyes and didn't say anything.

His lack of response told me everything I needed to know, and I lowered my head. I sat in the car for a little while longer until I saw lights being turned on in the house. My mom came out onto the back porch, and I knew she was waiting for me to come inside.

"I guess you can take my car. I will, well, I don't know what I'll do yet, but I'll get it back later. Thank you for driving."

"You will be ok." He said this so sweetly. I didn't want to say anything, so I just nodded.

I got out of the car and walked up the steps to my mom. My feet felt like I was dragging them through mud, and I felt I had aged a lifetime. Jeff waited until I reached my mom before driving away.

She waited solemnly for me to reach her. "Baby girl." I saw my dad's shadow through the door as I fell into her arms.

"Evie just called. She told me what happened. She wanted to make sure you made it home ok."

I laughed at the irony. Then, I looked at her and asked, "Is he ok?" My voice begged her to tell me yes.

"We'll know more tomorrow," she said.

I knew in my gut he wasn't ok, and my stomach clenched up. I stepped back from her, wrapped my arms around myself, and howled in pain.

My dad came silently out onto the back porch, wrapped me in his arms, and walked me into the house. He set me gently on the bed in the back bedroom, and I curled into a ball and took several deep breaths to calm myself down.

Mom followed behind him, took my shoes off, and covered me with a blanket. She left the room and came back a minute later with a glass of water and an aspirin. "Take these."

I got up on one elbow and washed the aspirin down with the water. Mom took the glass from me, set it on the night stand, and curled up behind me on the bed. She rubbed my back and whispered over and over again, "Everything will be ok. Everything will be ok."

My heart hurt, my head hurt, my whole body hurt. I wanted to go back and start the day over. I felt heavy and burdened. Eventually, my exhaustion overtook me, and I fell asleep.

∞

I woke in the morning to a quiet house. I felt all out of sorts. The smell of coffee from the kitchen turned my stomach, and the cheery sunlight I could see through the window seemed to be mocking me. Mom came in with a mug of coffee and set it on the nightstand next to me. I felt an unimaginable emptiness. "Did I dream it?" I knew, even as I asked, that I hadn't.

"No, baby, you didn't." She sat on the side of the bed and just looked at me with sadness and concern.

I sat up a little straighter in bed and reached for the coffee. I took a sip and tasted vanilla creamer. I needed the caffeine and the sweetness.

"What do I do now?" I asked her quietly.

"Do you work today?"

"Honestly, I can't remember."

"Call and tell them you need the day off." She was taking charge, and I was so grateful. She continued, "I am going to help Martha. She will need support and people around her to help her make decisions."

I started to cry. I'd thought I was empty of tears by then, but they came so easily.

"Now, stop. There is nothing you can do. Stay here. Take a shower. The Reids need to figure out what their next steps will be, and you need to focus on you."

"What about Evie? Should I call Evie?" I sounded desperate.

"Give it some time. I will call you later." She gave me a kiss, and then stood and said, "Now, get up and take a shower. You won't do anybody any good crying in bed. Least of all yourself." She kissed me again on the forehead and walked out. Ten minutes later, I heard the crush of gravel as my parents drove away.

I stayed under the covers a little longer and finished my coffee. I knew I couldn't stay in bed all day, so I got up and wandered into the living room. The house was so quiet. For most of the summer, I had enjoyed the peace. Now, it felt empty.

I wanted to call someone, but I didn't know what to say. I thought about calling Julie, but decided against it. Jason had been her high school sweetheart, and I wasn't prepared for what she might want to say to me.

I finally did as my mom had instructed and took a shower. I spent a long time under the hot water and cried some more. I blow-dried my hair, put a little makeup on, and dressed in white capris and an off the shoulder peasant blouse.

I thought it would make me feel better to take care with my appearance, but then I saw myself in the mirror and it looked like I had dressed for a date; and that made me cry all over again. Taking an afghan off the couch, I curled up in the recliner. My eyes were tired and sore from crying, and I soon fell back asleep.

A short while later, the ringing of my phone woke me from my nap. I reached for my phone on the coffee table, and saw it was my mom. I tapped on the green phone icon to answer.

"Hi, Mom," I said sleepily.

She was clearly in her efficient mode when she said, "Hello, sweetie. I called to tell you about the arrangements."

No one had even told me he officially died. "Is he gone?"

I heard her clear her throat, as if to keep the tears down. "Yes, baby girl, he is." She sounded sad, and less businesslike.

"He died on the way to the hospital. They think he took the corner too fast and saw a deer. With the fog, it was probably difficult for him to see in front of him, and when he swerved to miss the deer, he ran into the tree. Most likely he didn't see the tree, either. It happened very fast. Nick said Jason was unresponsive when he arrived at the crash scene. He called 911 immediately."

This was all happening so fast. I choked back a sob and told her to continue.

"The service will be at Center Church in three days, and he'll be buried in the family plot. The wake will be at the Reids' house immediately after." She paused, then said, "Evie needs you. Can you drive?"

"Yes. I can. Give me a few minutes to get myself together, and I will be over shortly." I hung up and took a few deep breaths. I realized that Jeff still had my car, so I'd have to take my dad's Lincoln.

I went in to the bathroom and splashed some cold water on my face. It was splotchy and my eyes were puffy, so I took a few minutes to fix my makeup. After putting some Visine in my eyes and reapplying my mascara, I grabbed the keys to my dad's car and drove to the Reids' house.

The driveway was full when I arrived, so I had to park out on the main road. The short walk up the drive to their house gave me time to pull myself together. I

148

took a few more calming breaths when I reached the door, and then I reached out to ring the doorbell. Evie came to the door and pulled me into a huge hug.

"Thank you for coming, Shaye. I'm so glad you're here. It's just so awful." She burst into tears in my arms.

I held her for a few moments until her tears had slowed and then we walked into the great room, holding hands. There were others just standing around talking quietly. My mom sat on the couch next to Mrs. Reid, holding her hand. Mr. Reid and Nick were talking to someone wearing a dark suit and looking very serious. I assumed he was the pastor, since everyone else was wearing casual clothes.

I tried not to seek Nick out, but I was drawn to him. I walked over to where they were standing and said, "Mr. Reid. Nick. I am so sorry!"

Mr. Reid pulled me into a hug and said, "Thank you, dear girl. I am so glad he met you. You were a bright spot in his life."

I looked at Nick and saw his eyes tear up. He nodded at me and said, "Shaye, thank you for coming."

"Again, I am so very sorry." I put more emphasis on my words, so that Nick would know I was sorry for so much more. "Please let me know what I can do to help." And with that, I walked over to Evie, Mrs. Reid, and my mom.

We stayed for a few hours, and then left the family to be alone.

∞

The day of the funeral was another bright and sunny one. The island seemed peaceful and reverent. I felt like an outsider.

I rode with my parents to the church, and quietly followed behind them as we walked up the path to meet the Reids. Evie looked achingly beautiful with her black hair and her black dress. Nick was wearing a black suit and black tie. I had never seen him in a suit before. He looked like a stranger.

That impression deepened when he glanced at me, and I saw that he was a different person. His hair had been cut short again, like it had been when I'd met him. His eyes had turned cold, like Jason's eyes had been when I first met him. He had difficulty looking at me, and he turned away. My heart ached, and my stomach was in knots. Not only do I have to grieve Jason, but now I have to grieve the loss of Nick too.

The church was full. Jason had been loved by so many people from the island. The graveside service was family only, so I went with my mom to the Reids' home to help prepare for the wake.

My mom was all business, and I was so grateful. "Shaye, you make sure everyone has food and something to drink. Do not let Evie ever be by herself, and wander around the house every now and then to make sure no one is alone."

I was numb, so I just nodded.

People were arriving back at the house, and I greeted them at the door, inviting them in. It felt strange to be the one doing this but it kept me busy, and this way I didn't have to talk to anyone for too long.

The Reids rode back to the house with my dad in the Yukon, and I met the family at the door. My dad was so solid and kind. He was never far from Mr. Reid's side. He stood by him, supporting him, and ensuring he wouldn't break down until later when he was in private. My dad understood his need to be strong, and I was so proud of him for taking care of his friend.

The day passed by in a blur. I heard people talking and laughing and telling stories. I hugged Evie while she laughed so hard at a story someone told that her laughter turned to tears.

I filled drinks and coffee cups. I washed dishes and cleared tables. Staying busy helped me stay numb. The sun was starting to set, and the beauty of the oranges and pinks and yellows made me ache. I couldn't keep the numbness up anymore, and I went downstairs to cry.

At the bottom of the stairs, I went into a room on the left, shut the door, put my back to the door and started to cry. I put my hands over my face and slid down to the floor.

My heart was breaking, not just for me, but for Nick and Evie and Mr. and Mrs. Reid. I felt responsible for their feelings. If I had been a stronger person, a better person, a less confused person, this may not have happened.

"Shaye," someone said quietly, hesitantly, from the corner of the room.

My head popped up at the sound of Nick's voice. "Nick. I'm sorry, I didn't see you when I came in." He had been sitting on the bed in the darkness; even now I could barely see him.

I struggled to get up off the floor. "I will leave you alone, I'm so sorry.

He stood and walked towards me. I stared up at him, and realized I loved him, but now everything was changing. I choked on a cry. "Nick."

Everything I felt was expressed in saying his name, and he bent down to kiss me. The kiss was hard and anguished, and I continued to cry. My tears mixed with our kiss, and my heart shattered. I felt his grief and his pain; I wanted to absorb it all away from him.

He pushed me back up against the wall and lifted my dress. He unzipped his pants and lifted me up. I wrapped my legs around his waist. He was inside me so fast I barely had time to think about where we were.

As much as I knew we were trying to ease our pain together, I also felt I was home with him. I didn't know how this was going to turn out, but I knew I didn't want to be anywhere else but with him.

We were as quiet as we could be when we finished, and his head was buried in the crook of my neck. I heard him crying softly. We held each other gently for a few moments, reality slowly seeping back into the private space we'd created.

He let me down softly, and I pulled my dress back in to place. He zipped up his pants and pulled himself together. He looked at me with such tired eyes. I reached out to touch his face, resting my palm against his cheek.

"Nick," I said, simply.

He closed his eyes again, reached up to put his palm over the back of my hand, and shook his head slowly back and forth. With a deep inhale, he backed away from me and then exhaled, waiting for me to move out of the way of the door. When I stepped aside, he opened it and left.

I went to the bathroom in the hall and cleaned myself up. Staring at myself in the mirror, I saw someone I didn't recognize. My eyes looked vacant, older than my twenty-two years, and my face was splotchy from crying. I straightened my dress and finger-combed my hair, and when I felt a little more composed, I went back upstairs to look for my mom.

I found her in the kitchen talking with Suzi and making another pot of coffee. "Mom, I need to go," I told her.

Whether she saw my distress or chose to ignore it, she said, "Okay, sweetie, I will ride back later with your father."

I looked over at Suzi. "Bye, Suzi, I will come see you before I go back to school."

"You do that darlin'. Take care of yourself." She reached up to grab me and I leaned down to kiss her cheek.

I found Mr. and Mrs. Reid in the living room and I said my goodbyes to them and Evie. Evie held me tight, and I had to dig deep within myself to stay composed.

Grabbing my purse and the keys, I let myself out the back door. When I got to the car, I looked back at the house hoping to see Nick, but he wasn't anywhere around. He was nowhere to be seen, and I felt deflated, empty and exhausted.

I started the car and headed home. Our hearts were not going to heal today. I knew we both needed time, and I needed to move forward.

The next few weeks passed by slowly. The weather was starting to turn, and the skies were gray. I completed my registration to go back to school, which would start right after Labor Day.

Labor Day was usually the last big weekend, and I wanted to head back before the crowds arrived. A few of the restaurants stayed open for the winter, but the resort cut back to a skeleton crew that could work the front desk, clean the rooms, and wait tables a few nights a week.

I worked a few more shifts at the resort. Jeff said he was going to stay for the winter to finish writing his book.

We were sitting out on the back deck on a Tuesday night drinking a beer together when he told me. My legs were up on a chair in front of me and my ankles were crossed. I tucked my chin into my fleece jacket and looked at him over the collar.

I chuckled a little, and had to lift my chin up so that he could hear me say, "I didn't even know you were writing a book."

"None of you asked me much about myself." He stated matter-of-factly. "Honestly Shaye, none of you ever asked me much of anything." His tone was self-deprecating, and I wondered briefly how he viewed me.

"Huh," I said, "I guess we didn't. That was unkind of us. I guess I just thought you were a private person and didn't want to share."

I saw him in a whole new light, and was grateful he had stayed my friend. "I'm sorry we didn't get to know you better. You were just always around. I guess we took you for granted. Sorry about that."

"I didn't mind, Shaye. You were all fun to hang out with and Julie and Evie were incredibly entertaining." He laughed, and then said quietly, "I'm sorry about Jason."

He obviously did not know about me and Nick, or he wouldn't have said that. He seemed like a pretty solid guy, and he probably would have gone off on me if he had known. I nodded, gave a sheepish grin and remained silent.

He lifted his legs up and mimicked my position. We looked out at the remaining boats in the marina and contemplated our own thoughts.

"When are you leaving?" he asked after a few minutes of silence.

"Friday morning. I'm pretty much packed. My parents will be up a few more times in September, and they will close the house up for the winter," I said, taking a sip of my beer.

"Are you going to stay in touch with Evie and Nick? They got pretty close to you too this summer." He was genuinely interested, but I felt it like a weight.

I answered as non-committedly as possible. "I'm going to try."

We stayed on the deck until it got too cold for me. I said goodnight and drove home. The house seemed quiet and sad. So many memories were wrapped up in this house, good and bad. I mourned the loss of my summer and my friends. I was changed and broken. I would carry the burden of responsibility for his death with me forever, but I prayed I would heal enough to get past it someday.

∞

The next day, I worked the breakfast shift and headed down to the bakery afterwards to visit with Evie. I pulled into the parking lot in front of the bakery and went next door to Foolish Amy's Pizza Garage. I ordered a slice of Canadian bacon and pineapple pizza and a diet coke. I took my lunch out onto the deck, waved through the door to Evie, and sat down to eat. Evie came out about ten minutes later.

"Ugh, I am tired," she said when she sat down next to me. She grabbed my pizza and took a bite. Her mouth was full when she said, "God, she makes the best pizza," and she took another bite.

"Do you want me to get you a piece?" I asked her as I took a sip of my drink.

"No, I'll just eat yours." She finished chewing and said, "When are you leaving?"

"Friday morning." I paused to see her reaction, then continued, "I am almost finished with my packing, and want to get off the island, and back to the city, before the crowds arrive."

"Yeah," she agreed, "this will be the last big rush for the summer. I'm thinking about heading up to Glacier Resort this winter to work the ski shop with the kayak guys. They have apartments for their seasonal staff."

I knew she wouldn't go. She wouldn't leave her family right now. This was her flight response; she needed to make sure I knew she was ok.

"That sounds like it could be fun," I said, a little too enthusiastically.

"Maybe I will come visit you." She sounded sad when she continued, "Or you could come up?" She waited for my response.

"I could do that."

We sat quietly for a few moments, and then I asked about her family.

"Mom is functioning, and dad is putting a lot of pressure on Nick at the firm." I tried not to jump at the mention of Nick, and was glad I didn't because she continued, "My dad is giving him a lot of accounts and work and cases and, well, I think he is trying to bury him in work so that he won't think about Jason. And, so he won't go back to Seattle."

"Is Nick here?" I asked as casually as I could.

"He left a couple of days ago to get his things and get out of his condo lease. He should be back today or tomorrow." Evie took her coffee and stood up. "I have to go back to work, Shaye." She sounded so final. I wasn't sure what I was supposed to do.

I stood up, walked around the table, and hugged her. "I will miss you, Evie." She was tense at first, and then she relaxed and hugged me back.

"I will miss you too, Shaye." She gave me one last sad smile and turned to go back into the bakery.

I had one more stop to make, and I would do that tomorrow. I called my dad on the way home to make sure he knew I was coming. He told me that my old room was ready for me, and that when I arrived, we would all go out to dinner and talk about what was next for me.

The entire island seemed to be grieving. The skies were dark, and the trees drooped under the weight of the rain. I drove back to the house and continued cleaning up. I went out for a run, and when I got back to the house, I took a shower, put on some yoga pants and a sweatshirt, and poured myself a glass of wine.

I turned the CD player on and sat in the recliner to relax. The CD was playing Blake Shelton's "I want to go home." I teared up and stared off into the forest beyond the house.

I wasn't going to cry anymore. I had a plan, and I was moving forward. Nick hadn't talked to me since the funeral, but tomorrow I would talk to him. I couldn't leave without saying goodbye.

I fell asleep in the chair. When I woke, it was dark and cold. I stood and went to the back bedroom. I pulled the covers up over my head and immediately went back to sleep.

The next morning was still gray and rainy. I stepped out of bed and went to shower. I dressed in

159

black leggings, a red T-shirt, and an oversized sweater that went down to mid-thigh. I pulled on my UGG boots and grabbed my brown barn jacket off the coat rack. On my way to the Reids' house, I stopped at the south-end gas station and got a cup of coffee.

Pulling in to the Reids' driveway a few minutes later, I parked next to Mrs. Reid's Cadillac Sedan. She must have seen me coming, because she opened the door before I got there.

"Shaye, come in. I am so happy to see you. How are you?"

I hugged her and stepped into the house. "I'm good. How are you?"

She shut the door behind me, and we walked into the kitchen together. She responded, "Every day is a new day, and we will heal." Her gracious tone made me hope that one day that might be true.

"I am so sorry for your loss." I had said this to her at the wake, but now that it was just the two of us, the sentiment felt more personal, more sincere.

She patted my hand and looked at me with understanding. "I know you are."

"I'm leaving tomorrow morning."

"I'm glad, Shaye. You need to finish your schooling and find your place in the world." I was trying not to look for Nick, but she must have sensed that I was a little on edge.

"Nick went out for a run," she said to me. "He should be back in about twenty minutes if you want to wait and say good-bye."

160

"I think I will head down to the beach and wait for him. I could use a walk." I went out through the glass doors to the deck, and walked down the steps to the beach. I walked a ways down the shore, and saw him in the distance running back towards me. I sat down on a log and waited for him.

As he approached, I felt my chest tighten and tried to hold back the tears. Not only was he so beautiful to look at, but I loved him, and I'd never told him. He probably knew, but I had never said the words. Now, it was too late.

He saw me on the log and slowed his run to a walk as he got closer. He put his hands on his hips and walked towards me, slowing his breath.

I stood up, put my hands in my pockets, and said, "Hi."

He showed no emotion when he said, "Hello."

"I wanted to let you know I'm leaving tomorrow."

He just looked at me and said, "Ok."

I didn't know what I'd expected him to say, but it certainly wasn't just 'ok.'

"That's it? Just 'ok'?" My head jerked back, and I spit the words at him.

"What do you want me to say, Shaye?" He still had his hands on his hips, and now he looked a little mad. I could take mad from him. I couldn't take disregard.

I looked directly at him and said, "I don't know what I want you to say." This conversation wasn't going the way I envisioned. "I thought we had something special, and I'd hoped at least to get a sense of where we stand before I leave."

The fog was rolling in and was creating a blanket around us. I put my hands in my pockets as if I could tuck into myself, and I glanced up at the house to see if Mrs. Reid could see us.

"I can't give you that, Shaye." Nick crossed his arms and lowered his head. "I can't do this with you right now. I can't." His shoulders sagged, and his voice was low. "I just..." he was grasping for words. "I just can't think straight with you near me. I can't organize my thoughts."

He looked back up at me, pleading with me to understand. Then he dropped his eyes to the sand. "I'm in so much pain. This grief is... it's overwhelming me, and I can't. I just can't."

He looked back up at me with sad eyes, shaking his head a little like he was trying to shake the memory of us out. He let out a deep breath and then added, "Not right now."

I didn't want to argue with him. My shoulders dropped, and I resigned myself to the fact that I wouldn't get what I needed from him. Not today, anyway.

"I understand." I took a step closer to him and looked him in the eyes. I saw all the love he'd had for his brother, and all the pain he was feeling. I also saw deep inside him that he wanted to love me, and just didn't know how to anymore.

I reached for his arms, but he remained unyielding in his stance. I put both my hands on his forearms and put my head to his chest. He put his head back and looked up at the sky. Then he dropped his arms and stood back from me.

"Good-bye Shaye," he said very quietly.

I took a moment to just look at him. To see if there was any space left for us in him, but when he didn't waiver, I sighed. "Good-bye, Nick." I turned and walked back up the path to the house.

When I got to the house, I saw Mrs. Reid standing at the windows. I don't know if she had been watching, and I didn't ask. I wanted to walk around the side path to avoid a conversation with her, but she opened the door, so I had to go through.

"You found him," she said to me, and I wondered if she even understood the impact of those words.

"Yes."

"Time heals all, Shaye." She patted me on the arm and walked me out.

"Good-bye Mrs. Reid. I pray your family heals soon." My eyes were glassy, but I didn't cry.

I gave her one last hug before I got in my car and drove away.

The next day, I gritted my teeth when I saw yet another grey sky through the window. My car was packed, so there was nothing left for me to do but get dressed and head out.

I locked the door behind me and drove into town. I had a few hours to spare, but I wanted to make sure I would get in line and not miss the ferry. I took my time in town saying goodbye to friends and locals I hadn't seen yet. I stopped in at the bakery, but Evie wasn't in yet.

Ready to put this summer behind me, I drove down to the ferry dock and got in line. I was pretty far back and was feeling a little anxious about whether I would make the boat or not. I got out of my car and walked down to the dock, counting cars as I went. When I reached the first car in line, I had counted 97. This ferry was supposed to take 105 cars, so I relaxed a little. I looked through the used books in the ticket office and decided on a Kathleen Woodiwiss romance novel.

When I saw the ferry approaching the dock, I headed back up the car line to start my car. As a child, I'd always loved the starting of the car engines and the anticipation of boarding the boat. I felt the same sense of expectation today, mixed in with a sliver of hope, as I waited to leave.

All the cars getting off the boat drove past in a line, and once they had all departed, the boarding line started to move.

As I got closer to the front, I saw the ferry was almost full. There were five cars in front of me now, and the dock workers were bringing them down slowly, one at a time. The dock worker flagged down one more vehicle, and then I was first in line.

I could see them squeezing the car in on the left, and then they flagged me down the ramp. I was the very last car to make it onto the ferry. They brought the orange mesh across the back of the boat to secure the cars, and the ferry started to pull away from the dock.

The water churned under the boat from the thrust of the motor, and the smell of the salt water hit me as I got out of my car. I stared at the dock as the ferry pulled away.

As the ferry rounded the tip of the island, out of sight of the dock, I tucked my hands into my coat pocket, turned away, and went upstairs. I hoped this chapter of my life was over, and I hoped I never had to open it again. I hoped the future would bring something sunnier, and I hoped I never again felt the overwhelming heartbreak I'd found here. I hoped I never had to return to this island.

PART 2 – September, 2016

11

I couldn't believe I was returning to Lopez Island.

After Suzi's call a few days earlier, I was in a brain fog. I was on my way into the office to talk to Don about needing time off to go to the island. I would ask him to fly me up. There just wasn't time to take the ferry, and Suzi was already putting a car at the float plane dock on Lopez Island for me. I pulled into my parking spot at the Seaplane terminal and stared out at the water. I had done a very good job focusing on my goals for the past eight years, and now the memories of that summer came flooding back.

After I left the island that day, I headed straight to my parents' house in Seattle, on Queen Anne Hill. They lived in a Tudor-style home on an old money street overlooking the city center and Puget Sound.

My parents were gracious, generous, and loving while I stayed with them. I spent a lot of time with my mom taking walks along Olympic Way and Queen Anne Ave. My dad did his best to be home with us for dinner, and every now and then he would bring me Godiva chocolates, which were my favorite.

I dove right into my schoolwork. For that last remaining school year, I don't remember doing anything except school, homework, sleep, repeat.

I was going to graduate from the University of Washington with a degree in Marketing, and while most of my classmates were joining Fortune 500 firms, I just wanted to finish school.

The following May, my dad called and asked if I wanted to go look at a building site with him. He owned a construction firm that built warehouses and manufacturing facilities. I guess that was why it was so easy for him to build our island home.

"The Seahawks are building a new training facility, and we are going to bid on the project. I want to go take a look at the property. Come with me. You need to get out and socialize." He was gruff, and didn't wait for an answer. "Meet me down at Kenmore Air Harbor in twenty minutes."

"Wait, what? We are flying? Why can't we drive?" I loved to fly, but it seemed a little excessive to fly to a building site.

"Traffic is horrible this time of day, and it is on the south end of Lake Washington. I don't have time to wait today." I didn't want to point out that he never had time to wait.

"I'll meet you there, but you owe me dinner afterwards."

"Done," he said and hung up.

The float plane base was a small building that would be easy to miss if it wasn't for the large billboard sign on its roof that read "Kenmore Air Harbor" with a large Yellow float plane on it."

I parked in the gravel parking lot, walked into the lobby, and checked in with the customer service agent. "I'm here to meet Dan Richards? I'm Shaye Richards, and I think he chartered a plane for us?"

She looked at me with crazy eyes and said, "Ok. Hold on a minute. My system is really slow, and we are really busy today with people flying to the islands for the weekend. Give me just one minute."

I didn't want to hear about the islands, so I said, "I'll just wait over here until you're ready." I went to take a seat in one of the plush leather chairs by the window.

Decorated with beautiful dark blue carpet, the lobby was a comfortable waiting area for the travelers. The walls were painted a lighter blue, and the trim around the doors and windows was cherry wood. It was tasteful and elegant.

The windows looked out over Lake Union, and I could see all the planes lined up on the dock. The company flew predominately de Havilland Beavers and Otters, each plane carrying eight to ten people. They were incredibly sturdy planes for taking off and landing in tricky locations in Alaska. Kenmore Air Harbor used them for flying in and out of lakes and islands in the Pacific Northwest.

Five minutes after I arrived, my Dad showed up. I saw him come through the front door like a hurricane and go straight to the customer service counter.

Watching him, unseen, I saw him as others might: commanding, focused, and with little time to waste.

"I'm looking for Tom Wilde. Is he here?" He had a booming voice, and just about made the young girl cry. "I'm Dan Richards, and we have a flight with him this afternoon."

Tom must have heard my dad's voice, because he walked out of a back office and said, "Dan, how are you? You ready to go?"

I recalled then that my dad's company had built this terminal about ten years before. I was a teenager then, so I wasn't paying much attention to my parents.

My dad responded that we were on a time crunch and wanted to get going. I stood and slowly made my way to the two of them.

Tom saw me approach from his side, turned to me and said, "You must be Shaye. It's a pleasure to meet you." He reached to shake my hand.

I said, "It's nice to meet you, too."

"Let's head down to the dock. We'll take the Beaver today, and she's all ready to go." He led us down the ramp to the floating dock, and I was fascinated by the planes. They looked stately and strong, like work horses lined up to serve an army. I felt butterflies in my stomach, and a physical pull to the airplanes. Something inside me was cracking, and I was feeling a new sense of purpose, as if the bubble around me was popping open and I could see the world outside of my misery.

My dad and I climbed in, and Tom asked me if I wanted to sit up front.

"Sure," I replied, and watched as my Dad climbed into the seat behind me.

Tom handed me a headset. "We can talk, and you can listen to ground control."

I had been in the planes a few times as a kid, but I never got to sit up front. This was a new way of flying for me, and I felt important. Tom started the engine, and it whirred to life. It sounded like a big diesel truck. The line guys threw the tie rope out into the water, and Tom gave the engine some power. Turning out towards the middle of the lake, we were bouncing around a bit from the waves. Tom lined the plane up in the middle of the lake, careful not to head toward boats that were moored. He was playing with some of the equipment, adjusting nobs and his seat. Glancing over at me, he looked at me questioningly. I nodded enthusiastically, smiling, and he pushed the throttle all the way forward. The plane roared to life, and he pulled the control yoke all the way to his stomach. The pontoons bounced a bit on the water, jostling the plane a bit, but Tom was handling the yoke with ease. It was exhilarating! I felt excitement and giggles bubbling up inside me. It was an unfamiliar feeling to me, and I was thrilled to be experiencing this today. The turbine engine was rumbling, and I felt alive for the first time in months.

He leveled the plane out, pushing the yoke forward a bit. I knew from listening to my Dad that we were coming up on "the step." The plane was similar to a water skier, ploughing through the water and then lifting up and out to fly on top of the water. The float plane skimmed across the water like an airplane on a runway, and we were picking up speed. Ten seconds later, the nose of the plane came up, and we were airborne. I felt like a little kid. This was so much fun, and I wondered why I hadn't flown in years. It was exhilarating, and I giggled with delight.

We landed on Lake Washington in front of the building site ten minutes later, and I told my Dad I would stay with Tom and the plane.

Tom tied the plane to the dock, and we sat together and talked. I was fascinated by his stories of Alaska and some of the other locations he had flown into. He said he would be happy to fly me to the islands anytime I wanted to go back.

"I don't think I will be going back," I said, pausing before I added, "At least, not for a while."

He was silent for a bit, and then said, "Your dad told me some of what happened, Shaye. I'm very sorry."

"Thank you."

"My brother died in a plane crash when we were young." He paused until he had my attention. "I was the pilot, and we were going lake fishing. I misjudged my approach, and we flipped at the shore." He was quiet for a moment, and then he continued, "It took me a long time to forgive myself—a long time for me to want to get back in a plane."

"Oh my God! I'm so sorry," I said with sincerity. I also knew he was trying to tell me something: something important about life.

He was calm as he spoke, and I couldn't help but feel a kindred connection to him.

"Thank you." He looked out at the lake, remembering. "My point is that flying is who I am, it's what I love to do. Now, I'm more careful, less reckless. And older." He chuckled to himself and paused for another moment. He looked over to me and continued. "We all have a story, Shaye. We all have something we need to work through. You will be ok."

Suddenly, I felt the need to tell him everything. He seemed so caring and kind. We were just sitting there talking, and it seemed like a natural time to tell him my story.

I told him about meeting Jason, Evie, and then Nick. I told him about how lovely their parents were, and how much I wanted to be with Nick. I told him I was afraid of hurting Jason, and just never found the right time to tell him. When I was finished telling the story, I felt as if I weighed less. It may have been my imagination, but I felt the sun come out. It may have already been out, but I felt like I was finally beginning to heal. I had closeted my feelings for the past year while I was finishing school, and after I told Tom the whole truth, I felt I could breathe a little easier.

Thirty minutes later, my dad walked down the dock with a man equally as big as he was. They shook hands, and I heard my dad say, "Thank you for the tour."

My dad climbed into the back of the plane, and ten minutes later we were airborne again and heading back to the terminal. Tom maneuvered the plane close to the terminal and jumped out to tie the plane to the dock.

A line guy came frantically running out towards us, as we walked up the dock and said, "Chief Wilde, Chief Wilde! Janie just quit, and I don't know how to use the reservation system."

Tom looked at him with a confused expression on his face. He put his hand out, palm up, to calm Chris. "Hold up a second, Chris. Janie in customer service just quit?"

We all started walking up to the terminal building, Tom's pace a little faster than before. My dad was next to Tom, and I was following behind.

"Yes sir, right after you left. She said the job was too stressful, grabbed her purse, and left." Chris was running behind him as he spoke.

"Well, shit!" he swore.

"I'd like to work here," I blurted out. "I can learn fast, and I'm smart." That last part sounded kind of lame, but I continued, "I graduate in a few weeks with a marketing degree, and I haven't found a job yet. I would like to work here, Mr. Wilde. I would really like to work here."

I don't know where all those words came from, but they felt right, and so did the idea of working in this place.

Tom and my dad stopped and turned to look at me. I continued, "I mean, if you need a replacement for Jane, or Janie, whatever her name is." They were both staring at me, and I suddenly felt as if I was crazy for speaking up. "I know I don't know anything about this business, but..." I paused for a bit, took a deep breath and said more calmly, "I would really like to work here."

"Shaye, you're hired," Tom said to me, and turned to continue walking into the building.

I think I squealed and ran to my dad. I gave him a huge hug, and he said, "About time, little lady. About time." He had a huge grin on his face.

That weekend, I started working what they called "the line." I learned how to tie the plane up, and how to jump on and off of the pontoons. I learned how to pump gas and pull planes into position. After I graduated, I started working flight reservations, calling cabs, and making hotel reservations for passengers. I moved out of my parents' house, and into a shared house with two other girls, just above the lake.

A few times, I saw Nick's name on flight manifests, and I planned those days off, or left when his plane landed. If Tom noticed, he didn't say anything. Evie had called a few times, and I never returned her calls. I had a few calls from numbers on the island that I didn't recognize, and I never answered those, either.

After two years, I was managing the reservations desk, and a year after that, the management added the customer service positions to my team. I was happy and fulfilled, but I still wasn't dating. I just didn't feel ready to open myself up to being hurt again. My mom was starting to worry about me, but I just kept pushing forward with my job.

When I had been with the company five years, I brought forward my idea to start an adventure series. We would fly to, and lead, fishing expeditions, up to the Northern tip of Vancouver Island. The campaign was so popular and profitable, the company promoted me to

Marketing Director, and I moved into an office with a view of the lake.

I felt like I had finally reached a place where I was safe. The weight in my heart had not lessened, but on the outside, I was doing everything right. I bought my own house in Ballard, and I felt that I was as happy as I could get.

Life was calm, and I had settled in to a routine that was peaceful and predictable.

Then, early this past summer, I received a call at work from my mom's brother, Jack: my dad had suffered a massive heart attack, and died instantly.

Apparently, my dad had just returned from a business lunch and had commented that he was going to his office. My uncle told me that my dad looked tired, so he didn't bother him. Later in the day, he went to check on my dad and found him slumped over in his office chair.

We had a celebration of life for him in Seattle, but my dad wanted to be cremated and have his ashes spread over the beach on the island. So my mom, brother, and I flew up one weekday after the service to have a private ceremony. I really didn't want to go, but I felt an obligation to honor my father's wishes, and wanted to support my mom and brother.

I did my best to sneak on and off the island. I tried not to feel selfish, but I wasn't ready to reconnect with the people there. My mom understood my feelings, and was careful not to bring attention to the fact that we were there. She also wanted that quiet time together as a family to grieve for my dad.

It seemed to me that just when one hole in my heart had started to close, the death of my father opened another one. My father had always worked a lot, so we weren't incredibly close, but he was still my father, and I always knew I would be provided for. Maybe not emotionally, but certainly financially.

I don't know how long I sat in the parking lot remembering the past, but looking at the clock, I saw I was late for work.

Walking into my office, I put down my purse and then went to get a cup of coffee. I walked over to Don's office and rapped my knuckles on the door frame. Don had pictures all over his office of himself and famous actors and actresses. A lot of them came through here on their way to private islands or vacation homes, and he made a point of getting photos with his favorites.

He said, "Come in Shaye. How can I help you?" As always, he was polite and to the point.

I sat down in the chair in front of his desk and said, "I received a call from my dad's attorney yesterday. I need to go to the island for a few days."

His face registered a moment of surprise. While Don and I had never officially talked about my life on the island, Tom was Chief Pilot, and I was certain he had shared pieces of my story with him.

He responded, "Okay. How much time do you need?"

"I'm not sure yet. I have a meeting in his office Monday morning at nine a.m. Any chance I can get a ride on the nine o'clock flight Saturday morning?" I paused to gauge his reaction and when I saw he was listening attentively, I continued. "I'd like to be home Monday night if possible, or Tuesday morning. I'll call you after I know more."

He nodded and said, "We can get you on the flight Saturday morning. Why don't you plan on spending a few days up there? You deserve a break, and you can come home on a flight Wednesday afternoon."

I stood to leave his office, but he stopped me, "You let me know if you need anything, Shaye, anything at all."

"Thank you, Don, I appreciate that." I turned to leave his office. I had work to finish before I left that weekend.

I was up early Saturday morning. Nervous energy prevented me from sleeping late, so I got up and went for a run. I ran down to the Starbucks at the marina, had a cup of coffee, and then jogged slowly back to my house.

I packed a small travel bag and drove to the float plane dock. I arrived at about eight fifteen, and spent a few minutes going through my emails and finalizing some advertising schedules. I was trying not to think about going back to the island, so I just stared out the window until Chris came to get me for the flight. Chris was now a pilot, and a very good friend.

Walking down the dock, I handed him my bag and climbed into the backseat. Chris looked at me and said, "There are only three other passengers today, if you want to sit up front."

"No thanks, Chris, I think I will sit back here today." I needed time to think, and I didn't want the chatter from the headset to interrupt my thoughts. I felt apprehensive about returning, but it also felt like it was time. Knowing I would have to see one of the Reids helped me feel ready to start to face the past.

The flight was uneventful; we landed around ten o'clock in the morning. After Chris secured the plane, I jumped out and told him I would see him later that week.

As I walked up the dock towards the resort, I started hyperventilating. Looking up at the resort, I saw Jason the way he was the very first time I saw him that summer, sitting on the railing.

My stomach clenched, and I had to take a deep breath. Apparently, my memories weren't buried deep enough.

I got control of my thoughts as I continued to walk up the dock. The old Ford pickup was parked a few spots down from the kayak shop, and, predictably, when I got to the truck and opened the door, the keys were in the ignition. Uber and rental cars were not transportation options on the island, so residents were inclined to lend their vehicles out to friends who were flying up for the weekend. They would leave them in the parking lot at the resort, where the planes landed.

Driving into the village, I noticed that not much had changed. The trees were a little taller, and they were starting to change color with the arrival of fall, but other than that, it was if time had stood still. Foolish Amy's Pizza Garage was still around, and I noticed the door was open, so I stopped in to say hello.

"Amy?" I called out and walked tentatively into the restaurant. She popped her head out from the kitchen where she had built a brick oven.

"Can I help you?" Her eyes focused as she realized who I was. "Oh, my God! Shaye! You're back?" She came around the counter and squeezed me tightly.

Her enthusiasm caught me by surprise, and I half hugged her back. "For the weekend, yes. How are you?" I asked her.

"I'm good. I'm really good. Have you seen Evie yet?" She reminded me of Evie with her bubbly personality. But where Evie was dark and thin, Amy reminded me of a red-haired Varga girl. She was as tall as me, but curvy like Julie, and with a much better disposition—from what I remember.

I responded that I hadn't, and that I would catch up with her later. I then asked, "Is there any chance I can get a pizza to go? I need to head to the store for a few things, and then I can swing by on my way back and pick it up."

"Absolutely! Ham and pineapple?" she asked.

I couldn't believe she remembered. "How did you remember that?" I was very surprised.

"Oh, Sugar, it's what I do." She winked at me and laughed.

"I'll be back in about thirty minutes to pick it up. Does that work?"

"Of course."

I left the restaurant and peeked into the bakery, but I didn't see Evie, so I got into the truck and drove to the store.

When I parked in the store lot, I called Suzi to let her know I had the truck, and that I would be in the office nine o'clock Monday morning. It was Saturday, and she didn't answer, so I left a message.

I grabbed some fruit and easy-to-eat raw vegetables. There was probably canned soup at the house, but I picked up a can of minestrone anyway, along with some creamer and ground coffee. I wasn't sure if there was coffee at the house, and that was something I certainly could not do without.

My pizza was ready when I went back. I thanked Amy, and told her I would stop by again before I left the island.

"There's a band tonight if you want to come out." She sounded hopeful, but not too optimistic, that I would say yes.

"Not tonight, but thank you." I said good-bye, picked up my pizza, and headed south to the house.

The house was cold, so I built a fire and changed out of my travel clothes. I heated up the pizza and sat down at the kitchen table to eat. After I had settled in, I called my mom to tell her I'd made it safely to the island.

"Oh good. I'm glad you made it," she said. "Call me Monday afternoon and tell me what he said."

I was a little confused about the meeting, so I asked her, "How come you aren't here, mom? It didn't really click with me until earlier today that you weren't here with me."

She responded, "I was just there last week. I met with the Reids when I was there, and I have everything I need. Your father prepared well, and we are all being taken care of."

"What about Jake?"

She laughed, "Well, nothing is ever enough for him. Don't worry about your brother." She sounded a little cryptic, and since I wasn't in the mood for drama, I decided not to pursue that conversation.

I laughed a little, and she continued, "What do you have planned for tomorrow?"

"I went to the store on my way in today and picked up a few things. I might go to Watmough Bay and go for a hike. I don't know yet, though, maybe nothing." Standing up and holding the phone between my ear and my shoulder, I walked to the sink with my plate. I covered the remaining pizza and put it in the refrigerator, then walked into the living room.

She sounded sad for me when she said, "You should call Evie and Julie while you are there."

I grabbed the afghan and curled up in my favorite chair. "Not yet mom. I will, but not yet."

We said our good-byes, and I sat staring out the window. Tomorrow was reserved for me, and then I would be prepared for Monday.

I woke early Monday morning and went for a run. This was the first run in eight years that I didn't see a car or a Starbucks or another person. It was soothing and peaceful; I remembered how much I loved to run through the woods and down dirt roads.

When I got back to the house, I put a pot of coffee on to brew while I took a shower and got ready for my meeting. I decided on my black skinny jeans, tall brown boots, a cream-colored knit sweater, and a brown poncho jacket. My hair was shorter than it had been when I lived here before, but it was still long enough that I could put it in a messy side braid. I grabbed my brown Coach tote bag and my keys and left the house.

Driving to the north end of the island, I felt simultaneously apprehensive and curious. I just wanted to get this over with. I had a life to get back to, and obviously, there wasn't anything here for me.

I drove into town and took a short road off to the left from the grocery store. Mr. Reid's office was in an old building that overlooked the channel to the bay. It was built in the late 1800's, and still had the original wood floors and cylinder glass windows. It made me smile that he had not made any changes.

The door creaked when I opened it.

"Hello? Is anyone here?" I called, shutting the door behind me. I walked in a few steps, and then Suzi came out from the back room. There was a staircase to my left that led up to a handful of offices. To my right was a large conference room that looked out to the channel. In the back was the kitchen, and a room they had converted to storage.

Suzi carried a mug of coffee and a plate of cinnamon rolls. "Well, look what the cat drug in." She was smiling at me. She put the plate and mug down so that she could hug me.

"Actually, I don't believe it was a cat." I smiled at her and hugged her back. "It was a Pitbull, and her name is Suzi."

She stepped back from me, reached up from her height of five feet, grabbed my cheeks, and said, "Now, darlin', it was your daddy that summoned you. But I sure am glad to see you." And then she kissed my cheeks.

I wanted to get this over with, but I also didn't want to be rude, so I asked her how she was doing.

"I'm fine, girl. Staying busy. Keeping that Evie out of trouble. That other one too." I thought she meant Nick, but she continued on, "I swear, Julie needs to be on a leash. I'm not sure who leads who down the rabbit hole, but those two are still thick as thieves. At least Evie matured enough to actually buy the bakery, so she isn't out as much anymore, but Julie is restless and needs something to do. And by 'do,' I don't mean Nick."

185

My stomach turned into a knot, and my throat closed up. Julie and Nick? What the heck? Okay. I couldn't focus on that right then. I reminded myself that I was here to get this over with, not reignite my relationship with him.

"Is Mr. Reid here? I would like to get this over with." I didn't mean to be abrupt, but her statement about Nick and Julie reminded me that I wasn't part of the island. I really wanted to get off this rock and go home. I was going to call Don as soon as this was over and have him fly me out of here.

"He is. Let me call him down." She went over to her desk and picked up the phone. She pressed a button, and he must have picked up because I heard her say, "Mr. Reid? Ms. Richards is here." She paused for a second, and then she said. "Ok. I will let her know."

"Let's get you settled in here, Shaye." She walked into the conference room, and I followed behind her. "Can I bring you a cup of coffee? A cinnamon roll?"

I put my bag in a seat at the table and said, "Coffee please. With cream."

"Okay, I will be right back." She left and shut the door behind her. I crossed my arms in front of me and turned to stare contemplatively out at the channel until I heard the door open behind me.

I turned and started to thank Suzi, but it wasn't Suzi.

"Shaye." It was all he said.

My heart stopped. I felt the room going black, and I couldn't get enough air. I thought I was going to pass out. I looked back out the window as if he would be gone when I turned back around. When I did, he was still there.

I opened my mouth to say something, to say anything, but the words wouldn't come out. Looking like a guppy, I finally closed my mouth and just stood there.

He had sounded so official and impersonal when he'd said my name. He stood there waiting for me to say something. My name hung between us in the silence as I looked him up and down.

God bless him, he looked so good. He was bigger now, broader and fit, and his face had gotten leaner. I'd thought he looked like a man before, but now I saw that he had still been a boy. Now, he looked like Nick the man. His hair was still short and cut the same way. His face was tanned from the summer sun, and it made his blue eyes almost glow. He wore a white button-down shirt with the sleeves rolled up onto his forearms. His pants were a flat-front navy slack, and he had on a brown belt with it and brown shoes. The man standing in front of me was someone I would totally go for in the city.

I knew I had to say something soon, so I simply said, "Nick." That was all I could get out, and it seemed woefully inept.

"How was your trip up? Did you get settled alright?" he asked as he sat down, and gestured with his hand for me to do the same.

My head was still spinning. Was this really happening? Were we really having this conversation, as if it hadn't been eight years since we had seen each other? I wanted to scream at him, 'Settled with what?

Settled with my heart? Settled in my life?' I chose to just go along with this conversation that seemed like an episode of the Twilight Zone.

"It was an uneventful flight up, and yes, I got settled just fine, thank you." I responded in the same tone, void of any emotion.

"Great. Shall we get started?" He gestured again to a seat at the table. I slowly lowered myself down.

He fanned out the files he had brought in with him, and started in on a bunch of legal talk that I didn't understand. He talked about assets and terms of the will, never once making eye contact with me. I watched his mouth move and his pen scroll across a piece of paper. I was so drawn to him, I fantasized about climbing over the table and kissing him. He put on a pair of glasses, and I let out a little squeak.

He paused and looked up at me. "Are you ok?"

I gave my head a little shake, and responded, "Yes. Please continue."

Continuing on, I heard him say something about my mother and my brother, and then, with a tone of finality, he said, "Lastly, all I need from you is agreement to the terms of the will."

I had been staring at his face and chest, and realized I missed everything he had just said. "I'm sorry, can you repeat all that?" My face flushed, and I felt stupid.

"Shaye, were you paying attention at all?" He looked frustrated.

"Yes. I mean, no, not really." I was a little embarrassed, but mostly I was confused. "Where is your dad? I thought I was meeting with your dad. Suzi said I was meeting with Mr. Reid." I paused for a moment, then said with even more confusion, "And my mom didn't say anything."

He leaned back in his chair, crossed his right ankle over his left knee, and put his right elbow on the arm of the chair. He was biting the end of his pen and staring pensively at me. It was distracting.

"I am Mr. Reid, Shaye. And my dad only works part-time now. My mom and he wanted to travel more, so I took over. We have a small team in Seattle down on Western Avenue, and two attorneys here in the islands. Suzi does all of our billing and scheduling, and I run the business. Would you like different counsel?" He said it as if he didn't have time to waste on my misapprehension.

"I... no, its fine. I'm sorry. I had different expectations, and it caught me off guard." I deflated a bit knowing I sounded like a petulant child, and tried to act more normal. "You obviously had time to prepare to see me, and I only had two seconds."

"I didn't need to prepare to see you, Shaye." The words felt like a slap. "Would you like me to start over?"

Holy Mother! Did he really become that much of an ass? My newly awakened attraction vanished, and I put my business face on. "Yes, please, if you would." I listened to him say that my mom would get the house in Seattle and my brother the car. The business transferred to my mom, and she had already been advised on the business's current condition and future plans.

He continued with, "There is money in a trust for your children and your brother's children. And the house on the island goes to you."

He paused and looked at me, gauging my reaction. The air got thick, and I wasn't sure I heard him correctly.

"I'm sorry, what?" I seemed to be apologizing a lot this morning. "I get the house?"

"Yes," he said.

"Why?" I was confused. He looked at me like I was a nutcase, and probably wondered why I wasn't understanding any of this.

He took his time responding. "I cannot answer for him, but I imagine he thought it meant something to you."

"But, what do I do with it?"

"There is a contingency to the terms." He paused, and I sensed this was something I was not going to like. "In order to keep the house, you need to live here for one year."

I stood up abruptly and shouted at him, "What are you talking about? Live here? On the island? In the house?" I was livid. "What on earth am I going to do here? I have a job and a house and a life in Seattle." I started pacing in front of the windows, trying to calm myself down.

He was still calm and unemotional. "If you choose not to live here, the house and the property will be turned over to the Center for Whale Research."

I busted out laughing, "A conservation? For whales?" I laughed again at the ridiculousness of the idea. "My dad did not have a philanthropic bone in his body. Was he senile? Did he have mental problems I didn't know about?" I knew I sounded a bit hysterical, and I didn't care.

"He was quite sane, Shaye. He knew exactly what he wanted. I don't think he wanted it this soon, but it is what it is, and these are his wishes." He leaned forward again and steepled his fingers.

"Jesus, Nick!" My fight or flight response was kicking in, and I was going to go off on him now. "How can you sit there after eight freaking years and just read that will like you don't even know me? Do you have any idea what this is doing to me? We don't talk for all this time, and our first conversation is the reading of my dad's will? A ridiculous will I might add. And you, you sit there like this is just another business transaction. Can you put any feeling or warmth or compassion into this discussion?" I emphasized my last words, "At all?"

I stopped to take a breath, and calmed myself down. I knew he wasn't going to answer, but I felt a little better for acknowledging the elephant in the room.

He appeared to relax a bit and let his guard down. "You are right Shaye, I did have time to prepare to see you, and this isn't easy for me either." He paused for a second, and I saw a brief flash of pain in his eyes. "That doesn't change the terms of the will or the fact that you need to make a decision."

I was grateful for the small display of compassion, as well as his pragmatic statement.

"I just don't know how I'm supposed to do this." I was talking to myself, and I walked to stand in front of the windows. He wasn't responding. He was waiting for me to say something, to make a decision. I felt like my whole world was collapsing around me. Everything I had run from was now, literally, standing in front of me.

Reaching a place of resignation, I turned from the window and sadly said, "When do you need a decision?"

He wasted no time responding. "By Friday."

"Friday?" I exclaimed, and had to calm myself again. "Why so soon?"

"The terms state that you need to take possession by the first of the month immediately following the reading of he will."

"October first is next Tuesday." I was stating the obvious.

He responded, "Yes, and we need time to notarize and finalize the transfer of ownership."

"A whole year?" I asked again, quietly, already knowing the answer. It seemed like forever.

"A whole year." He was looking at me intently.

"And if I leave next September 29th, I still lose it?"

"Yes."

I didn't want the house, but I also didn't want to lose it. First and foremost, I needed to breathe. Second, I needed to calm down so that I could think clearly.

"Ok then. I will call you by Friday with an answer." I tried to be all business as well, but inside I was a mess.

He stood to leave and said, "It's good to see you, Shaye."

I didn't know how to respond, so I just nodded and gave him a sardonic smile. He left the room, and I stayed just a few more minutes to gather my thoughts.

The door opened again, and I turned to see Suzi with a cup of coffee.

"You knew?" I didn't bother with pleasantries.

"Now, Shaye, would you have come?" She was a feisty old bat.

"Apparently, I wouldn't have had much of a choice, would I?" I stared her down.

She shook her head sadly at me and said, "You have a choice Shaye. You always have a choice. It's whether you can live with the outcome that is causing you frustration."

"UGH!" I groaned out loud. "Why am I back here?"

Suzi didn't answer, and I didn't expect her to. I told her I would talk to her later this week, and I grabbed my things and left. It was then that I noticed the Black Range Rover parked outside. Of course. I had been looking for the BMW, so it made sense that it hadn't occurred to me that he'd be there.

I drove down to the end of the bay where I could get cell service and called my boss. He answered right away.

"Shaye, how are you?" He sounded happy. I was so grateful to hear his voice.

I responded I was fine, and then relayed the story to him.

He busted out laughing and said, "I always liked your Dad."

I told him I didn't really think it was that funny. I told him I didn't know what I was going to do yet.

"You'll figure it out." He had stopped laughing, but I could still hear the smile on his face.

"Can you come get me tomorrow? I can't think up here." I didn't tell him that I had seen Nick, or that Nick was with someone I once hadn't cared for. "I need to make some decisions, and I want to be removed from here when I do it."

"Sure thing. I'll put you on the eleven o'clock off the island." He sounded efficient.

"Thanks, Don. I will see you tomorrow." I hung up and headed back to the house to pack.

When I got to the house, I saw it differently. I saw it as mine. I knew in my heart I wouldn't give it up. I just needed my brain to catch up.

Feeling like Scarlett O'Hara from *Gone with the Wind*, I thought to myself, 'after all, tomorrow is another day.'

I landed back at the Kenmore terminal a little after twelve the next day, and immediately went to my office to check my emails. After I was satisfied that I was caught up, I went across the street to the taco truck to get lunch. When I got back, Don waved me in to his office.

He jumped right in. "Have you decided what you are going to do?"

I chuckled at him and said, "You should meet Suzi, the lawyer's administrative assistant. You both just get right to the point."

"No time to waste, Shaye. We have to keep moving forward. Now, what's the plan?" He leaned forward with his forearms resting on the desk in front of him.

"I'm not ready to lose the house," I said. "I'm not ready to keep it, but I know for sure I'm not ready to lose it." He was listening intently, so I continued, "This house was a family home. I spent my summers there growing up, and..." I paused to find the right words to convey how it changed my life. "Well, I grew up there." I thought that statement would cover it, even though he might not know the full extent of my words.

I continued sharing my plan. "I am required to live on the island, in the house, for a year in order to keep it. I am sure I can go off island when I need to. It's not a house arrest or anything. It feels like it right now, but it's not."

He laughed at that and leaned back in his chair. I had thought this through carefully last night and again on the plane, and I was hoping he was going to go for it. "What I propose is that I set up an office on the island. I will work just like I always do, just from up there. I can meet the planes and take care of the passengers when they arrive. The only difference is that you don't get to see my smiling face every day."

"When do you need a decision?" It was the same question I had asked Nick, and I prepared myself for the same level of shock from Don that I'd had.

I said as calmly as I could, "By Friday. I need to be there by the end of the month."

"Jesus Christ, Shaye! He didn't give you much time, did he?"

"I know exactly how you feel." I laughed at his vehemence. "Well, in fairness to the dead, he set it up that I take possession by the first of the month after I was notified. If I had gone up earlier this month or late next week, I would have had more time to decide."

He laced his hands behind his head and leaned back, smiling. "Well, ok, then."

"Ok then, you will think about it?" I wasn't sure what he was saying.

"Ok, you can go," he said.

A part of me wanted to jump up and scream from excitement. The other part of me felt my stomach drop.

He continued on about how we could work out the details over the next week, and he asked me when I thought I would go.

"I need to pack up my house and get my clothes and things together. I'd like to try and leave by the end of the week so that I can get settled over the weekend." I told him I would work with the resort to get office space near the dock. I was still a little shocked that he had agreed to the plan.

"Take care of yourself, Shaye. Your job is safe with us." He looked back at his computer, and I took that as my dismissal.

I went back to my office, shut the door behind me, and sat down at my desk. I pulled the paperwork out of my bag and found Nick's cell number.

He answered after two rings, "Nick Reid."

I heard wind in the back ground, so I assumed he was outside. "Nick, its Shaye."

"Hi, give me a minute, I am just walking back in from the bakery." I heard a door creak open, and then it was quiet. "Ok. I am here. How can I help you?"

He was all business again, and I said, "I have made arrangements to be there." I realized my statement wasn't particularly clear, so I tried again "What I mean to say is that I accept the terms of the will, and I will be there this weekend."

"That was a quick decision." He sounded surprised.

"There really wasn't any other answer. It was my home. I'm not going to let it go. I may not like the terms, but I'm not going to give up the house." I wanted him to understand my decision was about the house, not him.

He was silent a minute. When he spoke, it wasn't what I was expecting. His voice was soft, and it felt like warm butter pouring over me.

"Shaye, I'm sorry about yesterday. I was an ass." I didn't know what to say, so I waited for him to continue. "Even though I knew you were coming, it was harder to see you than I imagined it would be."

All I could say was, "Thank you."

"We should talk when you get here." He sounded resigned and patient. This Nick made me nervous. It had been easier to stay numb or angry.

I knew we would need to talk at some point, and it was probably better sooner than later. I couldn't avoid him up there forever, so I responded, "That would be fine."

"Is Monday morning good for you to come back into the office to sign some papers?"

"Can we make it later in the day? I would like a little time to get settled." I needed to work, and get my office set up at the resort.

"Sure, come around 4:30, and then we can get dinner afterwards." He wasn't asking.

I thought to myself 'crap, crap, crap.' Out loud, I said, "Great, sounds good." And before I could change my mind or say something foolish, I said I would see him the following week.

"See you next week, Shaye," he said before he hung up.

∞

The week went by quickly. I called the resort about space, and they said they had a storage room on the side of the office I could convert. I told them that would be fine. I cleaned out my office so that it could be used as a conference room or a break room if necessary. I rented out my house to a couple from San Diego. The husband was starting a job with Amazon, and they needed some time to figure out where they wanted to settle down. A year lease was perfect for them.

All the pilots and my co-workers hosted a good-bye lunch for me that Friday. It felt strange, since I wasn't quitting. It was a very nice gesture, though, and I appreciated all the well wishes.

I took my time leaving work that day. It was still light until almost 7:30 at night, and I sat out on a bench on the floating dock until the shadows started creeping over the hill behind me. I walked back to my office, grabbed my bag and a box of books, and walked to my car. Don was still in his office, so I stopped to say good-night.

"Check in next week when you are settled. Take your time, Shaye. We're still here for you." For once, he wasn't rushing me.

"Thanks, Don. I will call you early next week." I nodded because my arms were full, and then I walked to the front door. I pushed it open with my back and walked to my car.

I could see the cars moving quickly on the Interstate on the other side of the lake—people going about their day, moving from one place to the next. I thought briefly how quickly my life had changed. This was the last time I would leave this office, for a while anyway, and I simultaneously felt a sense of loss and anticipation. It was time.

I slept soundly that night and got up early to run. I made sure my Ford Explorer had a full tank of gas, and then I drove up Interstate 5 to the ferry dock. I was going to try and catch the noon boat, so I left around 9 a.m.

It was a beautiful, sunny day. The air was crisp, and the earthy smell of the leaves that had fallen to the ground was evidence that fall had arrived.

The ferry ride was uneventful, and I felt at peace. I stood at the front of the boat as the ferry chugged through the water. I'd always loved the sound of the boat rattling like a drum band, and the clickity-clack of the water hitting the hull. I raised my face to the sun and thought that I finally might be ok. I thought that maybe this year, my insides might heal and finally match my outsides.

I used my time over the weekend to stock up on groceries and clean out the house. My mom had already taken my dad's clothes, and the bathroom was empty of all toiletries. I unpacked and assessed the furniture situation. I decided I would leave things as they were for now.

I went into my dad's office and sat down on the couch to look around. Behind his computer, I saw a picture of my family and the Reids. It was taken the night they were here for dinner, that summer Jason died.

I stood up and walked to it. I looked closely at me and Nick and Jason. Jason had been off to the side, sitting on the railing. He was smiling, and his mom was next to him. Nick and I were off to the left of my dad, and Evie was on my left. She was laughing and looking across us at Jason.

Nick and I were standing close together, my hip pushed up against his side, and he had one arm around me and was trying to scoop Evie into the picture. My right hand grazed his thigh, and my head leaned back into him.

"Oh my God! How could I not have seen this before?" I said out loud.

I tried to think back to that night. I didn't think I had been overly forward, but my mom had said something later that night about being careful. I put my hand to my mouth. Had Jason known? God, I was so young, so stupid. I gently put the picture back behind the monitor and went to finish my cleaning.

Monday morning came, and I started my day like I always did. I still had a job, and, regardless of being on the island, I needed to stick to my routine. I went for a run, made my coffee, and headed to the resort. I needed to get my office settled and check in with Don.

The storage room definitely needed some work. I just didn't feel like tackling it that day, so I decided I would work from the lobby. I called Don and told him I needed to order some supplies and some furniture, and he told me to order whatever I needed. Sometime during the day, a waitress came over.

"Ma'am," she said, "do you need me to bring you anything?"

When had I become a ma'am? "Oh, no, thank you, I'm fine. But thank you for asking." I went back to work.

She continued to stand in front of me.

"Well, it's just - It's just that the lobby is usually for our guests, and you've been here for almost six hours."

I looked at the clock on my computer and saw that it was almost three in the afternoon. "Oh, my goodness, I am so sorry."

I stood up to introduce myself. "I'm Shaye Richards. I work for Kenmore Air Harbor, and my office is the storage room over there. It isn't ready to go, so I thought I would sit here and work."

She looked a little startled by my outburst, so I reached out my hand. "It's nice to meet you."

"I'm Candy Miller. It's nice to meet you too." She was baby-faced, and I thought to myself that I couldn't remember looking, let alone being, that young.

"You know what? I could use a diet coke, and maybe a cup of soup. I have dinner plans in a few hours, and I don't want to eat too much." It was definitely information overload for her, so I stopped talking and just smiled. Then, I realized I probably looked crazy, so I added, "Thank you so much for asking."

She brought my soup and diet coke. I continued working until a little after four o'clock, and then I drove up to Nick's office.

I walked into the office and waited in the hall. The office smelled like furniture polish and pumpkin spice. Suzi had a fall candle burning, and it made the room feel cozy.

I waited a few minutes before Nick came down the stairs. God bless him, again, he still looked just as good. He was in the same outfit I had seen him in last week, only this time the shirt was lavender, and the pants were black. I thought to myself that only a confident man could wear a lavender shirt.

"You're early." He stopped in front of me and put his hands on his hips. He was standing too close, and I backed up a step.

"I was finished for the day, and I guess I am used to driving times that take longer than two minutes." I was trying to make fun of myself to ease the tension I felt.

"Ok, right." He looked around like he needed something but couldn't remember what it was. "Give me a few minutes and I will be right back. Why don't you wait in the conference room? Do you need anything? Water? Coffee?" I replied that I was good, and that I would wait for him in the conference room.

This was a completely different Nick than the one from last week. This Nick made me nervous. He was friendly and normal. He came into the conference room a few minutes later with a stack of papers.

"What is all that?" I was a little overwhelmed.

He looked at the pile and then at me. "You need to sign these documents."

"All of them?" I think my eyebrows hit the middle of my forehead.

He laughed. "Yes, Shaye, all of the documents, but not all the pages. Some of these documents are pages long; you only need to sign one page for each."

He went through each one and I signed them. I didn't understand most of what he was saying, and stopped him at one point to ask, "You do know what you are doing right? You aren't taking all my savings or my first-born child, are you?"

He stopped for a minute, and then he said, "Do you have a child?" He seemed so sincere that it caught me by surprise.

"No, it was a joke, Nick. A joke." I tried to make light of it, but the moment passed, and he continued on with the documents.

By the time we were finished, it was almost six o'clock. My eyes were tired, and I was starving.

"Can we eat now? Please?" I asked as I reached up to stretch.

Nick gathered up all of the documents, and I saw him covertly glance at me when I stretched. He went up to his office with his papers and came down a few moments later with his keys and a sport coat. "Ready?" He grinned at me.

He locked the office door behind us and we walked across the gravel parking lot to the Bay Café. "This is close, so I thought it would be ok."

"It's fine. It's perfect."

The Bay Café was in another old building and had only twelve tables. It was always crowded in the summer. People made reservations weeks in advance, and flew up from Seattle just to eat there.

Tonight, there were only four other people eating, and the waitress sat us at a table in a secluded corner. It was still light outside, but the lighting in the restaurant was dark, intimate. Battery-operated votive candles were lit and placed all around the restaurant.

The waitress came back to our table, and I ordered a red wine. Nick ordered a Jameson's Irish whiskey, neat, and we both ordered the Pecan encrusted salmon with mango salsa and vegetables.

When the waitress left, we both spoke.

"I want to apologize," Nick said.

"I owe you an apology," I said at the same time.

Nick laughed and said, "You go ahead."

"I'm sorry about my behavior the other day. I know you were just doing your job, and I was acting like a child. It was unexpected—both the house and seeing you. I was caught by surprise. I'm sorry." I was watching him swirl his ice. His head was bent as if he was thinking, and he raised his eyes to mine.

"You are forgiven." He was smiling at me, and it was boyishly charming. "It's not really necessary Shaye. You were right. I knew you were coming, and I had time to think about it." He sounded sincere, and I could tell he had a lot more to say. "I'm sorry I was rude to you. Even though I saw your dad frequently, he never mentioned you. He was always business. The only reason I knew you were working at Kenmore Air was because he picked me up one day and made a comment that we should say hello to you." He was looking at me intently, "But you weren't there that day, and he never mentioned it again."

I took a sip of my wine and fidgeted with the ring on my right hand.

He continued, "I noticed after that you were never there when I flew in. I knew you still worked there because, now that I was paying attention, I saw your picture on the wall with the other managers."

I couldn't tell him that when I saw his name on manifests I would leave for the day or work from home. I wasn't about to call myself out just yet, so I let him keep talking.

"I didn't know anything about you anymore. For all I knew, you were married, or had forgotten about us. I expected you to walk in, sign over the house, and waltz back out." His frustration with the situation came through in his voice. "I had to guard myself against whomever you had become. If you never wanted to talk to me again, or if—if I might still love you."

We were silent for a moment, looking at each other. I took another sip of wine just as our waitress brought our dinner.

I said, "I'm sorry, Nick." I prayed he would realize that I was sorry for so many things. He smiled a little sadly and took a bite of his salmon.

He swallowed and took a sip of his water. "I came after you."

I choked on my food and had to drink some water. "What? What do you mean?"

"The day you left. I came to the dock." He looked like he did that day on the beach, the day before I left, and I felt my heart squeeze. "I felt like such a shit for the way I talked to you that day. I didn't want you to leave with those being our last words. I didn't want you to leave at all, for that matter, but I knew you had to."

My heart was racing, "Nick, what are you saying?"

He repeated, "The day you left... I came to the dock. I woke up that morning, and I knew I had to see you. I knew I needed to say things—better things, healing things. I got dressed and drove as fast as I could to the dock, but the boat was pulling away. I saw you get out of your car, but I guess you couldn't hear me over the wake of the boat. I came to the dock, Shaye. I came to the dock."

I had stopped eating, and my eyes were tearing up. "All this time, I thought you hated me."

"No, Shaye. I never hated you." He was poking his dinner with his fork. "Jason's death was just so painful. I couldn't forgive myself for a really long time."

"It's been eight years, Nick. Eight!"

"I did try and call. Evie and I both waited awhile. We had our own grief to process, but we did try and contact you."

"I know. I was so angry, and I didn't know you'd come to the dock. I tried so hard to avoid you and put you out of my mind."

He was nodding in agreement. "I figured you were done with us... done with me."

"I understand." We were both absorbed in our own thoughts. "I couldn't do much more than exist until I took the job with Kenmore Air. I'm so sorry."

We sat quietly for a moment. Each of us reflecting on that day so long ago. After a minute, I asked, "What did you do after I left?"

"Do you really want to know?"

"Yes, please." I looked at him with kind eyes.

"The *whole* story?" Now he sounded like he was warning me. Whatever it was, I had to know. I thought it might have something to do with Julie, but I also knew we wouldn't be able to move forward, even as friends, if I didn't know everything.

"Yes."

His chest rose as he took a long, calming breath and continued. "I arrived at the dock just as it was pulling away. I tried to get your attention. I knew I wouldn't be able to talk to you, but I wanted you to at least see me. I wanted you to know that I wasn't a total asshole.

We both chuckled at his self-deprecating tone, and he continued. "I saw you get out of your car, and then turn to go up to the inside deck. At first, I thought you were dismissing me because you hadn't even acknowledged that you'd seen me. As I replayed that scene over in my head later, I thought that maybe you hadn't seen me at all."

"I didn't see you. I remember feeling empty. Vacant. I know I looked towards the dock, but I didn't really see it." I shook my head, as if trying to bring that day into focus, to conjure up the memory. "I remember feeling like I needed to toughen up."

He was nodding in understanding—as if it all made sense now.

He continued with the story. "When the boat rounded the corner, I remember feeling deflated. I felt like I just had nothing left in me. I sat in my car staring out at the water for a really long time, and then drove to see Evie. She saw me right away when I pulled in and came out with a coffee and a scone."

He started laughing when he described Evie's face. "She saw me and said, 'God Bless, Nick, you look wretched.' She was so funny, and it was so like Evie that I just hugged her. She couldn't hug me back because she was holding my coffee in one hand and the scone in the other."

"I stepped back from her and then sat down on a bench. She sat down next to me, and I told her you had come to the beach to see me the day before."

"Did she know about us, Nick?"

"I think she knew some, but couldn't process the truth of it." His face took on a pained look when he added, "Or didn't want to.

"I told her you had tried to connect with me the day before, to make peace, and I had treated you horribly. I remember her looking at me strangely, almost accusingly, and asking, 'Why was she trying to make peace with you?'"

"I couldn't hide if from her, Shaye. I had to tell her. I knew if I didn't tell her, we would never be close again." He looked lost and sad.

"Was she mad?" I asked him. I had wrapped my arms around myself.

He looked thoughtful when he said, "No, not mad. Hurt. Disappointed. Sad for all of us. But not mad."

"What happened next?"

"I told her about when we met, and how I just couldn't take my eyes off of you." He was looking directly at me.

I felt warm all of a sudden, and tried not to move.

He shook his head in disbelief and laughed a bit when he said, "I told her I couldn't believe my bad luck when she introduced you as Jason's 'friend.' She was never very subtle. I told her we just kept ending up together. I told her it felt like we were supposed to be together."

"Oh my God. Nick, please, this hurts." I didn't think I could hear anymore.

"I wanted her to understand, Shaye. I wanted her to not hate me the way I thought you hated me when you left." He was almost pleading with me. He seemed to be asking forgiveness.

This was an incredibly difficult conversation, but the gates were open, and we couldn't stop now. "Did she understand?" I asked him.

"Not at first. She said we were both stupid, and maybe Jason would still be alive if I wasn't such an asshole. Not for loving you, but for pushing you to make a decision—for sneaking around and not being responsible. We were both stupid for not telling him sooner. She wasn't saying anything I hadn't already thought of myself. But we were young; that's what I told myself, to justify our behavior.

"I was broken and messed up, and I worked all the time. I couldn't separate my thoughts about you and my guilt about Jason. They were all tangled up together." He was on a roll with his words and our food had grown cold. "My dad needed me at the firm, so I just immersed myself in work. It was easier than feeling. Evie was hurting too, but she just kept right on going, in her Evie sort of way." He paused and smiled in remembrance.

"One night, I guess she finally had enough of my dark mood, and her dark mood, and she said, 'we were going out.'" He was staring off into the distance, and I knew he was reliving that night.

"It was the weekend before Memorial Day, and there was a band at the bar. Evie and I took my car that night. I was still staying at my parents' house, and she was living in the cottage on the property."

"We got wasted. I don't know how much I drank, but we just kept doing shot after shot after shot. I think she danced on the bar, and we made spectacles of ourselves, but we both needed it. We needed to be together, and we needed to start healing." I could feel the pain rolling off of him.

"By the time I finished drinking, Evie was already slumped over in a booth. I went to get her, and Pete, the bartender, said he didn't think I should be driving. I think I cursed at him, so he came around the bar to stop me from leaving. He said to me, 'Listen, brother,' and I blew up. I punched him and screamed at him that he was not my brother. Evie barely registered what was happening when I picked her up and carried her out."

The waitress interrupted. "Excuse me for interrupting. Here's the check, when you are ready."

We glanced around us and noticed the restaurant had closed. Nick pulled out his wallet and paid her. "We'll leave shortly. We lost track of time."

"No worries, you can sit for a while. We still need to clean up. And, we always eat dinner together after

212

closing, so you are welcome to stay as long as we do." She smiled at us and took the check.

Nick had been yanked from his thoughts when the waitress came over. He seemed to be staring off into space.

I didn't want to continue putting Nick through this anguish, so I said, "Do you want to go?"

"No, you need to know." He cleared his throat and continued. "When I got to the parking lot, Officer John was there. I don't know if someone called him from the bar, or if he was already in the parking lot. Regardless, he was there, and he said to me 'Let us drive you home, Nick.' I told him I was fine, and I put Evie in the passenger seat. He then told me that if I got in the car with intent to drive, he would arrest me."

Nick started laughing. "I think I told him to eff off and started to get in my car. The next thing I knew, I was being pulled up by the back of my shirt and slammed against the side of my car. John put cuffs on me and walked me to the police car."

My hand was now covering my mouth in disbelief. That entire year I was zoned out in my own self-pity, Nick and Evie were up here suffering. "Oh Nick." I didn't know what else to say.

"It's not a bad story, Shaye. It was a turning point. He took me in and locked me up, but he didn't arrest me. He just wanted me to sober up and be safe. I passed out, and the next thing I remember was that it was morning, and my dad and Evie were on the other side of the bars waiting for me to be let out.

"My dad took us out to the beach. He had coffee and almond butterhorns. The three of us sat on a log and watched the sun come up. None of us said anything at all. Then Evie said, 'I miss him.' And that was it. Evie and I broke. We cried and cried. It had taken almost a year, but our hearts finally broke, and we just sobbed with our dad."

I was watching Nick tell the story, and I felt the tears running down my face. I wiped them with the back of my hand and waited.

"The three of us went back to my parents', and my mom was there making breakfast. Bless her heart. She just looked at the three of us and said, 'Everything all better now?' It made the three of us all laugh so hard I couldn't catch my breath. It was so inappropriate, and yet it brought so much levity to the darkness that had been surrounding us."

I laughed, because I could see his mom's face and hear her voice saying those words.

"A few days later, I was riding my bike to work and stopped to see Evie at the bakery. She said that I should call you. That I should try to talk to you. I agreed, and called that day. You didn't answer, so I waited a few more days and tried again. You didn't answer, *again*." He emphasized the last "again," indicating to me that he knew I was avoiding him. "An entire year had gone by, and I thought if you didn't want to talk, I would let you move on."

"You didn't leave a message." I realized my mistake as soon as the words were out.

"Yep. And there you have it." He wasn't mad, but there was a tone that said, 'See, I was right.' "Evie called, too. She missed you."

"I'm so sorry, Nick. Sorry for all of us." He still hadn't brought up Julie, and I didn't want to leave here tonight with anymore misunderstandings or second guesses.

He was leaning back in his chair with his ankles crossed and his hands linked over his stomach. I was getting a little lost in looking at him. I knew I needed to guard my heart again, but at least we could be friends. At least we could move on, even if it wasn't together.

"Is that all?" I asked quietly.

He looked directly at me. "You want to know about Julie?"

I didn't respond. I just waited.

He sighed heavily. "It was about five years ago. I was going back and forth to Seattle." He added that sometimes he would take the ferry if it was a longer visit. "I had been seeing Jackie every now and then, but she was always a city girl. The island life wasn't going to work for her, so she moved on. We are still friends, but I hardly ever see her.

"My parents had gone on a cruise to Jamaica. I was still at the house, and Evie was still in the cottage." He took another deep breath as if he didn't want to tell me this. "I made dinner one night for me and Evie, and she invited Julie. I had never given her much thought before. She was Jason's high school sweetheart." He paused and asked, "Did you know that?"

"Yes, I knew. We didn't get along well at first. She grew on me though." I was trying to remain neutral about this situation. I couldn't fault Nick for what happened.

He continued. "It was all very casual. She stayed for dinner. We drank some wine. Evie went back to her cottage. Julie and I just kept talking, and we ended up in bed." He stopped so that I could gather my thoughts.

I knew it was coming, but I didn't expect the punch I felt in my stomach. It was a good thing I didn't eat all my dinner because I almost felt like I was going to throw up. I needed to hear everything so that I could move on. I told him to continue.

"It lasted a few months, and then just stopped. I think she was trying to replace Jason with me, and I wasn't Jason. I'm not what she wants, and, more importantly, she isn't what I want. She is more like a sister to me now. Looking back, I think she was just bored."

I laughed, "That's what Jason said about her."

"Really?" He chuckled as well.

"Yes, the first time I saw Jason that summer, she was hanging all over him. He looked disinterested, but was still pacifying her. I asked him about her later, when we were having coffee together, and he said, 'She's just bored.'" I smiled at Nick and we sat in silence for a few minutes.

Nick went on, "So there you have it. Julie is trolling the islands again. Every now and then, she comes around and wants to get a drink or dinner." He laughed again, "It makes Suzi nuts, but, really, Julie is harmless."

My feelings were all over the place about what Nick had told me about Julie. I wasn't entitled to feel jealous, but a part of me felt like she had taken something from me. Logically, I couldn't fault them. It didn't change the fact that it stung.

Nick was looking at me, gauging my reaction, and when I showed none, he changed the topic and told me about my dad. "Your dad came to me a few years ago to make changes to his will. I told him he was crazy for setting it up this way. I said it would make you angry, but he was insistent it be this way." He smiled apologetically at me and said, "I'm sorry you had to come back under these circumstances."

He was referring to my dad's death, and I simply said, "Thank you."

Nick sat straight up again and said, "And there you have it. Here we are. Here you are, and now we move forward." He had gone back to business, and I realized this had not been a date. It was a cleaning of the slate. He wanted to continue with his life the way he had built it. We were going to be here together for the better part of a year, and he didn't want it to be awkward.

"Thank you for telling me your story." I smiled at him.

"You are welcome." He smiled back at me.

We talked a little more about the island, and then he walked me out. The intimacy of our dinner together was gone, and he told me he would reach out to me if there were any legal problems.

He leaned in to kiss me on the cheek and said, "It is really good to see you, Shaye."

I breathed him in, and realized that I had never really gotten over him. He smelled the same: like warm sand and a cedar forest. I wanted to wrap myself in him, but this wasn't the time. I needed to keep my emotions together.

"You too, Nick." I said back to him. I got in my car, waved and headed back to my house. I was going to have to guard my heart with him. We were grown now, and another heartbreak would destroy me.

A few days after my dinner with Nick, I finally settled into my office and was working on some new campaigns for weekend packages. I had been avoiding most people, and even tried to slip in and out of the grocery store unnoticed. I went to the bakery one morning to try and see Evie, but she wasn't there. I was disappointed in myself that I actually felt kind of relieved.

From my office window, I could see to the end of the bay where the planes approached, and the gravel parking lot between the kayak shop and the resort.

I saw the eleven o'clock plane come in, so I walked down the dock to help tie up the plane and meet the passengers. I was happy to see it was Chris on this flight, and I gave him a big hug when he jumped down out of the pilot seat.

"Chris! It's so good to see you!" I said, and my tone was a little high-pitched.

"Shaye, it has only been three days. Are you that hard up for adult conversation?" He was laughing, and not buying into my over-dramatization of cheer.

I groaned. "Three days? God! It feels like forever. Let me help with your passengers." I stepped onto the pontoon and opened the passenger door. "How are you guys doing today? Welcome to the island." Wow! I must be really hard up for friends. I really did sound overexcited.

Chris was shaking his head at me and tying up the rope. I helped the passengers down the steps and onto the dock. Then I climbed into the plane, unfastened the luggage net, and handed the bags and backpacks down to Chris. There was a twenty-five-pound luggage limit per person, so people always traveled light.

The passengers walked up the dock to check in with the resort while I chatted with Chris. After a few minutes, I said good-bye, watched him climb back up into the plane, and then untied him. Holding onto the rope, I dragged the plane around so that he was positioned to taxi out. When he was clear, he started the engine, and the propeller started to turn. I waved him off, watched him taxi out into the bay, and then I headed back to my office.

When it was almost lunch time, I called in an order to the Bay Café and drove into town. I stopped at the print shop to get some office supplies, and then at the bank, before going to the café.

I went into the café, and the hostess asked if I was a party of one.

"No, I'm here for a to-go order? Last name is Richards."

"Ok. I will be right back."

She walked into the main dining area and around the corner to the kitchen. I glanced around the restaurant and saw Nick having lunch with the County Judge. Nick was smiling at me. I waved tentatively at him and then looked away. I did not want to engage in conversation.

All of the sudden, a voice boomed across the restaurant, "Shaye Richards!"

I felt my cheeks turn bright red. I could not escape now, so I walked over to where Nick was sitting with Judge Miller. Nick looked casual today. He was wearing khaki shorts, a blue T-shirt, his Teva water sandals, and a baseball cap. He looked manly, and I tried not to stare.

"Judge Miller, how are you?" I leaned down to give him a hug.

"Good, good. I heard you were back. I'm so sorry to hear about your father. He was a good man. A good *businessman*."

I wasn't about to say, "And yes, he was also batshit crazy because he made me come back here." Instead I smiled and said, "Yes, sir, he sure was."

He continued, "Nick, you know Shaye, here." He pointed at me with his fork.

Nick was grinning with amusement, and then he said in a lazy southern way, "Yes, sir. Shaye and I go way back. In fact, Shaye had a big crush on me when I was boy." His eyes were laughing at me. I felt my face flush again, and I looked at him in shock. "Followed me into the woods, she did." He winked at me.

What on Earth? This fake southern accent made me want to punch him.

The Judge then said, "Look at her now! You should be crushing on her, not the other way around. Those big long legs and that pretty blond hair. You two would make a handsome couple. Pretty blue-eyed babies, too."

Nick looked at the Judge, "Maybe I am, judge. Maybe I am." Then he looked at me and said, "What do you think, Shaye? Do you think we would make pretty blue-eyed babies?"

I could see he was playing with me.

I was equally embarrassed and turned on. "I don't think so, Nick. I'm not into donkeys."

The Judge howled with laughter and took a sip of his tea. I turned to the Judge and said, "It was a pleasure to see you again sir." Then I turned and left the restaurant.

I was halfway back to my office when I realized I had forgotten my lunch. "Crap, crap, crap!" I said, hitting my steering wheel with the palm of my hand.

I certainly was not going to go back and get it and risk running into them again, so I went to the resort restaurant and ordered a cup of soup to take back to my office.

I had just sat down when Nick entered the front door. I saw him turn to the receptionist and ask her a question before turning and looking in the direction of my office.

As he started down the hall, I made eye contact with him. Then I got up from my chair, walked around my desk, and slammed the door shut.

I heard him laugh on the other side of the door and knock gently. "Shaye, I'm sorry. That was rude of me. I brought your lunch. You forgot it."

I spoke through the door, "That was mean, Nick." I added, "And unnecessary."

"Open the door, Shaye," he said more softly.

I opened the door and glared at him. I wasn't going to let him in. I stood there with my left hand on the door frame and my right hand on the door.

He said with a drawl, "I don't know If you remember or not, but Judge Miller is from Georgia, and he likes to talk about the pretty girls. I was just mimicking him." He was trying to apologize, but I was still mad.

"It was embarrassing. Talking about me like I was a breeding horse. And did you actually wink at me? I am embarrassed for you." I was frowning at him.

"Shaye, I have to see the man at least twice a week. I need to play along with him and keep the peace. He's the County Judge. It wasn't personal."

He looked like a repentant little boy. I felt myself softening towards him, and I needed to snap out of it.

"Give me my lunch," I said, putting my hand out.

"Forgive me." He held the to-go box away from me.

"No." Now I was being the petulant child.

He put his head back and laughed. "Oh, my God, Shaye!" He smiled at me. "You are so gorgeous; do you know that?"

I took that moment to grab my lunch from him, and said, "Go away." I shut the door.

I heard him chuckle from the other side of the door. A few minutes later, I saw his Range Rover head back towards town.

Sitting down at my desk, I opened my lunch. I had lost my appetite and my will to work. I opened my office door, walked to the kitchen, and tossed my lunch in the trash. Then I went into the bar. "Eric, can I get another diet coke from you?" Eric was one of the full-time waiters/bartenders at the resort. Since my office was in the building, he and I had become friends.

"Diet Coke, here ya go." He handed a to-go cup over to me.

"Thanks, Eric," I said, and walked back down the hall.

I worked for a couple more hours, and when I finally got up to stretch, the sun was starting to go down and dinner guests were coming in to the restaurant. I shut down my computer, locked my office door, and headed home for the night. I stopped by the grocery story to get a bag of salad and some tortellini and vodka pasta sauce.

When I got home, I changed into my usual yoga pants and T-shirt and put the pasta on to cook. I had cleaned out a few more things and had bought new sheets for the beds. I realized I needed to work on the kitchen next.

I poured myself a glass of red wine and walked into the living room to put some music on. I put a CD in the stereo, making a note to myself that I needed to look into Wi-Fi and a Bluetooth stereo system. There wasn't much of a music collection. My dad had all country CD's, which I found very odd since he always listened to classical at home.

I found the Nickelback CD, 'Dark Horse', which was obviously mine, and put it in the CD player. I didn't remember being that angry back then, but it seemed to fit my day, so I turned up the volume and started jumping around the room.

The volume was so high that I could feel it vibrating in my chest. I was letting out the frustration of the day and screaming 'burn it to the ground' as loud as I could. It felt more than good: it felt cathartic. I jumped up and down and whipped my head like I was a rock star.

I slowed my jumping a bit, but I was still whipping my head. My eyes were closed, and I was just feeling the music. When the song ended, I fist bumped the air and shouted, "Yes!"

Slow clapping came from the hallway. "Well, that was interesting."

Startled, I fell back against the couch. "What the heck, Evie! You scared the crap out of me." My heart was racing, and I took a moment to catch my breath.

"Two things," she said. She came over to the couch and sat down next to me. "First, your front door was unlocked, and I could see you kangarooing in here." She pulled her feet up under her and continued, "And second, I'm angry with you." She punched me hard in my left arm.

"OW! Evie, seriously?" I snapped at her.

"Yes, Shaye, seriously!" She jumped up off the couch and proceeded to yell at me. "You have been back for almost a week, and you haven't even called me."

"I'm sorry, Evie. I came by one day, and you weren't there. I know it's no excuse, but I kind of needed to get settled here first before I started getting reacquainted with people," I said, trying to sound remorseful.

"I'm not 'people,' Shaye." She sounded really hurt, and it broke my heart.

I looked at her sadly, and then opened my arms. She came back to the couch and we hugged. I said again with more emotion, "I'm so sorry, Evie."

After a moment, we pulled apart, and Evie said, "Nick told me you had dinner together the other night."

"We did. It was nice." I was trying to not give too much away. I couldn't make eye contact with her, and I saw her staring intently at me.

She started to smile slowly, and said, almost as if she had just uncovered a secret, "You still have a thing for him." Her voice became lilting as she teased me, "He's pretty handsome now, isn't he? He's like a real man."

"Evie, stop! It doesn't matter."

"So, you do have a thing for him!" She shouted, giddy like a child.

"No! I don't." I got up off the couch to check the pasta. I had forgotten all about it, so it was probably a soggy mess.

She followed me into the kitchen. "It's okay, you know. He told me." She had turned somber, and I could tell she wanted to be real with me.

I took the pasta off the stove and drained it. I asked her if she wanted to stay and eat with me.

"Sure. I will set the table while you finish up." She took forks out of the drawer and grabbed two bowls from the cupboard. I was fascinated that she knew where everything was. Thinking back, I realized she had spent a lot of time down here that summer.

We sat down to eat, and I picked up the conversation where she had left off.

"It was a long time ago, and people change. People grow and have new relationships." I paused to see where she would take that conversation; I was not disappointed.

"You mean Julie?" She looked incredulous. "Please. That was a blip." She rolled her eyes.

I laughed, "A blip?"

"Yeah, you know? Something that shows up quickly and disappears so fast you aren't really sure you saw it? A blip."

She was totally committed to her statement, so I said, "Ok then, a blip." And I put it right out of my head.

We continued eating, and I said to her, "Nick and I were wrong. We were wrong for what we did."

Evie looked at me sweetly. "No, you weren't, Shaye. I saw him with you. He was always near you, hovering. I never thought much about it until after you left, but then it made sense. I think I knew long before the accident. And it wasn't your fault. Jason had demons of his own; he should not have been driving. I miss him. I do. But I still have Nick and my parents."

She paused, then added, "And Julie."

We both laughed.

She continued, "And now I have you back." She put her fork down and grabbed my hand. "Nick and I healed a while ago. For the most part, we are good. I hope you are there, too. Or that you get there soon." She smiled at me, and I felt a tear fall down my cheek.

"Now!" She exclaimed, jolting me out of the moment. "There is a band this weekend, and you need to come out with us."

I laughed and said, "Maybe."

She batted her eyelashes. "Nick will be there."

"Well, then no, I won't make it." We both laughed again.

Evie stayed for a little while longer. We talked about the house and the crazy stipulation. "It is kind of odd, don't you think? That he would make you have to stay here for a year?" She tilted her head and looked at me questioningly.

"I guess so. What I find stranger is that I feel as if my life in Seattle doesn't exist anymore. It feels like it is already gone." I looked at her in resignation. I wasn't sad or happy. I just was.

She helped me clean up the kitchen, and then she said she needed to go home to sleep. She had to get up at 3:30 AM to start baking and needed to get to bed soon. I hugged her good-bye and went back inside. Out of habit, from living in the city, I locked the front door behind her. Then, just because I could, I unlocked it before going upstairs to bed.

∞

Friday flew by. We had a number of extra flights because of the weekend, so I was exhausted by the time I got home. I took a bath, drank some wine, and went to bed early. I'd called Evie from the office before I left at the end of the day and told her that I would come out Saturday night.

"Yes!" she'd said, and I could hear the happiness in her voice. "Why don't you meet us about eight o'clock? We can get a booth before it gets too crowded."

"Who's the 'we'?"

"Me, Nick, Julie, and you. Nick is bringing a friend from the firm in Seattle, and Amy might show up later. The Pizza Garage is usually really busy on Saturday, and she doesn't leave until late. I guess that's it." She sounded happy.

I told her it sounded like fun, and that I would see her Saturday night.

I slept in until nine Saturday morning, and the house was freezing when I got out of bed. Fall was coming, and I had forgotten how cold it could get in the forest. I found a pair of those slippers the airlines give you when you fly first class. In the closet was an Eddie Bauer flannel of my dad's, and I put that on, too. I went downstairs to make coffee and start a fire. I could turn the heat on, but the fireplace was so much cozier.

When the coffee was done brewing, I took my cup and curled up in my favorite chair. The house was warming up, and I was waking up. In a little while, I would go for a run.

The day passed by easily, and I ended up taking a nap on the couch. I had not been this lazy in so long. It felt decadent, and (apparently) I needed it.

I took my time getting ready to go out. Since I was leasing out my house, I had most of my clothes from Seattle with me. I wanted to look good, so I chose a gray turtleneck mini-dress which had a pleated skirt, and black over-the-knee suede boots. Pulling my hair back into a low ponytail, I put hoops in my ears that I could show off. I wore smoky eye makeup and red lipstick. I felt good, and I know I looked even better. Part of me wanted to outshine Julie, but the other part just wanted to feel good about myself as a girl.

When I got to the bar, it was already crowded. I looked around and saw Evie and Julie sitting in a booth with another guy I didn't recognize. Evie caught my eye and waved me over.

"Shaye, come sit down." She looked beautiful. She had flat-ironed her hair, and it hung to the middle of her back. She was wearing black Palazzo pants and a black off-the-shoulder beaded blouse. With her blue eyes and pale skin, she looked stunning. She was down-to-earth and pleasant, and she didn't even know how pretty she was.

Julie sat next to her, looking smug and beautiful. She wore a red one-piece halter-top jumper that showed off every curve she had. I wanted to hate her for her figure, but she really was quite lovely. At least she knew how to show it off.

230

Evie yelled over at the bartender, "Mac, bring me another Blue Moon."

I slid in the booth next to her and said hello to Julie. "It's good to see you, Julie."

"You too, Shaye. Whose boyfriend are you going to steal this time?"

I figured she must be drunk already, and I really didn't want this crap from her.

I responded, "Well, Julie, I thought I might go two for two with you."

She looked at me in surprise, understanding registering on her face that I knew about her and Nick.

Evie slapped my arm and said, "Shaye!"

The guy across from us inhaled. I looked at him with a huge smile and introduced myself. "Hi, I'm Shaye Richards, boyfriend-stealer. I'm currently on house-arrest in order to receive my inheritance." I stuck out my hand and he took it.

"Ethan Archer, wingman to Nick Reid and currently unattached, so no stealing necessary." He was laughing, and I felt an immediate kinship with him. I was certain that he would have my back.

Julie shoved him and said, "Let me out."

He stood to let her out, and she stormed off.

Evie turned and said to me, "Do you really need to provoke her?"

I was stunned. "Uh, yeah. I hate to sound petty, but she started it."

"Yes, but you already know how she is." Evie was defending her, so I brushed her off. I turned to Ethan

231

and asked him what had brought him to the island that weekend.

"I work for Nick in Seattle. I'm originally from Jackson, Wyoming, and Nick thought I might want a weekend in the islands. I have never been here before, and he thought it would be a nice break for me. Evie picked me up at the seaplane dock this afternoon, took me to dinner in town, and here we are."

He was quick and to the point. He reminded me of Don. Because today was Saturday and I didn't work, I had not seen him get off the plane. He looked like a cowboy, and I had difficulty imagining him in a suit. He wore Ariat western-cut jeans and cowboy boots. His shirt was a dark blue, long sleeve Henley, and there was a Carhartt jacket hanging on the hook behind him that I presumed was his. He had thick, wavy, copper-colored hair and brown eyes. I thought he was very nice to look at.

"Speaking of Nick, where is he?" I turned to Evie and asked.

"Speak of the Devil, he just walked in." She nodded in the direction of the door.

He was shaking hands with a few of the guys at the bar. He turned to us and jerked his chin up to acknowledge he had seen us. He must have come from work because he was wearing suit pants that were tailor-fit to his body, a button-down shirt, and a tie that he had loosened. I was struck again by what a beautiful man he had become. This Nick was not a boy, and my lady parts had taken notice.

He worked his way to our booth. When he stood in front of us, Ethan rose to meet him. "Nick," he said.

"Ethan, you made it." He glanced between us, and I couldn't make eye contact with him.

"Sure did. Evie has been a great host. Took me to dinner, showed me around town, and introduced me to Julie and this lovely lady." He was referring to me, and I felt my face flush.

Nick glanced at me, and he bit his lower lip. Then he said in a friendly tone, "Really? That's great. Shaye works for Kenmore Air. You might see her at the dock when you leave Monday morning."

I heard the underlying message in his words to back off from me, and it instantly pissed me off. He'd invited his friend for the weekend, but now jealously was creeping in, making him snarky. Ethan didn't seem to notice, or, if he did, he didn't comment on it.

At that moment, Julie decided to rejoin the group. She walked up to Nick, slid her right arm around his waist and put her left hand on his stomach. "Nick, you made it."

She glanced at me triumphantly, and I knew she was intentionally messing with me.

It was nauseating to watch Julie play up to Nick just to get a rise out of me. I rolled my eyes at her. It was all I could do not to laugh.

Nick casually extracted himself from her, saying, "Hey, Julie, back off."

He looked at Ethan, jerked his head towards the bar and said, "Join me for a beer." The two of them walked away from our table, and Julie stalked off to another group of friends, seemingly un-phased by Nick's dismissal.

I turned in the booth to face Evie straight on, and said, "What's going on?"

"What do you mean?" She was acting too innocent.

"Don't be coy, Evie. The tension in this place is off the charts."

She responded, "I think you are projecting, Shaye. We are supposed to be having fun." She took a sip of her drink and refused to look me in the eye.

"Look at me!" I said sternly, under my breath. She turned to me and I said, "Julie is bitchier than she has ever been, and is peeing all over her territory. Nick practically dismissed his friend, you are all chipper and ambiguous, and poor Ethan is just stuck in the middle. What am I missing?"

"Fine." She let out a heavy sigh. "I think Nick invited Ethan this weekend to take Julie off his hands."

I threw back my head and laughed. "Oh, that's rich."

I glanced up at the bar where Nick and Ethan were sitting. They looked like good friends deep in conversation. I turned back to Evie. "Poor guy."

Evie said, "Which one?" and we both started laughing again.

A few more people stopped by to say hi, and I enjoyed re-connecting with the locals. I realized how much I had missed them, but also how much I had changed. I wasn't a lost girl anymore. I was more centered, and calmer.

"Excuse me for a minute, Evie, I will be right back." I stood up from the booth and headed towards the bathrooms.

I was washing my hands in the sink when I looked up and saw Julie behind me in the mirror.

"Hey, Julie. Sorry about earlier. I wasn't trying to be mean."

"How long are you staying this time, Shaye?" She was calm, but I could see vulnerability in her eyes.

"Look, Julie, we were starting to be friends before..." I started to speak, and she cut me off.

"Before Jason died." WOW! Ok. So, she hit that right out of the park.

"Yes, before Jason died." I didn't want to argue with her. "I'm sorry you lost your good friend."

"He was my boyfriend, Shaye." She had a little more heat in her words.

"No, Julie, he wasn't. And you can't replace him with Nick." I was getting angry, and a little tired of her high school behavior.

She lowered her head, and I suddenly felt sorry for her. She raised her eyes to me. "Try not to hurt anybody else this time around." And with that parting shot, she walked out of the bathroom.

I stayed in the bathroom to compose myself before walking back into the bar. I caught Nick's eyes as I came out. He raised his eyebrows in a question. I rolled my eyes and shook my head a little, and he went back to talking with Ethan.

I stood at the end of the bar, staring out at the people and marveling at their joyfulness.

The band started playing Patsy Cline's 'Crazy'. I looked up to find Nick looking at me. Our eyes locked, and he started walking towards me.

Taking my hand, he walked me to the dance floor. He took me in his arms and started swaying with me. He spun me around a few times, and then dipped me backwards. I smiled and laughed at him, so he spun me around again.

He had his left arm around my waist, and his right hand was holding my hand against our chests. He pulled me closer. I let go of his hand to wrap my arms around the back of his neck. He tightened his hold around my back with both hands and pulled me tighter to him.

I raised my face to his neck, and he lowered his cheek to my cheek. We were pressed so closely together, I could feel his heartbeat. I felt like I was inside him. We continued to sway together, and I felt that if he let go of me, I would fall. I felt him kiss my hair and heard him whisper, "Shaye."

I turned my head and pressed my mouth to his neck, inhaling the cedar and lime scent of him.

It was the longest and shortest two minutes of my life. When the music stopped, I stepped away from him, my chest heaving, and a question in my eyes. People around us were clapping for the band. I looked at Nick, thanked him, and turned away.

Evie was chatting and laughing with some friends, and I leaned down to tell her I was leaving.

"What? Why? You've only been here a few hours."

"I know, but I'm not used to late nights. I'll catch up with you this week." I gave her a hug, grabbed my jacket, and left. I did not look back. I did not slow down. I went right to my car and drove the ten miles to my house, where this time, I locked the door.

Monday morning, I was standing down on the dock waiting for the nine-a.m. flight to arrive when I saw Nick's Range Rover pull into the resort parking lot. I saw him get out and look towards me, but he didn't wave. He was wearing cargo pants, his Timberland boots, a pullover, and a baseball hat. He did not look like he was going to work. It was cold out, and I was bundled up in a Helly Hanson sailing crew jacket and khaki shorts. I was wearing boots and a baseball cap as well.

Ethan was with him, and as he climbed out of the passenger side, he gave me a quick wave and then opened the back door to grab a duffle bag. He was dressed for work, and he looked like a completely different person than the guy at the bar the other night.

I saw the two of them shake hands, and then I watched Ethan walk down the dock towards me.

Climbing back into his car, Nick sat and looked out his front windshield in my direction. He had both his palms wrapped around the top of the steering wheel, and after a few seconds he lifted his fingers and gave me what looked like a quick wave. I gave him a quick wave back, and then Ethan was in front of me.

He had a big grin on his face when he saw me. "Shaye! Good morning!" He put his bag down on the dock and gave me a big bear hug.

"How are you?" I asked him. Standing back, I smiled up at him and put my hands in my coat pocket.

"Good, I'm good. Nick took me to the bakery this morning before dropping me off. Man, those cinnamon rolls are the best." He was rubbing his stomach.

"Yeah, Evie makes some yummy treats," I laughed.

"We missed you last night. I was expecting to see you." He acted as if I knew what he was talking about, so I played along.

"Yeah, I am still trying to get settled in my house, and don't go out much." I was hoping he would elaborate, and he did not disappoint me.

Ethan continued, "Nick said the same thing." I could feel my blood pressure rising, and wondered why Nick would lie to Ethan. Ethan went on about the Vineyard and how beautiful the property was. The private dinner was apparently "to die for," and he felt really welcome. "Nick really pulled out all the stops for me."

"That's Nick," I smiled tightly at him, "a very gracious host."

I heard the turbine engine of the float plane taxiing up through the water. I could never hear them land, and it startled me a bit. I grabbed the line from the strut and pulled the plane so that the pontoon was aligned with the dock.

One of our newer pilots jumped out and greeted Ethan. "Ethan Archer?"

"Yes sir." He shook his hand.

"Ready to go?" the pilot asked him.

"Sure am." He turned to me and said, "It was really nice to meet you, Shaye. I hope I get to see you again."

"You too, Ethan, have a good flight." I watched him climb into the back seat, and the pilot shut the door. The pilot got in the plane and gave me a thumbs-up, and I untied the line.

I walked back up the dock and went to the restaurant to get a coffee. I was so mad that I didn't really want to talk to anyone, so I went and sat in my office with the door shut.

After a bit, I realized I wasn't really mad. I felt hurt, and I felt left out. I wasn't going to confront Nick for lying about my whereabouts last night. I needed to think about why I felt excluded, and why I cared. It was times like this that I resented being here, and resented my dad for putting me in this position. I needed a connection with the city, so I called Don to check in.

The receptionist answered, and I was feeling so formal I forgot that she knew me, "Shaye Richards for Don Sanders please."

"Hi, Shaye, it's Jessica." She sounded hurt that I didn't acknowledge her.

"Oh, hi, Jessica. I didn't recognize your voice." I felt like such a liar, and I dropped my forehead into my hand. "How are you?"

"Good. How are you? How is the island?" Oh, dear Lord. I did not want to have a friendly conversation with her.

"I'm good," I responded curtly.

"We sure miss you around here," she continued.

"Thank you. Is Don in?" I wanted to get off the phone with her.

"Oh sure, let me transfer you." The line went quiet, and then I heard Don answer.

"Shaye, good to hear your voice. What's the plan for the week?" Always reliable, Don, getting right to the point.

I told him about the adventure series that would include kayaking and camping. He liked the idea, and said he was coming up this weekend.

"Great! What can I get ready for you?" I asked.

He told me Tom was coming, and would keep the plane overnight. "I think Jane and I will stay at the resort. Check it out for our future adventure passengers." He sounded as if he was excited for a night away.

"Oh, you're bringing Jane!" I was so happy to hear this news. Jane was his wife of 40 years, and I adored her. "I can't wait to see her."

"Make reservations somewhere for dinner. We should land between five and six in the evening."

"Perfect! I will see you then."

He hung up, and my mood remarkably improved. I called the Bay Café and made reservations for Friday night at six-thirty p.m. for four people.

The week passed uneventfully. I had settled into a routine, and it felt really good. I woke between six and six-thirty and went for a run. I got to my office by eight-thirty, and then I met the nine a.m., one, three, and five p.m. flights. I locked up after the last flight and went home to make dinner. It was predictable and safe, and it was starting to feel real.

Friday morning, I walked down to the dock to meet the nine o'clock plane, and I saw Nick pull his Range Rover in next to the resort office. He was dressed in a suit, and I saw him grab his briefcase out of the backseat of his car. He looked so handsome. I had to remind myself that he had not included me in the invite to dinner at the vineyard, nor had he contacted me since our dance at the bar.

He disappeared into the office and came out to the dock a few minutes later with a to-go cup of coffee. "Good morning, Shaye." He smiled at me and seemed overly enthusiastic.

"Good morning, Nick." I was wearing khaki shorts, a Kenmore Air polo, and my Keens, and I felt mousy next to him. He looked so sexy in his suit, and smelled like lime and soap. I couldn't look him in the eye, so I stared out into the bay, waiting for the plane.

He made an attempt at small talk and said, "Have you had a good week?"

I replied, "Yes, I have. Did you have a nice dinner with Julie?" I could have choked myself. I felt stupid for sounding bitter.

The plane arrived, and I went to grab the line.

Behind me, Nick said, "It wasn't dinner with Julie." He sounded frustrated, and continued, "It was dinner at the Vineyard with Ethan and Julie and her parents. I am trying to hook them up."

I tied the plane up. Since there wasn't anyone getting off the plane, and Nick was the only person getting on, it was a quick stop.

I held the line, looked at him, and said, "Ok."

He raised his eyebrows. "Ok?"

Staring him down, I said flatly, "You need to get on the plane."

He chuckled and said, "So, not OK?" He paused for a minute, and then said, "Fine. I don't have time to talk about this now." He stepped on the pontoon, threw his bag up into the plane, and stepped back off onto the dock.

He stood right in front of me, grabbed my face with both his hands, and leaned in to kiss me. He breathed me in. Closing my eyes, I started to fall into him. He backed up and said, "We'll talk tonight." He looked me in the eye, and then gave me another quick kiss.

He climbed up into the plane and shut the door. I stood there in shock with my fingers pressed against my mouth. The pilot knocked on the window to get me to drop the line. I shook myself out of my daze, dropped the line, and gave him a thumbs up. The turbine engine started, and I watched the plane taxi out and take off.

My head was reeling. I didn't know how to respond to what just happened. And, I suddenly remembered my boss was coming for the night.

"Oh, dear God!" I said to myself. "I need to check the flight manifest."

I ran quickly up the dock, across the lawn, through the resort back door, and into my office. My computer was still running from earlier, so I clicked on the system that would bring up all passenger flight logs. I scrolled down for five o'clock, and sure enough, there was Don Sanders, Jane Sanders, and Nick Reid. "Shit!" I said out loud. I did not need them together in an enclosed space.

But there was nothing I could do other than pray that Nick missed the flight, or that he came home early. I went about my day doing exactly as I would have any other day. Nick was not on the three o'clock flight, so I assumed he would be on the plane with my boss.

I dressed for dinner in a light peach halter maxi dress and nude sandals. I brushed out my hair and put a little more makeup on. A little after five, I saw the plane approaching, so I walked down the dock to meet Don and Jane. When Jane stepped off the plane, she saw me and squealed, "Shaye."

I continued down the walkway to give her a big hug, enveloping her tiny frame.

"Shaye. It's good to see you. You look lovely."

"Thank you. It is so nice to see you."

I saw Tom unloading overnight bags, and then he climbed back in to secure the plane.

Don came over next and gave me a hug. "I agree, Shaye. I think the island agrees with you." He sounded really happy. I thought maybe he had been drinking on the plane, but we don't allow that, so it had to be something else.

He continued on, "We met your friend Nick today. Nice fellow." I was starting to feel panicked, like something really awkward was about to happen.

I watched Tom get out of the plane and pull it around to the other side of the dock so that he could tie it down for the night. Nick walked towards us at the sound of his name.

Don said, "We invited him to dinner with us. We thought it would be nice to get to know the island folk a little better, as well as some of your friends." My stomach dropped.

I put a smile on my face and said, "I only made reservations for four. It's really difficult to add people. Maybe another time?"

"Nonsense. Tom said he would much rather go down the street and get a burger from the local pub."

I looked to Tom for help—but he just shrugged at me. I glanced over at Nick, who looked really pleased with himself.

I continued to smile and said, "That sounds lovely. Thank you, Nick, for joining us for dinner." Then I addressed Tom. "Tom, it was nice to see you. Enjoy your *burger*." My emphasis indicated he was going to be chopped meat the next time I saw him. He knew about Nick and Jason, and I felt somehow betrayed.

"My car is right this way, Mr. Sanders." Nick motioned for us to follow.

"I can drive. Nick, you can meet us there," I said.

Nick mimicked Don and said, "Nonsense. We can all ride together." He grinned at me like he was enjoying my discomfort immensely. "It will save on gas."

I rode in the back seat with Mrs. Sanders, and we talked about how, even though she enjoyed the city, it was always nice to get away for the night. She was looking forward to a peaceful night's sleep, and a scone from the bakery in the morning.

We were early for our reservation, but they were ready for us, so we all went in and sat down. To any onlooker, we looked like two couples having dinner together. I took several calming breaths, praying I would get through the meal without having a panic attack.

Don ordered a bottle of wine to share. Once we had ordered dinner, Don said to me, "Nick tells us he is an attorney."

I nodded and said, "Yes, that's correct."

Nick was leaning back in his chair a bit, watching the conversation between us.

Don addressed Nick. "We may want to talk with you about some business with the company."

Glancing back and forth between the two of them, I said, "Well, I think Nick does mostly Wills and Estate planning, if I'm not mistaken?"

Nick looked at me, put his arm around the back of my shoulder, and said, "Actually, Shaye, my dad was an Estate Planner. I am in Corporate Litigation." He turned back to Don and said, "I would be happy to discuss business with you, Mr. Sanders. Maybe tomorrow. I wouldn't want to bore the ladies tonight."

He was using his kiss-ass voice, but the way he looked at me when he said "Corporate Litigation" was something else entirely. I felt all my eggs screaming,

"Yes! Blue-eyed babies—YES!" I sucked in air and took a long sip of my wine.

"Fair enough, son, fair enough. And please, call me Don."

"Yes, sir, Don," Nick said, and took a drink of his wine.

Our dinner arrived, and we all commented on the beautiful presentation. Don asked for the salt, and Jane *tsked* him. Nick ordered another bottle of wine for the table. I tried to relax and enjoy the company.

When we had settled in with our meals, Jane commented to me and Nick, "You two seem to have known each other for quite a while."

It wasn't really a question, and Nick and I glanced at each other to see who would speak first. I raised my brows at him.

Nick took that as permission, and said, "Yes and no. My father was her dad's attorney, and from that relationship, our parents became friends." He looked thoughtful as he started telling the story, not knowing how much they knew, or how much I was willing to share. "I remember her briefly from when she was younger, spending the summers up here. I grew up here, so it wasn't as if I ever saw her in the city."

I glanced up at Jane. She seemed to be giving Nick her undivided attention.

Nick continued, "I do remember the brief times that I saw her, she was always running: running through the woods, running on the beach, running to catch me on my horse." Nick turned to look at me, and I saw sweetness in his eyes. Then, something in his look

247

changed. I realized he was going to tell the story. He was going to tell Don and Jane our story, and I had to just hang on.

"I really only got to know Shaye about eight years ago," Nick started in. I saw Don glance at me. I know he knew part of it, and I think he might have sensed more was coming. I saw concern and a question on his face as to whether this was ok or not. I nodded briefly to him, letting him know it was ok—that I was ok.

Nick continued, "I came home for the fourth of July and met her at the bar with my sister, Evie."

Jane asked, "The one you told us about on the plane? The one who owns the bakery?"

"Yes, Evie introduced me to Shaye, and then introduced Shaye to me... as Jason's friend." He chuckled, remembering. "It wasn't hard to figure out that by 'friend,' she meant girlfriend."

Jane laughed, and then she realized. "Oh, no. Was this the brother who died?"

"Yes, Jason was my brother who died." He spoke softly to Jane.

Jane looked at me and said, "Oh, Shaye, I am so sorry. I had no idea."

She reached across the table and grabbed Nick's hand. "And Nick. I am so sorry for your family's loss."

He said, "Thank you. As my mother likes to say, 'time heals all.'" We all paused for a minute and reflected on that statement.

Then he turned back to me. Before he spoke, he made sure I was looking directly at him, and he said, "What makes this story even sadder is that I fell in love with Shaye that summer. Then she left the island and never came back."

I felt my eyes well up. I saw out of the corner of my eyes, Jane's mouth fell open, and Don put his fork on his plate.

Nick continued as if they weren't there. He never stopped looking directly at me, as if we were the only two people in the world. "She captivated me. I couldn't stay away. I quit an internship to be on the island, just so I could be here with her. At first, she was just so lovely to look at. Then, I realized how smart and caring she was. And I loved her. We were young and made some mistakes—costly mistakes. But it didn't change the fact that I still wanted her." He paused for a moment, holding my gaze. "Then she left."

He looked back at Don and Jane. They were dumb-struck. Jane had her hand to her mouth, and I looked at her with tear-filled eyes.

She looked at me and said, "Jason?" I knew what she was asking.

"Yes, he knew." My throat had closed, so it was difficult to get the words out.

"Oh, you two. What a horrible time for you." She was so empathetic, and so kind.

I wiped my tears and said, "Well, as Martha says..."

We all laughed a little and said together, "Time heals all."

Don was looking at us and nodding. I think the emotional stuff was a little much for him. "It's nice to see you are still friends." He was serious, but I also think he wanted to move on. "Now, let's order dessert."

We were all grateful for a break in the mood. I felt closer to Nick, and to Jane and Don as well. I could feel my heart healing, and every time we talked about Jason and that summer, the pain lessened. I hoped that one day I would be able to think of Jason and celebrate him.

We finished dinner, and Nick drove the Sanderses back to the resort. Their room was back up behind the main lodge, with a lovely view of the bay.

Nick helped them with their bags and said good-night. I got out to hug Jane, and then got back in the front seat and rolled down the window.

Don turned to me, "Shaye, take the day off tomorrow. You deserve it."

I laughed, "It's Saturday, Don. I intend to." He laughed with me.

Nick drove me back down to the resort restaurant and parked over near the kayak shop. The shop was closed, and there weren't many lights on this side of the building. Nick turned off the car, and we sat in silence for a few minutes. The marina lights were twinkling off the water, and tension filled the car.

I turned in my seat to look at him, and he turned and said nothing. I felt like a teenager. He put one arm over the steering wheel, and the other on the console between us. He was caging me in, and the only way out was forward.

I moved over the console and climbed into his lap. I grabbed his face and started kissing him. My hands were everywhere—moving over his face, his chest, down between his legs, where I could feel how much he wanted me.

He must have noticed that I was trapped on his lap by the steering wheel, because the seat started to slide back. When the seat had gone back as far as it would go, he raised his hands to my face and pulled me in. He looked directly into my eyes, and said, "Shaye."

Then his mouth was on mine again. I felt his tongue dive into my mouth, and I thought about all the things that tongue could do. I ground down on him. I was so filled with lust, I didn't even notice he had undone my halter.

He cradled me with one arm while the other hand found its way to my breasts. He started kissing me down my neck and loving my other breast with his mouth. I leaned back, adjusted my legs so I could straddle him, and closed my eyes. I pushed myself down harder on him, and when I leaned back, my back pushed down on the horn. It was so loud, it startled me. I opened my eyes and put my hands up in front to cover myself. He looked at me with surprise on his face, and then we started laughing.

In a voice one would use to scold a child, he said, "Jesus, Shaye, you need to calm down." I saw the smile in his eyes. I couldn't stop laughing. I pulled my halter up to tie it behind my back, and he cried, "Noooo. Don't put those away."

I tried to crawl off him, and he turned serious. "Please. Just sit here for a minute. Please."

I relaxed again and put my head down on his shoulder. He was holding me, placing gentle kisses on my head. A few minutes later I lifted my head, kissed his chin, and whispered, "I need to go."

He held his arms back and up to let me untangle myself from him, laughing in the process. I managed to make it over to my side of the car and pull myself back together. I looked at him, smiled primly, and said, "Thank you for a lovely evening."

He put his arm over the back of the seat and said, "You are welcome." He continued to look at me for a moment, and then he said, "About this morning."

I held up my palm to cut him off and opened the car door. "Nope. Not right now. Not after this lovely moment." I got out and shut the car door. He got out and started walking me to my car.

"You look a little disheveled and distraught. Are you sure you can make it home?" He was teasing me.

I was grinning at him, "I'm fine, I can make it home."

He put his hand to his heart and said, "Are ya sure? Because I can follow ya home. Make sure y'alright." He was pulling out his Southern accent, pretending to be the gentleman that I knew he was not.

"I'm fine, thank you." I was backing towards my car.

He took a few steps toward me and said, "Positive?"

I shouldn't have been laughing, but I was. I used my best "bad-dog" voice, held up my palm again, and said, "Stay!

He laughed and put both his arms up. "Okay, I got it." But he was smiling.

I got in my car, backed up, and then drove down the bay road. I saw him in my rear-view mirror. A faint smile was on his face as he watched me go. He was still standing in the parking lot, watching me as my tail-lights disappeared around the corner.

I didn't see Nick all week, and I started to feel anxious about what had happened in the car. I kept checking my phone for texts, but there was nothing. I tried to concentrate on work and keep myself busy, but I had a tingling sense that we had unfinished business. I was on edge waiting for it.

By the end of the week, I was restless. So I drove into the village to see if there was anyone at Foolish Amy's Pizza Garage, but didn't see anyone I knew. I drove down towards the local pub to see if I recognized any of the cars, and I didn't, so I kept driving. I felt a little lost. Then I thought I should go see Julie. That thought disappeared as quickly as it arrived.

I headed home, and I thought that maybe I would stop in and see Evie. When I got to the fork in the road, I had to pull over and think. I was completely second-guessing myself. I wanted someone to hang out with, but if Nick was there, I might look desperate. If he wasn't there, would I be disappointed?

"Oh, for goodness sake, Shaye, just go." I said out loud to myself, annoyed at my own indecision.

I drove to the Reids' property. There were two cottages on the property, and Evie lived in one of them. They were about halfway down the driveway and set back from the road a bit. The cottages were small, and built in a Bavarian style, with decorative wooden panels framing the windows and doors. Carved flowers graced the fascia board, which was painted a rich cream to complement the dark wood exterior. They reminded me of the Hansel and Gretel cottage.

To get to them, I followed a circular drive that went in front of both. When I pulled in to the tiny parking space in front of Evie's cottage, I saw that all of the windows were dark. Through the trees, I could see that all the lights were on at the main house. I thought, what the heck, and drove the rest of the way.

I didn't see Nick's Range Rover, so that was a good thing, but now that I was there, I realized that I really did want company. I sat in my car for a minute or two, and then Mr. Reid opened the back door. He waved at me, so I opened my car door and stepped out.

"You can't just sit out there all night."

I smiled at him as I walked across the driveway and into the house. "I guess I really can't, can I?"

"Shaye! So good to see you." Mrs. Reid said to me as I stepped into the kitchen. "It is about time you came to see us." I did not realize how much I had missed her until she hugged me, and I started to cry. "Oh, you poor thing! Oh, sit down, sit down. Evie, get the girl a glass of wine."

It was only then that I saw they had been sitting around the kitchen table playing cards. There was a huge bottle of wine on the table, and a plate of pumpkin spice cookies.

"Hi, Shaye," Evie said. "Do you want a glass, or should I just hand you the bottle?" She laughed teasingly at me as she got up and grabbed a glass from the shelf.

"I am so sorry, it's just been so long since I have seen you." I said this to Mrs. Reid. "I guess I didn't realize how much I had missed you." I took a seat at the table. Evie brought a glass and poured me some wine.

"Do you want a cookie?" Evie said to me as if I was a child.

I swatted her hand away, laughed, and said, "No, thank you, I'm fine now."

Mr. and Mrs. Reid were sitting across from us, and Mrs. Reid said, "We were playing cribbage. Do you know how to play?"

"I do, and I am a master," I said proudly.

They all laughed at me. As we played, I cast covert glances at them to see how they looked. For the most part, they looked happy. A little older, but happy. I tried not to stare, but I saw so much of Nick and Jason in their father, it was hard to look away. Mr. Reid was a very distinguished-looking man, and I saw that Nick would be one day, as well.

We played cards and drank wine until past nine o'clock. At one point, Evie burst out laughing. "Remember, Mom, when you took me and Nick and Jason off-island to go shopping for summer clothes and swimsuits? I think Jason was six or seven, I was nine, and Nick was eleven. You wanted to stop in at Bed, Bath, and Beyond for beach towels or something, and there was a huge caged-in area with beach balls in it. Remember, Mom? Oh, my God, ok, hold on." Evie had to pause and collect herself before she could continue. "Remember it was caged in with those wire-type fences that clip together? Jason saw this big pile of beach balls and decided he wanted to jump in it."

I was watching Evie tell this story, and the look of joy on her face already had me laughing.

Evie continued with her story. "Nick was looking at the candy, and I was holding your hand, and all of the sudden Jason screams, 'Watch me, Mom!' and takes a running start and jumps into the cage of balls. The force of the balls pushed the fence apart, and the all the balls went rolling out into the store." Evie was clutching her stomach and laughing so hard, she could barely get the words out.

"You were so embarrassed, and Jason was just floundering about on the ground with the balls. Remember? He thought it was the funniest thing!" Evie wiped the tears of laughter from her face. "Man, he was so funny."

They told a few more stories, and then I helped them clean up the kitchen. Mr. Reid went downstairs to the TV room, and I stayed to talk with Evie and Mrs. Reid. I wanted to ask about Nick, but so much time had passed, and now it seemed awkward. I said my goodbyes, and Evie walked me to the door.

She looked right at me when we got to the door, grabbed my hand, and said softly, "Nick will be home tomorrow."

I blushed a little as I said, "Evie, I didn't come here tonight for him."

"I know you didn't." She was smiling sweetly and tilting her head. "Nevertheless, he will be back tomorrow."

I hugged her tightly, said goodnight, and drove home.

Saturday was a sunny but cold October morning. I pulled on black leggings, my Eddie Bauer hiking boots, and a wool beanie. I had a tank top and a long sleeve shirt on, and I grabbed my puffer jacket on the way out the door.

I decided to skip my usual morning run and get out and hike instead. It was such a beautiful day that I didn't want to miss any of it. I felt light and happy.

I drove into town to get a coffee, and then headed back south towards Shark Reef Road. I wanted to hike the half mile to the shore, and then work my way down to where the seals would be sunning.

I had gone about two miles when my tire blew. I pulled over and pulled out my cell phone to call someone. All of the sudden, I didn't know who I was going to call. I sat on the side of the road, paralyzed.

My mind flashed to the last time I was stranded, when I ran out of gas and called Jason at the bar. That was the night Nick and I made love on the floor of my living room. I was staring off into space thinking about that night when I saw Nick's black Range Rover pull around the corner. I wasn't even surprised to see him.

I stepped out of my car as he slowed his down.

"Do you need help?" he asked from inside his car. He had his Ray-Ban aviators on and a baseball cap, and he was smiling.

"I do." I smiled back. "I have a flat tire."

"Were you going to call someone, or just sit here on the side of the road?"

I laughed and said, "I was getting around to it."

"Let me pull my car over," he said, and turned his car around behind me.

Stepping out of his car, he said, "Pop the back."

I opened the back hatch, and he reached in to get the spare.

"You know, you are really bad with vehicle maintenance." He was teasing me, and I couldn't help but just shrug my shoulders and grin at him sheepishly.

He went to work changing my tire, and only mumbled a couple of words every now and then if he needed me to hand him something. He was wearing khakis and a black t-shirt, and when he lifted the tires, his biceps flexed. I think I was drooling.

When he finished, he said, "You need to drop this off at Roy's garage." Not to be confused with the Amy's Pizza Garage; Roy was a mechanic. "He needs to take a look at it and maybe replace your tire. I will follow you, and you can drop it off."

He seemed to think I had nothing better to do, so I said, "I was actually on my way to Shark Reef. Do you think I can drop it off on Monday on my way to work?"

"I don't think so. I should probably come with you to the Reef—make sure you don't hurt yourself." His grin was wicked, and I couldn't resist him.

"Fine. I'll follow you," I told him. I got in my car and followed him to the garage.

We dropped the tire off at Roy's, left the car, and then drove together to Shark Reef.

He reached for my hand. I slid mine into his, and stared out the window at the fields of hay rolling by. The roads were winding and narrow on this side of the island, and the fields soon edged up against the forest.

He slowed as we approached a small parking area and parked in front of a fallen log. The park was secluded and private, and easy to miss if you weren't looking for it.

It was still cold out, so Nick grabbed a flannel shirt and a zip-up hoodie from his back seat. I stepped out of the car and relaxed against the hood while he got dressed.

He walked around in front of me, tilted his head slightly, smiled, and asked, "You good?"

I smiled and nodded at him, happy and content at the turn in my day.

He held out his hand to me, and I took it. We walked the dirt trail under a canopy of fir trees. Other than the sound of the wind rustling the branches above, it was completely quiet. Every now and then as we walked, we heard a seagull caw. With every step I took, I heard my boots crunch on the dirt. The path narrowed, and Nick dropped my hand and walked behind me. Tree roots crossed the path, and I was careful not to trip.

We walked in silence until we got to the edge of the cliff. The trees were left behind us, and I stopped to raise my face to the sun. I closed my eyes, raised my hands up in a V above my head, and took a deep breath. I felt Nick come up behind me and wrap his arms around my middle. I leaned my head back against his chest and covered his arms.

He whispered, "I missed you."

I whispered back, "I missed you too."

He let me go, and we climbed over ledges and rocks. We poked sea anemones in tide pools, and waited for the seals to pop their heads out of the water. I was sitting on a boulder, hanging my legs over the water, and Nick was down on a small shore, throwing rocks, when he said, "My mom called me this morning and said you came by last night."

I turned and looked over my shoulder at him. His eyes were shaded by his sunglasses, so I couldn't read what he was fishing for. He wasn't asking a question, but I answered, "Yes."

"I went to Seattle this week. I have a corporate case that is getting a little heated, and it was too much to manage from up here," he said while he continued to throw rocks. "I had just gotten off the ferry and was headed home when I ran into you."

I just looked at him and said, "Ok." He didn't elaborate, and I didn't ask.

I jumped down off the rock to the beach next to him and said, "I enjoy being with your family."

"Good," he grinned at me, picked me up, and threw me over his shoulder. He gave me a pat on the butt, and ran up the trail until I got too heavy for him to carry. He dropped me on the trail and put his hands on his knees to catch a breath.

I pushed him on the shoulder and said, "C'mon, I'm not that heavy." He laughed and gently backed me up against a tree.

"You are beautiful!" he said, and he bent down to kiss my cheek. And then he was off, running to his car.

I was a fast runner, but he was much faster than me. When I got to his car, he had already finished an entire 20-ounce water bottle. He reached in the back of his car and handed me one.

"I'll take you home, summer girl." He pulled the brim of my cap down and, for the first time in a long while, the memory attached to those words didn't hurt.

When we got to my house, I asked him, "Do you want to come in?"

"Yes."

I was prepared to hear yes or no, but when he said yes, I was really pleased. I smiled at him. "Okay, good."

He followed me into the house.

"I am going to take a quick shower. There is beer and soda in the fridge if you want one. I'll be right back."

"I'll be right here." He watched me as I started towards the stairs.

My shower took about five minutes. I put on a pair of yoga pants and a tank top. I couldn't do much about my hair, so I put it in a bun on the top of my head.

I heard the stereo turn on, and the Blake Shelton CD came on. It was cued up to "Boys 'Round Here," and I laughed at him when I came around the corner from the stairwell.

He was dancing, and he was so unbelievably sexy, I couldn't help singing along and dancing with him. He heard my singing and turned to sing with me. I was singing the girl's part, and trying my best to look sultry. We were being silly, and I felt like the missing pieces were finally clicking into place.

When the song ended, I was out of breath from belting out the tune. I laughed and walked into the kitchen to start dinner. I popped back around the corner and said, "Do you want to stay for dinner?"

Remembering the last time he stayed for dinner, I felt myself flush to my roots. The heat in his eyes was enough to keep me frozen where I was standing.

He came slowly towards me and said, as if reading my mind, "Do you remember what happened the last time I stayed for dinner?"

He caressed my cheek with the back of his hand. Every part of me was tingling, and I couldn't respond. He wrapped his arms around my middle, picked me up so my feet were off the floor, and gently put me in my chair.

He knelt down in front me and reached for the waist-band of my pants. I finally came to my senses, swatted his hands away, and nervously laughed. "Nick, I'm not going to have sex with you right now."

He lightly pushed my hands away and said, "I never said we were going to have sex." He looked mischievous and sexy as he pulled my pants off. "No panties, Shaye? Shame on you." Then he put his mouth to me. I didn't even have time to think.

I let him love me until I couldn't think at all. I ran my hands over his shoulders and reached up to grab his head. I pulled at his hair and pressed him closer as I rode the beautiful wave of pleasure, and melted beneath him. My legs trembled as his tongue pressed against me one hard, final time, and I let go, crying out his name and throwing back my head.

As I lay there in an exquisite fog, he nuzzled his way up my belly, came up on top of me, and kissed me hard. I held his head, and when he pulled back, he was smiling.

"I'll be right back," he said, and jumped up off the floor.

I felt a little self-conscious, sitting there half-naked, until he came back with a pair of my boy-short underwear and a bathrobe. "Put some clothes on, woman," he teased, but he looked at me as if he would prefer that I stayed naked.

I stood up and got dressed. "So, are you staying for dinner?"

He threw back his head and laughed. He sat down on the couch where there was room for both of us and patted the seat next to him. "Come 'ere. I have something important I want to tell you."

I hesitantly sat down next to him. I felt a chat coming on, and I steeled myself to it.

"Relax," he said, and poked my bun.

When I had settled back against the cushions, he leaned into me, looked me intently in the eyes, and said, "I can't stay for dinner."

I hit him in the arm and said, "Oh, my God! Seriously? I thought this was going to be an 'it's not you, it's me' talk." I hit him again and added, "You're mean."

He laughed at me, "No, really, I do have something to tell you, but I need to get home and can't stay. I told my mom I would come over for dinner." He was caressing my face with his fingers.

I was confused for a minute, "Wait, what? 'Come over for dinner?' Not, 'be home for dinner?' Don't you live there?"

My face registered my confusion, and he said, "God, you are so cute." He leaned in to kiss me quickly. Then he said, "Shaye, I am a thirty-three-year-old man. I don't live at home anymore." He was smiling at me, and I sat up a little straighter.

"Then where do you live?" I asked.

"I bought the lot next to my parents' and built a house."

"Huh. I guess I hadn't thought much about it." I looked out the windows.

He scooted a little closer to me and said, "I have an idea."

His voice was silky, and I was getting turned on all over again.

I rolled my shoulder towards him, creating some visible cleavage. Trying to seduce him, I said, "What's your idea?"

He leaned in and whispered in my ear, "I think we should try dating."

I pushed him back, "What?"

"I think we should try dating," he repeated in a normal voice, grinning.

"Do you mean like boyfriend and girlfriend?" I asked him.

"Yes, Shaye: like boyfriend and girlfriend." He was very serious, but he was still grinning.

"I..." I paused for a minute to think. "How do we explain it?"

He sat up straighter, and his smile dropped a little. "Explain what?"

I felt flustered. I hadn't gotten this far in my thought process regarding me and Nick, and I was a little dazed.

I said softly to him, "Explain how we got together."

"Don't do this again, Shaye. Don't do this. It isn't anybody's business." He was stern in his plea.

"Nick. I'm not quitting on us, I promise. I just hadn't gotten that far in thinking about us." I looked him in the eye, and then kissed him sweetly on the lips. "Yes. Yes, I will be your girlfriend."

He reached under my bathrobe and rubbed his hand all the way up the side of my thigh. He squeezed my butt. "Good."

After that, Nick came by my office every day. If it wasn't in the morning with coffee, it was at lunch with something from the Bay Café. Sometimes, he would sit in my office and watch me work, and sometimes he would hang out on the dock with me when I met the planes. He was getting to know all the pilots by name, and they started greeting him before acknowledging me.

"Don't you have a job?" I asked him one day while we were sitting out on a bench looking at the boats.

His legs were straight out in front of him, ankles crossed, and he was reclining against the back of the bench. He turned and looked at me sardonically, "It's my firm, Shaye, and I can do what I want."

If people noticed us as a couple, no one said anything. And if they were talking, we didn't care. We ate at the bar or with his parents. Evie was always there, and I always drove home alone.

One Wednesday night, we were sitting outside on his parents' porch. The lights were dim, and we were sitting on a rocking bench. We had a comforter pulled up over us, and my legs were over his lap.

"I really enjoy being with your family, but when do I get to come to your house?" I was rubbing my hands on his shirt front, and every now and then I would reach out to rub his neck. He was stroking my thigh, and every few seconds, I would kiss his cheek or stroke the back of his hand. I couldn't stop touching him. He was being chivalrous and patient, and I was beginning to feel desperate for him.

He said, "Shaye, the Halloween party is at my house. Remember, I mentioned it to you a few days ago? You will be there, won't you?"

"Wow! I guess I hadn't connected the dots. I didn't get a costume yet." I grinned at him.

"I am going to Seattle tomorrow morning. I will bring you one back on Friday."

"What? Why are you going to Seattle?" I knew I sounded whiny, but I hadn't known he was going, and I hadn't seen his name on the manifest before I'd left work. I was going to miss him.

He scooped me up and brought me onto his lap. We hadn't done anything except kiss since last weekend, and I was getting really frustrated.

"I have to meet with the Board about a company we are counseling. There are some issues, and I need to be present." He nipped my neck, and I pulled the comforter up over our heads so that I could kiss him deeply.

I almost told him I loved him. I knew for sure that I did, but something was holding me back. I wasn't ready to let him know that I could give into him completely.

Instead, I said, "Bring me a naughty costume," and he laughed.

He was on the nine o'clock plane the next morning, and I kissed him good-bye on the dock. The island would feel empty without him, and I didn't know what I was going to do while he was away. I didn't want to barge in on the Reids again, so I ordered a salad to-go from the resort restaurant and took it home to eat by myself.

I looked around the house, and all of the sudden, I knew this was where I wanted to be. It wasn't about the house, it was about me and Nick. I wanted him. I resolved to tell him Saturday, and I slept peacefully that night.

When Friday arrived, I took my gray turtleneck dress to change into after work, along with my over-the-knee boots. I met Nick at the dock. It was getting dark earlier, and this would be the last week of the five o'clock flight. We ate dinner in the resort bar, and it was comfortable and easy to be with him. We were sitting at a corner table, so it was quiet and private.

Crossing my legs and leaning into him, I asked, "What costume did you bring me?"

He leaned back in his chair, folded his hands together, and made a point with his fingers. He looked so rumpled and sexy, I wanted to curl up next to him. He was still wearing his suit. He was also wearing his glasses, so I knew he was really tired. I knew I shouldn't keep him much longer, but I had missed him.

"It's a surprise."

"Are you going to tell me anything?" I tilted my head and leaned on the table.

He leaned back towards me and said, "Yes."

I grinned at him, and we laughed because he was always answering with just 'yes' or 'no.' I think it was the lawyer in him that didn't give away too much unless he had to. I waited him out.

He chuckled because he was figuring me out too. "Evie wants me to give the costume to her, and then you need to go to her cottage tomorrow between six and seven to get ready with her."

I laughed and leaned back in my chair. "What is this, high school?"

He responded, "It's Evie," and smiled fondly.

"Ok. Then what?" I went on.

He looked directly at me. "Then, you walk to my house."

A tingle ran through my body. I wanted nothing more than to have tomorrow night arrive quickly, when it would be just the two of us. He leaned across the table and kissed me. It was a gentle kiss, not passionate or demanding. It was full of promise and adoration. He stroked my cheek and said, "C'mon, I need to sleep. I'm done for the week."

We walked out to where he had left his car the day before. I had parked right next to him. He leaned against my door and pulled me to him, hugging me close. I turned in his arms and put my cheek to his chest. He was keeping me warm, and I could hear his heartbeat.

We must have stood there for a few minutes. I wondered how I had lived without him all this time. My life in Seattle seemed like a blur. I didn't know if this was going to work out, but I prayed it would.

I pulled back slowly. "We need to go. You are tired." I leaned up to kiss him on the cheek, and he buried his face in the crook of my neck.

He stepped forward out of the way of my car door and held it open while I stepped in.

"Drive carefully," he said, shutting my door.

I waved, backed up, and drove off. I was tired too, and I needed a good night's sleep.

Saturday couldn't pass fast enough for me. I had my coffee, and then went for a run. I took a shower, and it was still only ten o'clock in the morning. I groaned, and decided I would clean the house.

I turned the CD player on and started on the upstairs. I cleaned out the rest of the closets, did my laundry, and cleaned the bathrooms. I worked my way downstairs, and then started on the kitchen. I threw away chipped plates and bowls and Tupperware without lids. When I finished my cleaning frenzy, it was four o'clock, and I needed another shower.

I showered and dressed in leggings and a T-shirt. I slipped on an old pair of Birkenstocks that I found in the closet, and I packed an overnight bag. I put it in the back of my car, just in case.

At six o'clock, I drove to Evie's. She opened the door with a big grin. All her lights were on, and I heard dance music playing. I grabbed my bag and went into her cottage.

To the right was her bedroom, and to the left was a small kitchen and bathroom. The rest of the cottage was one big room with two sheets of glass in the corner that created a picture window to the trees outside.

"I am so glad you are here. I hate drinking alone," she said. I looked past her and saw Julie at the kitchen table doing her makeup.

"You aren't alone, Evie," I said to her.

She giggled and said, "I know, but there isn't a saying that goes, 'I hate drinking with Julie.'" She shut the door behind me.

"Hey, Julie." I said to her casually, but kindly.

"Hey," was all she said, without looking up from the mirror she was using. She was concentrating on her face in the mirror. She was so perfectly beautiful.

Evie bounced in front of me as she said, "Are you ready for your costume?" She was grinning like a Cheshire cat.

"Yes, please." I sat down next to Julie and watched her finish her makeup while Evie went into her bedroom to get my costume.

Evie squealed when she brought it out. "Here you go." She pulled it out of the bag and my jaw dropped.

"Is that an Elvira costume?"

"Yes! Isn't it fabulous?" She could not contain her smile.

"There's barely anything to it!" I exclaimed when she put it in front of me.

Julie glanced over at me. "I think that's the idea, Shaye."

The skirt had a slit up to mid-thigh and the front V reached down to the middle of my breasts. The dress was long-sleeved and had a high neck in the back. There was a lot of fabric, but it didn't seem to cover much.

Evie was laughing. "Oh, c'mon Shaye," she grinned at me. "You are going to look smoking hot. I can tape you in." She laughed again.

"Fine. But seriously, you better use multiple strips of that tape." I tried to look like I was scolding her, but she just squealed again and laughed.

Evie did my makeup and helped me with the wig. Julie was going as a tiger, and had a long tail she had attached to her wrist so that it would swing when she moved her arm. Evie was Little Bo Peep, and she looked adorable. I thought for a moment that she had lived in her brothers' shadows for so long, no one saw her as sexy, and she just perpetuated that image. She was stunning, and we were going to have to help her see that. But not tonight. Tonight was for fun, and for me and Nick.

"You guys ready?" Evie asked from the door that she was holding open.

"Ready," I replied.

"Ready," Julie said.

We walked across the Reids' driveway to a path that cut through the woods to Nick's property. It was a wide path, kept clean and clear of leaves and branches. I could see lights through the trees that I assumed were coming from Nick's house.

The path came out onto a road, and the sign said Pavey Boulevard. We took a right, and I saw Nick's house for the first time. It was magnificent, but I couldn't help but laugh.

"Evie?" I asked. My face registered confusion and humor.

"I know, right? So unoriginal." She laughed and continued down the driveway.

The house was the exact replica of his parents' home, only it was built from logs. It looked sturdier and more inviting, homier somehow. It sat up higher on the property and had a porch that went all the way around instead of just in front. All the trees had been cleared in the front, so he had an open view of the bay. I could even see a boathouse down below.

We walked in, and the party was already loud. People were everywhere. I heard laughing from the kitchen. As we entered the great room, I caught Nick's eye from across the room. He glanced down my body, and then raised his glass in a toast. I tilted my head and cocked my hip. Winking at him, I ran a hand down my front in a gesture of display.

Nick made his way towards me, and he reached out to grab me. He put one arm around me and leaned in to kiss me. I leaned back in his arm and smiled up at him. He was smiling down at me, and if anyone noticed, no one said a thing.

"Hey, Naughty Elvira," he said and bit my earlobe. Nick was dressed as the Man with No Name from 'The Good, the Bad, and the Ugly.' He looked like a perfect young Clint Eastwood.

"I didn't think you would take me seriously." I tapped him on the chest.

He laughed, "I'm a guy, I hear 'naughty,' and I stop thinking. Do you want something to drink?"

I replied, "Yes, Cape Cod, please." He kissed me again and walked off to get me my drink.

I glanced around the room at all the people I knew, and some that I didn't. I saw a few of Jason's friends, and was glad that they had stayed connected with the family. I saw one that I didn't like because Jason had always drunk too much with him. I steered clear of him and went to talk to another group of people I knew that worked at the bank. Nick brought me my drink, kissed me on the cheek, and said he would be right back.

The night wore on, and I was having a good time. Evie seemed to be playing hostess, and Julie was doing what she did best and flirting with several different guys. I saw Nick outside, leaning against the railing, and my eyes connected with him. I lifted my drink to my mouth, but I was so distracted by him that I missed, and the drink went down my chest. I looked down at my wet chest and glanced back up at Nick.

His eyes had turned dark, and there was so much heat in them, I thought I would combust on the spot. He pushed himself off the railing, muttered, "Excuse me," to the people he was talking to, and came directly for me. Grabbing me by the hand, he led me out the back door and around the side path down to the boathouse. I was laughing and trying to keep up as he tugged me along.

He took me into the boathouse, and I saw a water-skiing boat. I looked at him and said, "You've been keeping secrets from me."

He looked right back at me and said, "No secrets, Shaye."

And then he kissed me so long and hard, I felt I was drowning in him. He released me for a minute and stepped into the boat. He helped me get in after him, and then he pulled me on his lap as he settled into a bench seat. I straddled him and cradled his head as he licked my chest where the drink had spilled. My dress had hiked up around my hips, and his hands were working their way under my thong.

The door to the boat house opened and we both froze.

We heard Evie's voice as she said, "I think Nick keeps some extra cases down here."

And then she saw us.

She stared right at us and didn't say a word. The guy she was with looked embarrassed and just stood there as well.

Nick said, "Shaye got lost." He was grinning ear to ear.

"I got lost," I parroted.

Nick continued, "I went to find her."

I smiled and said cheerily, "He found me!"

Evie looked at us, and said with an exasperated yet teasing tone, "You guys are so stupid. You can't wait until later?" She turned to leave the boat house and called over her shoulder, "Hurry up and get back to your party."

After she shut the door, we fell apart, laughing. I had tears running down my face.

"How soon can I kick everyone out?" he asked, and we started laughing again.

I untangled myself from him, and we headed back up to the house. Nick held my hand as we walked up the steps that led to the back deck. There was a large group mingling on the deck, and Jason's friend Michael was getting loud and obnoxious.

"Hey, there's the host!" Michael slurred.

Nick stopped once he reached the deck, but he didn't let go of my hand. I didn't want to make eye contact with Michael, so I stepped back behind Nick just a bit. He shielded me behind him, and I could sense something bad about to happen.

Nick pasted a fake smile on his face and spoke softly, as if he were trying to calm a frightened horse. "Hey, Michael. You doing ok?"

He realized Michael was drunk, and was hoping to ward off anything unpleasant.

Michael continued, pointing his beer back at us, "Yeah, man, ya know, I've always wondered... what were you and Jason arguing about the night he died?"

I tensed up, and everyone around us went still.

Nick let go of my hand, dropped his smile, and went to try and steer Michael to the side patio. "Let's go, Michael."

Michael shrugged him off with his elbow, and pointed his beer at me. "Were you guys fucking around behind his back? Was that it? Did he catch you?"

I felt tears sting my eyes, and I turned to see Evie and Julie standing in the doorway. Evie looked sad that all of this was coming out, and Julie looked sick and betrayed. Whatever she knew, or thought she knew, before, was being confirmed. Even if I had been on my way back to building a friendship with her, that would come with greater difficulty now.

Nick grabbed Michael by the back of the neck, nodded at one of his friends and said, "Get him out of here."

I was shaking when Nick came to get me and walked me into his room.

His room was decorated in log cabin style furniture with a four-poster bed. The rug was plush, and he had a plaid comforter on the bed. It suited him.

He set me on the bed and went to his walk-in closet to change out of his costume. He came back out in a pair of faded jeans rolled up at the hem, and a blue Henley.

Kneeling in front of me, he removed my wig and caressed my face.

"I'll be back in a bit. Please don't leave." He put his head in my lap, and I kept my hands on the mattress and just nodded.

I realized he couldn't see my nod, so I said simply, "I won't."

After he left the room, I went to the bathroom to wash off my makeup, and then I lay down on the bed to wait for him.

I could hear voices out in the house and assumed Nick and Evie were cleaning up and saying goodbye to everyone. A while later, Nick came into the room and shut the door quietly behind him.

"Shaye," he whispered.

I had been lying on my side, and I rolled over onto my back. "I'm awake," I said.

He lay down on the bed beside me and started rubbing my forehead.

"I don't think this is going to work," I said into the darkness.

Nick got up on one elbow and looked down at me. His voice was soft when he said, "What are you talking about?"

My eyes filled with tears. "Don't you see? I am always going to be the girl who caused Jason's death."

His voice was low but strong. "No, you aren't. You're going to be the woman who belongs to me. Please stop thinking it was your fault. It was an accident, and I don't blame you, or me, for his death."

I could hear the pain in his voice, and that hurt me even more. He pulled me in close, and I snuggled into his chest. We stayed like that until I fell asleep.

The next morning, I woke to the sun shining through his windows. Nick was still sleeping as I quietly rolled out of bed and grabbed my shoes. I snuck out quietly and walked back through the woods to my car.

Evie's cottage was unlocked, so I snuck in to get my bag. I peeked in her room, and she was sleeping peacefully. She looked like Snow White, and my heart squeezed a little with what had become sisterly love.

When I got to my house, I took off my dress and climbed into bed. What an uncomfortable night.

I spent the rest of the weekend thinking about what I was going to do. The days were getting shorter, and there weren't as many tourists flying to the islands.

Not wanting to react or do something I would regret later, I tried to stay away from Nick, Evie, and Julie. I groaned at the thought of Julie. I needed to talk to her. I gave myself a few more days before deciding I would go to the Vineyard after work some time that week and see her.

Nick had called late Sunday night to tell me he was going off-island for a few days. "I'll call you when I get back, ok?"

"All-right. Are you flying? Will I see you in the morning?" I still felt raw from the party and wasn't sure what else to say.

"No. I'm driving, but I will come see you on my way to the ferry."

"Ok."

"Shaye, we're going to be ok. I promise."

I nodded my head, and then realized that once again he couldn't see me, so I simply said, "Ok."

After work on Tuesday, I drove up to the Vineyard to see Julie. From what I remembered from Evie, the Vineyard was over a hundred acres, and had been in Julie's family for generations.

I parked in the gravel lot in front of the tasting room attached to the winery, and went in. It was dark outside now, and the warm lights made the tasting room inviting.

There was a rock fireplace at the far end of the room that had two couches and two overstuffed chairs comfortably arranged in front of it. I saw Julie behind the bar with a clipboard and a pencil stuck behind her ear. She wore jeans and an Island Winery sweatshirt. She didn't look like the girl I was always fighting with. She was a few years older than me, but she looked like she could be my little sister, if I'd had one.

She heard the bell ring over the door when I entered, and she turned to see me. Her face fell a little. I wanted so desperately for her to be my friend. I wanted her to forgive me for betraying Jason.

"Shaye," was all she said, putting her clipboard down on the bar. At least she didn't dismiss me, so I took that as an invitation to talk.

"Hi, Julie," I started. She just continued to look at me. "I was hoping you had some time to talk." She looked at me for a beat longer, and then I saw the resignation in her eyes, and she came around the bar.

She sat down next to me on a bar stool, and then reached back over the bar for two glasses and an unopened bottle of Chardonnay. She expertly uncorked the wine and poured. This was a Julie I didn't know, and I was fascinated by her.

"Talk." She took a sip of her wine. I felt intimated by this girl, and I stumbled a little over my words.

"I, uhm," I cleared my throat and started again. "I wanted to tell you I was sorry. I haven't been as kind as I could have been to you. I think I was a little jealous." Her face softened, making it easier for me to continue.

"I felt like an outsider when I arrived, and Jason was just so cute and funny and charming. I enjoyed being with him. When I met Nick, it was like a hurricane-force wind hit me, and I fell hard. I didn't know what to do. I felt trapped, and wanted to do right by everyone." I chuckled at my foolish thoughts. "I wanted everyone to get along."

Julie looked at me disbelievingly. "Here's the thing, Shaye. You showed up here completely oblivious that these were our lives. You breezed in all tormented and privileged, and didn't even acknowledge that maybe there were stories that came before you."

"I'm not that girl anymore, Julie. I want to move past all that." I sounded like I was pleading with her.

She looked me directly in the eye and waited a few minutes. I got the feeling she wanted to make sure I was paying attention to what she was about to say.

"I loved him, Shaye. I loved him the way you love Nick." She laughed when I started to deny it. "Oh, please. Don't go all dumb girl on me now." I gave her a small smile, and she continued. "Everyone was grieving around me, and no one considered what I was going through. For the last eight years, I have been on autopilot being the same happy, flirty Julie, and no one even asked how I was doing."

I saw her differently now. She was right.

My throat was choked up when I said, "I may not stay on the island."

She paused, waiting.

I cleared my throat and continued. "I, uhm, I'm going to let the house go. Perhaps that way, everyone can move on."

She looked at me sadly as she jumped off the bar stool. "You should think a little more clearly about that." She went back behind the bar, and I took that as my cue that she was dismissing me. "I mean, why do you want to leave now when it's just getting good?"

"Julie," I said in frustration.

"Too soon?" She laughed at me, and continued in a more subdued tone. "Seriously, Shaye. I know how people see me and what they say about me. I don't care. As much as you may have thought I disliked you, I never really did. I always had the impression you were made of stronger stuff than this. Be an Island Girl, or don't be. Either way, get off the fence." As she went back to work, she muttered, "That's what led to all this grief in the first place."

She dismissed me, and I let myself out the way I had come in. Inhaling a deep breath of the fresh fall air, I noticed the fog was settling in, and it felt like the island was wrapping itself around me protectively. If I stayed mindful and in-the-moment, I would figure this out.

Thursday afternoon, I was finishing up my day when I saw Nick's Range Rover coming quickly down the bay road. He skidded into the resort parking lot, flinging gravel into the air.

He jumped out of his car and slammed the door. He was in his suit, and he looked frazzled. He disappeared out of sight from my window. The next thing I knew, he had entered the building and started down the hall towards my office.

He looked really angry, and I had no idea why.

"Hi, Nick," I said, trying to hide my amusement.

"What the hell are you doing, Shaye?" He threw the words right at me.

"Uh, working?"

"Julie called me this morning. She told me you said you were thinking of giving up the house." He had his hands on his hips, and his feet were spread apart. He was taking up the entire door frame, and I felt trapped.

I seethed a little inside and thought to myself, 'Effin' Julie.' I looked at him and said, "I was thinking about it."

"Why?" He pinned me down with his eyes. They were laser-sharp blue, and I couldn't move.

"You know why." My tone was desperate.

"No. I don't." He punched the door frame with the side of his fist. "Don't do this, Shaye! Regardless of how you feel right now, don't do it. Not yet."

I considered what he was saying. I knew we could work it out together, but at that moment, I didn't know how to respond, so I just sat there.

He must have misinterpreted my struggle to find words. He pointed his finger at me and said one word. "No."

"Excuse me?" My head jerked back, and I had to shake it to make sure I'd heard him correctly.

"Give it some time. You haven't given us enough time. Stay until after the first of the year, and then decide. Fight for us, Shaye. Don't let them win." His anger had deflated, and he looked so much like the man I loved. "We already lost him. Don't let his death destroy all of us again." My heart ached, and I knew I would not deny him.

Instead, I stood, wrapped my arms around him, and kissed him.

He nodded curtly, and then turned to leave. He drove away with much less speed than when he had arrived.

Over the next few days, I was busy trying to get proposals wrapped up before the holidays, and didn't see much of Nick. I didn't intentionally avoid him, but I also think he was giving me space to think about us.

I called Don the week before Thanksgiving to check in, and he asked if I was coming home for the long holiday weekend.

"Oh, thanks for reminding me. My mom called a few days ago about dinner, and I forgot to call her back. I need to tell her I am coming. Can you get me on a flight out Thursday?"

"Of course. Does the one o'clock work for you?"

"Perfect," I said to him.

"It's the last flight of the day, so don't miss it."

"Ok. See you Thursday." I hung up the phone and called my mom to tell her I was coming home for Thanksgiving.

"I'm so glad, sweetie. This is the first year without your father, and it will be nice to have you home." Hearing her voice made me feel better. I couldn't wait to get home and hug her.

"Have you made a menu yet? Who is all coming?" I asked her.

"We'll have the regular food, turkey, mashed potatoes. You know, Thanksgiving food. You can make something if you like."

"I would be happy to help."

"Your brother and Caitlyn will be here, Uncle Jack and Aunt Lisa, and you and me. Nice and quiet."

"That sounds lovely, Mom. I miss you." Her voice was lulling me. I was cradling my phone against my ear, and my head was in my hand. I had started to lean over on my desk. I really did miss her.

"Oh, I miss you too, sweetie. Anything you want to tell me?" I swear she had a sixth sense. I sat up straighter in my chair.

I wasn't ready to talk about Nick, so I said, "No, everything's good. We can talk when I'm there." I paused and continued, "So, can you pick me up at the float plane dock Thursday afternoon? I won't have a car."

"Of course. Text me before you take off." She told me she loved me and then hung up.

I put my phone down on my desk and stared out the window. Now that I had plans to go to Seattle, I was feeling a little stronger.

I picked my phone back up off the desk and sent a text to Nick. *Busy?*

He instantly replied, *Hey beautiful.*

My heart squeezed, and I felt like a shit for my next text, *I'm going to Seattle for Thanksgiving.*

I could feel him thinking. It was a few minutes before he responded, *Ok.*

What? God! I am such a child. I knew I had no right to expect more of a response, but it would have been nice. This is my family's first holiday without my father.

I tried one more time, *I will call you when I land.*

Crickets. Well, I deserved it.

I took my time getting ready on Thursday. I packed leggings and a red wraparound dress for dinner that night. I got dressed in jeans and a black turtleneck and left my hair down. After I put my UGG boots on, I pulled my Eddie Bauer down jacket from the closet, grabbed my carry-on bag, and went to my car. I locked the house behind me since I would be gone for a few days, and I drove to the float plane dock.

The water looked like glass. It was so flat that the remaining boats in the bay were perfectly mirrored in the water. The pilot would have a difficult time landing. Glassy water lacked the visual cues of choppy water, and the pilot would need to use all of his or her flight skills to come in safely.

I walked down to the dock to watch the plane fly , and saw Tom through the cockpit window. This was easy for him, so I no longer felt worried. He taxied in to the dock, and out of habit, I grabbed the line. I pulled the plane in as Tom jumped out of the pilot seat.

"Hey, there's my girl!" he greeted me and gave me a big hug.

"Hi, Tom." I handed him the line and he secured the plane. "Full plane today?"

"Yep. Just waiting for one more." He stood there smiling at me. "I'm going to have to put you in the back, if that's ok?"

I smirked at him. He was acting weird. "Of course, it's ok." I climbed up the stairs and put my bag behind me in the luggage bin. I buckled up and waited for our last passenger.

I heard feet stomping on the dock, so I knew the passenger was arriving, and then I heard Nick's voice. "Hey, how ya doin' Tom? Sorry I'm late, I needed to close up the office for the weekend."

Looking out to where they were standing, I saw them shaking hands. What the heck?

Nick came up to the plane and started climbing in. He greeted everyone, threw his bag in the back, and then sat down next to me. He was so big, he had to squeeze in. He had on his boots and cargo pants, and a heavy wool sweater. He had pushed the sleeves up to his elbows, and his forearms were brushing up against my middle.

"Hello, Shaye," he whispered in my ear. When he pulled back, he was smiling.

I was instantly suspicious of him, and I told him so by narrowing my eyes and not responding. He just laughed.

I put my ear plugs in, and put my head back to rest for the hour-long ride. Five minutes into the flight,

288

Nick poked my leg. I opened my eyes and rolled my head towards him. He looked down and indicated a note pad in his hand. He had written me a note:

You going to your Mom's?

I read it, then grudgingly took the pad from him and wrote back:
Yes

I tried to hand the pad back to him, but he wouldn't take it. He was waiting for something else from me. I sighed and played along. I wrote back to him:

Where are you going?

He took the pad back from me and wrote:

Your Mom's

My eyes snapped up to his, and he put a finger over my mouth. He mouthed, "Shhhhhhh." I turned to stare out the window. He reached down, grabbed my hand, and laced our fingers together.

I fell asleep with my head on Nick's shoulder and our fingers still locked together. Nick woke me when we were coming in to land; I saw the Space Needle through the front window. Tom landed effortlessly, and we taxied across the bay to the float plane dock.

My mom was waving frantically from the outside deck. She wore a quilted yellow barn jacket, so I couldn't miss her. I waved back, and she went back inside to wait for us.

"Shaye, sweetie. You made it." She took me in a tight hug.

"Hi, Mom." I hugged her back. "You remember Nick." I indicated him with my hand, but my tone was rhetorical. She had obviously been in contact with him.

"Don't be cute, Shaye. We have business to discuss, so I thought I would invite him to dinner." She turned to Nick and said, "Glad you could make it Nick, it's nice to see you."

"Nice to see you, too. Thank you for the invitation." He was polite and gentlemanly. I couldn't fault him for that.

We packed up the car and arrived at my mom's house ten minutes later.

"Nick, I have put you in the pool-house. There is a full-bath and mini kitchen, so you should be comfortable." Now that we were back in her territory, she was barking orders at us. "Shaye, you are in your old room. Dinner will be at seven." She stood in the hallway looking at both of us expectantly.

My bag was over my shoulder, and my hands were palm-out in my back pockets. Nick stood next to me with his bag in his hands, looking equally confused.

I looked at Nick, and then looked back at my mom. I said, "We will put our bags away and come help you?" It was both a statement and a question, and it seemed to be what she was waiting for.

She looked and me and said, "Excellent! See you in a bit." She briskly walked off.

Nick and I both laughed, and I showed him to the pool house. His eyes followed me, and it was making me very uncomfortable. When we got to the little house, I showed him the bedroom and where the bath towels were. We went back into the sitting room, and I showed him where the coffee was. He was taking up all the space in the little room, and I was getting a little heated.

He was a perfect gentleman, though, and didn't try to touch me at all.

After making sure Nick was settled in, I took my bag to my room, changed into a t-shirt, and went downstairs to help my mom. My brother and his wife showed up around six-thirty, so I went back upstairs to change.

I left my hair down and put my red wrap dress on. It was soft and slinky, and cut down just far enough to tease but not show. It was long-sleeved and had a tiny belt.

I decided not to wear the leggings, and went bare-legged instead. I was planning on wearing black flats when it was just my family, but now I wanted something a little sexier. I dug around in my closet for a pair of heels, and found a silver pair from prom. They had rhinestones across the top of my foot, and they wrapped around my ankle. I laughed out loud, and thought, *What the heck.*

Walking slowly down the stairs a little before seven, I saw my brother and Nick in the living room talking to my Uncle Jack. Nick wore a navy suit, and a white shirt open at the collar. The corded muscles in his neck were visible, and it struck me again how handsome he was. I wanted to be near him and never leave. I didn't think I would ever tire of looking at him. I waited until he saw me before I took the last step.

He saw me and held my eyes as he walked over to the steps. With my heels on, I was almost six feet tall, and I looked down at him from the step.

He reached out and squeezed my hips with his hands. "You are..." He paused for the right word, and started again. I saw him swallow before continuing. "You are enchanting." He pulled me to him. He pulled me so far, I came off the step, and he hugged me against him. I couldn't hide my feelings for him, so I just let it happen.

When he released me, we walked in to the living room together, and I hugged my Uncle Jack. My brother said, "Hey, Sis." I punched him in the arm.

I left the men to talk and went to help my mom. My sister-in-law was trying to make whipped cream from scratch, and was struggling.

"Hey, Annie Oakley, they sell that stuff in the stores now," I said to her. She snorted at me.

"It's not the same, Shaye," she said, and continued with her efforts.

At seven-thirty, we all sat down to dinner, and proceeded to have a lively evening. The conversation never stalled, the wine disappeared, and the food was delicious.

After dinner, my brother said he had an announcement, and tapped his spoon on his wine glass. "I would like to share with you that Caitlyn and I are going to have a baby."

He bowed like he had done something remarkable, and my mom squealed and stood up to hug them.

We all clapped, and I said, "Congratulations, you guys. I know you really want this." I looked at Caitlyn; she was tearing up.

Nick raised his glass and said, "Cheers!" And we all said, "Cheers!" Moving closer behind me, he followed up just loudly enough for me to hear, "To blue-eyed babies."

I almost choked. He patted me on the back and said, "You ok, Shaye?" I glared over at him. He was laughing.

My aunt and uncle left shortly after dinner, and Caitlyn and I helped my mom clean up. When the dishes were done, Caitlyn and my brother left, and my mom asked Nick and I to sit with her in the living room.

I had a cup of coffee, and I sat down on her sofa. I took off my sparkling sandals and pulled my legs up underneath me. My mom had lit a gas fire and turned off the overhead lights in the living room. With only the warm glow from the two end-table lamps, the room was cozy. Through the windows, we could see the lights of the city, which sparkled like a chandelier.

Nick was standing at the glass looking out at the city, and my mom sat down across from me.

"Is this an intervention?" I half joked.

Nick turned from the window and laughed at me, as if what I said was really funny. He stayed facing us with a smile on his face, amused.

"No, honey, I wanted to talk to you about the house." She started in, "Don't give it up." My eyes darted to Nick. He must have called her, and, in the process, must have wrangled an invitation to Thanksgiving dinner.

She continued, "I know your feelings of guilt are at the surface right now, but they will fade, and you will be grateful you have the house. Jason wouldn't want you suffering over him. He would want you to be happy, and he would certainly want his brother to be happy."

She looked at me with solemn eyes, and I felt myself tearing up. "Don't let his death be in vain. You aren't that person anymore, Shaye." She paused so I could absorb her words. The same words Nick had said to me a few short weeks ago. "Take the gift of life that you have and do something with it. Don't suffer any more for your mistakes." She looked back at Nick and said, "Both of you."

She stood and came to me. Leaning over me, she cradled both my cheeks in her hands. She spoke softly when she said, "Nick has something for you. Your father wanted him to wait until the year had passed, but I think it is important that you have it now. I love you, sweet girl." She kissed me on both cheeks, and then said, "I'm going to bed."

Then she wandered over, took one of Nick's hands, and patted him on his cheek with her other hand. She smiled at him and said, "Good-night, you two."

Nick watched my mom walk away, and then walked around to the chair she had been sitting in and handed me a letter.

"What is this?" I asked him.

"It's a letter, Shaye. People put them in envelopes, and the post office delivers them." He laughed.

"I know that, but what's in it?" I took the letter from him and waited for him to answer.

He sat down and said, "I was instructed to give it to you a year after you arrived..." He put his elbow on his knees and was clasping his hands in front of him. He glanced up at me with hooded eyes and said, "If you were still on the island." He paused, waiting. When I didn't reply, he continued, "When I talked to your mom the other day, she asked me to bring it."

"Do you know what's in it?" I asked him.

"I do not."

He waited silently while I opened the letter and started to read.

My darling Shaye,

I am smiling from above that you decided to stay on the island. The house is yours. It was always yours, and I hoped that one day you would come to realize that this was where you belonged.

Please forgive your mother and me for our antics. We were never sure if you would decide to return on your own. I know you think I wasn't paying attention to your life, but I was, and I hope you know that I love you. Your pain over lost love was our pain, and we tried our best to give you a safe place to land.

I cannot know for sure if your heart has healed. I pray you find your way back to Nick, and that your love story lasts forever.

Always in my heart,
Dad

I looked up at Nick and saw love in his eyes. Tears were streaming down my face, and I could not find the words to explain the letter, so I just handed it to him. He took it from me, read it, and I saw his eyes glass over.

He handed the letter back to me and waited.

I said, "This assumes I stayed the year?"

"It does."

"Does it free me from staying on the island?"

He waited a beat, looked at me directly, and said in a slower drawl, "It does."

He stood, never breaking my connection with him, and held out his hand. He was waiting for me to take everything he had to offer. I reached out and took it.

Turning to the sliding glass doors, we walked out onto the patio to the path that would take us to the pool house. Neither of us spoke; we just walked quietly together.

We reached the door to the pool house, and he turned to look at me. He brought my hand to his mouth and searched my eyes for permission. There wasn't any turning back for us now, and he wanted to know if I was ready for us.

I closed my eyes, leaned into him, and said, "Yes."

He kissed my forehead and opened the door. I stepped inside, and he shut the door behind me. I felt his front flat against my back. I closed my eyes and put my head back on his chest. I was already hot and flushed, but I didn't want to rush this.

He reached around and untied my wrap dress. The fabric fell to the side, and my dress opened in front. He leaned down and kissed the side of my neck, while his hands roamed across the front of my body.

I turned in his arms, letting my dress fall down my body to the floor. I wrapped my arms around his neck, and leaned up to kiss him. Softly at first, our lips just touched, and we melted into each other. He pulled me up against him and walked slowly back towards the bed, his lips never breaking our connection. The lamp on the side table had been left on, and the room had a romantic glow.

When the backs of my legs hit the bed, he put me down, and I scooted back on the mattress. I sat up, wrapped my arms around my knees, and just watched him. He took his jacket off, and then he slowly started unbuttoning his shirt. This began to feel playful, and I started to smile at him.

"You are taking too long," I teased.

He reached out, grabbed my ankles, and pulled me towards him. I squealed while he unhurriedly climbed up over me. Gently kissing me everywhere, he reached behind me and unfastened my bra. He threw it to the side and gave each of my breasts the adoration he had shown everywhere else.

I was melting. I was turning to liquid beneath him. I felt him run his fingers under the waistband of my thong, and then he grinned up at me.

"These are very sinful, Ms. Richards." He tried to sound scornful.

I purred back at him, "Only for a sinner, Mr. Reid." He laughed.

He took his time with me, touching me, loving me, his fingers caressing me between my thighs. My head fell back against the pillow, and I watched as his eyes turned dark with desire for me, and then I felt him leave me for a second.

I sat up on my elbows and watched him unbuckle his belt and take his pants off. He took his boxers with them, and stood before me.

He was glorious, and he was mine. I looked at him with love in my eyes, and then he came to me. There wasn't any time to prepare; he just took me, and we were lost in each other. He ravaged my mouth with kisses, and whispered over and over again how this was so right, how *we* were so right.

He cradled my head in his hands and held me close as he drove into me. He was ardent and attentive. I was intoxicated. Every nerve tensed as I pulled my legs up around him and let him take me. He stroked into me, gently, firmly, rhythmically, as he pushed us up and over the edge together.

When the stars and lights had diminished from behind my eyes, and I lay beneath him, sated and weak, I knew this was always meant to be. He rolled to the side and tucked me in next to him. He kissed me sweetly on the face, and we drifted off to sleep.

The next morning, I woke before him. I was still naked, and I grabbed the comforter up off the floor to wrap around me. The pool house was freezing, so I got up to turn the thermostat up.

Crawling back in bed, I shivered and burrowed myself down under the covers. I was watching him sleep, and my heart was aching with love for him. He was perfect. He was sleeping on his back, and the sheet was down to his waist. His hair was sticking up all over the place, and he had scruff on his chin.

This is what I want. Him. Forever.

He opened his eyes and caught me looking at him.

"Hello, beautiful!" His voice was raspy and seductive, and it did something to my insides. I wanted him to kiss me, everywhere, all over again.

"Hello."

He opened his eyes a little more and looked at me tenderly. He reached out a finger to brush the hair out of my eyes, and then turned on his side to face me directly. He tucked his left arm under his head and pulled his other arm up between us.

I was smiling at him, and in awe that he was here.

"I love you, Nick." It was easy to say. It was heartfelt, and I had been waiting eight years to tell him.

"I love you, Shaye." He smiled and kissed me.

Thirty minutes later, the phone in the pool house rang. I was trying to stretch, but Nick was pinning me down. We had both nodded off again, and the shrill call of the phone startled us.

He rolled off of me and reached out to get the phone.

"Hello?" he answered.

I saw him look at me like he got caught with his hand in the cookie jar. I looked back questioningly.

"Yes ma'am. Ok. Thank you. Yes, we'll be there." He was answering quickly to what I could only imagine were rapid fire questions from my mother. I had left my cell phone in the house, and I was sure she knew by then I was not in my room.

"My mother?" I asked.

"Yes." He raked his hand through his hair, and it stood up on all ends. He was adorable. "She said breakfast would be in 30 minutes."

"And?"

"And," he looked at me like he was in trouble. "Aaaand... she said, 'and please bring my daughter. I am sure she will be hungry.'"

I groaned out loud and blushed to my roots. Nick just started laughing.

"It's not funny," I said, half-offended.

"Yes, actually, it is." He pulled me towards him for a third time.

Needless to say, we were late for breakfast.

21

To: Shaye Richards
From: Nick Reid
Subject: Missing you
Shaye,
I hope you made it back safely to the island.
It will be very hectic here for a few weeks, so
please don't worry if I can't get a call to you.
You are always on my mind.
N.

Nick and I had spent the rest of the weekend in the city together. We did touristy things, like going to the Space Needle and the Pike Place Market, and we went on the Ferris wheel down on the waterfront.

We stayed at my mom's house. Every night, I would go to my room until my mom went to sleep, and then I would sneak down to the pool house.

Every morning, my mom would call the pool house and invite Nick to breakfast, and remind him to bring me, too.

Sunday night, he told me he was not going back with me in the morning. The corporate case he had been working on for the last few months was ramping up, and he needed to be physically present in Seattle.

My heart sank. I didn't want to be without him. My house was in Seattle, and I was living on the island. His house was on the island, and now he had to be in Seattle.

He said it would only be a few weeks, and that he would be home by Christmas, but that didn't make going back without him any easier. Already missing him, I replied to his email as soon as we landed.

To: Nick Reid
From: Shaye Richards
Subject: RE: Missing you

Nick,
I am safe and sound back on the island. There will be fewer flights now that the days are shorter.
I am having dinner with Evie and Julie tonight.
That's what I'm worried about. ☺
Shaye

Nick responded immediately.

To: Shaye Richards
From: Nick Reid
Subject: RE: RE: Missing you
Shaye,
I hope you make it out alive. Tell Evie to protect my treasure.
Nick

I kept myself as busy as I could. I chopped wood for the fire, and ran every day. It was getting dark by four-thirty, which was kind of depressing. I missed Nick, and I knew I couldn't keep hanging out with Evie and Julie. I felt like I was annoying them.

My relationship with Julie was mending. When I could get her alone, I really enjoyed talking with her. She was smarter than most people gave her credit for, and we were slowly becoming friends.

The weekend came and went, and I started wondering about what would have happened if I hadn't been dating Jason. Unable to sleep late one night, I sent an email. Late night emails were always a mistake.

To: Nick Reid
From: Shaye Richards
Subject: What if
Dear Nick,
I've been thinking... What if I hadn't been with Jason? Would we be together? Would Jason still be alive?
Shaye

He responded immediately.

To: Shaye Richards
From: Nick Reid
Subject: Don't overthink us

Beautiful girl,

Don't overthink us. I love you, and you love me.
Don't let the past win. We have already lost him,
and we can't change how we got here.
Please move forward with me,
Nick

That was all I needed from him: a little
reassurance that I wasn't up here on the island, in this
relationship, alone.

Evie came to my office Thursday with treats and a
coffee. I was so happy to see her, I just about squeezed
the life out of her.

"Good lord, Shaye. Get out much?" She plopped
herself down in my office chair.

"I miss Nick," I whined.

"Gross. I don't want to hear it." She pretended to
gag. Then she added, "Come to the resort Christmas
party with me this Saturday. It will be fun."

"We don't work for the resort, Evie," I reminded
her.

"So, what? I mean, it isn't like a private Christmas
party. It's at the pub, so it's just another Saturday night
out. Saying we are going to the resort party makes it
sound swankier, and we can dress up."

I laughed at her enthusiasm. "Okay, sure, I will go
with you. Sounds like fun."

She clapped her hands together and smiled at me.
"We will have *so* much fun."

I had been thinking about Christmas, so I tried to
hint at making plans. "I was thinking about staying on
the island for Christmas. Do you have plans yet?"

She let out an exasperated sigh, as if I should already know. "My parents' house Christmas Eve, and then Nick's house Christmas morning."

"That sounds nice." I tried to keep the melancholy out of my voice. Nick hadn't said anything about Christmas yet, and my mom was asking if I was coming home.

Evie looked at me and laughed. "Oh, Lord, Shaye. Don't be so mopey. You are expected to be there. My brother is so in love with you, he would chain you to his side if he could."

I looked at her expectantly and said, "Really?"

She stood up and said. "Girl, bye." I grinned at her backside as she walked away.

I was going through my closet Friday night when a text appeared from Nick. *"Why would you think we wouldn't be spending Christmas together?"*

He had obviously talked to Evie. I rolled my eyes to no one.

I was wiggling my fingers over the buttons, trying to decide what to say when another text appeared. *"We are spending all of our holidays together – we will always be together."*

Grinning, I texted back, *"I've just been so lonely without you."* I put a crying emoji after the last word. I saw the little dots bouncing across the screen and giggled, waiting to see how he would respond.

The dots stopped and then started again. A few seconds later, his response appeared, *"You're a goddess and I will be there as soon as I can."*

I jumped back from my phone and my heart thundered against my chest. He was flirting with me, and I was totally turned on.

A second later my phone rang, and I jumped again.

"Hello?" I was a little breathless.

"Shaye." All he said was my name, and I became a puddle.

"Why are you calling me?" Now I wanted to play.

He was somewhat serious when he responded, "I can't have you having any doubts that I want you, or that I love you. I can't be down here, thinking about you being up there, unhappy."

"I'm not unhappy; I just miss you. That's all." I laid back on the bed, stared at the ceiling and kept talking. "And sometimes I wonder what it would be like if I met you now, and we didn't have all these shared scars. Would we still be together?"

He continued, "But we do, Shaye. And wondering and worrying and second guessing doesn't change it." His voice was caressing me through the phone. I wanted him here with me.

I sat up and snapped out of my funk. "When will you be home?"

"Before Christmas. I promise." He sounded tired.

I took a deep breath and told him that Evie was taking me to a Christmas party Saturday night.

"That sounds like fun," he said with mock enthusiasm.

"Actually, I think we are crashing a Christmas Party, but whatever." I rubbed the back of my neck.

"Do you have something to wear?" I could tell he was talking because he knew I needed him, but his tired voice made me feel bad for keeping him.

"I was just looking through my closet." I stifled a yawn and said, "I think we are both tired. Can we talk tomorrow?"

"We can. I'll talk to you tomorrow."

I tapped the end button, tossed the phone on the other side of the bed, and lay back to stare at the ceiling again. I would worry about what to wear tomorrow. Tonight, I had what I needed.

∞

Saturday morning at around eleven o'clock, I drove to the store and then to the bakery to see Evie. I ordered an almond butterhorn and a coffee. The butterhorns were so good, I would need to run an extra mile or Nick would have a donut for a girlfriend when he got home.

Evie asked me to wait for her, so I took my coffee outside and sat on the deck. It was freezing out there, and I was grateful that I had put gloves and a beanie cap on when I'd left that morning.

My phone pinged with an incoming text. I pulled it out of my pocket.

Shaye.

It was from Nick. I saw the little dots bouncing, and another text came through: *You know I love you, right?*

What the heck?

Evie came out at that moment and said, "Ok, so here's the plan. Come over tonight about five-thirty, no six-thirty, and we will get ready together." Evie seemed completely oblivious to my current state and kept talking. "Julie is coming, too. And before you yell at me, it's time we all were friends again. She isn't a bad person, and she *is* my oldest friend."

She grabbed a bite of my butterhorn, and then snapped at me. "Shaye, did you hear me?"

"Yes, yes, I heard you. Five-thirty. Julie. Your house." I brought her back into focus.

"Fine. Five-thirty if you want." She took another bite of my treat, and then said, "I have to close up soon. See you tonight."

I went to my car and sent him a text. *Nick?*

I drove home waiting for my phone to chime, but there was nothing. I tried to call him, and it went to voice-mail.

I sent him a text. *I know you love me.*

The dots were popping again. Why didn't he pick up the phone? *It took us a while to find each other again, and I want you to know you are cherished.* More dots... *Where are you now?*

I texted back, *I'm at home, getting my things together to go to Evie's tonight.*

Have fun. Be safe.

I arrived at Evie's at about six p.m. Julie was already there, dressed in a gold jumpsuit.

"What on Earth are you wearing?" I exclaimed. I was still trying to be her friend, but the jumper was just too much.

Julie laughed at me. "Wait until you see what Evie picked for you."

I turned to Evie, "I'm wearing this red dress."

"Oh, no, you aren't. Come. Come see what I have for you." She was acting like the Wicked Witch of Oz, and I was a little nervous. If the next thing she said was, 'Come, my pretty,' I would have to leave.

She pulled out a black sequined tank dress that was cut low in the front and very, very short.

"What is it with you Reids and naughty black dresses?" I looked at her in shock.

She laughed. "I got it at the thrift store today. I think it was part of a costume." She was laughing so hard she had tears coming down her face.

"Evie, I am not wearing this. I can't even wear a bra," I said, nonplussed.

Julie overheard us and joined in from the other room. "I think that is what she was going for. If we look like her hooker friends, she can get away with looking like Snow White, and get in more trouble than the two of us combined." She didn't sound that concerned about Evie's wardrobe selections.

"I will try it on," I said, adding hurriedly, "but I'm not promising to wear it!"

I went into Evie's room to change and took my phone with me. I saw Nick hadn't texted me again, and I tried not to feel anxious. Taking off all my clothes except my thong, I slipped the dress over my head. It slid on like silk, and I actually looked pretty hot.

Walking out to the living area, I stood and waited for Julie and Evie to notice me.

Julie looked up, "Holy smokes, Shaye."

Evie sat down as if in a daze, "You weren't supposed to look *that* good."

Julie laughed and punched Evie in the arm. "That's what you get for being a pimp." She went back to doing her makeup.

We finished getting ready, and Evie put my hair up in a messy bun. She put way too much eyeliner on me, but I didn't care. I loved having girlfriends that loved me, in a place where I hoped I now belonged.

The bar was decorated for Christmas, and the red and green lights twinkled all around us. A tree was set up in the entryway, and the resort staff had put presents underneath. I kept an eye on Evie, because I wasn't convinced that she wouldn't try to take one. We put our coats in a booth, and then we danced and drank champagne.

I missed Nick terribly. He hadn't texted since that morning, and my heart ached for him. I sat down in the booth to text him and saw I had missed one. *Hi, baby, are you having fun?*

I immediately texted back, *Yes, but I miss you terribly.*

My chest was tight, and I just wanted to hold him right then. He responded, *I need to tell you something, Shaye, and it's very important.*

Oh no! I geared up for something horrible. Looking down at my phone, I typed, *OK?*

I'm going to marry you, Shaye.

I read the words and brought my hand to my chest. I couldn't breathe. The texts continued popping up.

I have loved you from the moment I saw you. Before you spoke, I knew we were meant to be together.

I didn't know how or when, but I knew.

More dots...

You are mine, Shaye. And I will always be yours.

My heart was racing. Tears were streaming down my face, and I grabbed a napkin from the dispenser on the table.

Then another text came through, *And if we were to start over tonight and meet for the very first time, I would still love you the very same way: completely and forever.*

My head snapped up, and I was too stunned to move. He was here. I could feel him. I knew he was there the same way I'd known my life would change on the day I'd first met him, eight years before.

My phone was silent a moment. My chest moved up and down, and my breaths came short and fast. I tried to calm down. My phone chimed one last time, *And we are going to make pretty blue-eyed babies... lots of them.*

I laughed. I stood to get out of the booth, and turned to see him standing there, against the wall, just as he had been eight years ago.

No one else existed in that room. No one but us. The sounds and people were all the same, but we weren't.

I felt Jason's presence, and his love, and I knew he had forgiven us. I knew he wanted us to be happy. Nothing stood in our way, now.

As I approached him, he put his foot down and stood up straight. We were just looking at each other and smiling. I could see how much he loved me, and my whole heart was reflected in his eyes. Any doubts I'd had about returning to the island disappeared in the love I felt between us. Our smiles grew wider the longer we stood there.

I put out my hand and said, "Shaye Richards."

He took my hand. "Nick Reid."

Play List

"Still Falling For You" - Ellie Goulding
"Boys 'Round Here" – Blake Shelton
"Burn it to the ground" – Nickelback
"The Cowboy in me" – Tim McGraw
"Crazy" – Patsy Cline
"Peel me a Grape" – Diana Krall
"Use Somebody" – Kings of Leon
"I Want to go Home" – Blake Shelton
"Body like a Back Road" – Sam Hunt

Acknowledgements

Special Thanks to Karlena Pickering for her beautiful photo of the boathouse on Fisherman Bay.

To Kenmore Air Harbor. Everyone should have a floatplane adventure in their lifetime.

Made in the USA
Columbia, SC
22 February 2019